"You are a foolish man,"

she said. "It is I who do not wish to harm you, and yet you stand here, filling your chest like a courting grouse, daring me to strike you down."

"Strike me down?" It was his turn to laugh. "You would kill me for kissing you?"

"I would not want to see you dead, James. You must not touch me as a man might touch a woman. I am called Double Woman Dreamer. Two men lie dead because of me, my husband and my brother. The power of a Double Woman can destroy a man's medicine."

"I have no medicine, Kezawin. I'm a scientist. You'll not dream me dead." He pointed to the sheath on her belt. "Unless you plunge that knife into my heart."

"I would need no knife to kill you, so you must take care not to touch me—even if I seem to want you."

Dear Reader:

Harlequin offers you historical romances with a difference. Harlequin Historicals have all the passion and excitement of a five-hundred-page historical in three hundred pages, and stories that focus on people—a hero and heroine you really care about, who take you back to and make you part of their time.

We have some great books for you this fall. I've highlighted a few, and I'm sure you'll want to look for these and our other exciting selections. Here's what you can look forward to in coming months: *Rose Red, Rose White* by Marianne Willman is a passionate romance set in medieval England. *Texas Heart* by Ruth Langan is the story of a young woman who goes in search of her father and finds love along the way. *Apache Summer* is the third and final book in Heather Graham Pozzessere's miniseries, and it features Jamie Slater. Lastly, in December, look for *Chase the Thunder* by Patricia Potter, which is an exciting Western romance and a sequel to *Between the Thunder*.

We appreciate your comments and suggestions; our goal is to publish the kinds of books you want to read. So please keep your letters coming. You can write to us at the address below.

Karen Solem
Editorial Director
Harlequin Historicals
P.O. Box 7372
Grand Central Station
New York, New York 10017

Medicine Woman

Kathleen Eagle

Harlequin Books

TORONTO • NEW YORK • LONDON
AMSTERDAM • PARIS • SYDNEY • HAMBURG
STOCKHOLM • ATHENS • TOKYO • MILAN

Harlequin Historical first edition September 1989

ISBN 0-373-28630-9

Books by Kathleen Eagle

Harlequin Historical

Private Treaty #2
Medicine Woman #30

KATHLEEN EAGLE

is a transplant from Massachusetts to her favorite regional setting, the Dakota prairie. As educator, wife, mother and writer, she believes that a woman's place is wherever she's needed—and anywhere she needs to be.

In memory of my mother, Mary.
Let it be.

Prologue

Paha Sapa, the Black Hills in the land of the Lakota
1819

Morning sifted through Kezawin's eyelids like a gray-clad intercessor. The dark dream fell away piece by piece, and the hideous high-pitched laughter faded. She forced her eyes open wide and covered her ears against the staccato hoof-beat of the dream's final retreat. *Too late,* came the husky warning all around her head. *Too late to cover your ears. You have heard. You have seen. You have chosen.*

Kezawin turned her head slowly, pressing her cheek into the matted curls of buffalo hair, and stole a look at the face of her sleeping husband. Iron Shell was a beautiful young man with a strong heart. For three years he had protected her and provided for her well, never complaining as he waited month after month for his wife to conceive. Now, in the gray light of morning, a terrible truth seized Kezawin's heart. She was barren. No life would quicken in the womb of a woman who dreamed as she just had. And the young husband who lay beside her, though he was as strong as any man, was endangered by her very presence in his bed.

Trembling, Kezawin eased herself from their sleeping robes. The morning chill touched her backside first. She balanced herself on the balls of her feet and her fingertips, shielding her breasts behind her knees as she backed away without making a sound. She must not wake him. She must not let him see her crouching and shivering in shame.

Slipping a robe over her shoulders, she uncoiled her body slowly as she found her moccasins with her toes. Carefully she reached for the buckskin dress that lay neatly folded on the tipi's plush buffalo carpet and clutched it to her breast beneath her robe. She could not pull the dress over her head and risk the sound of ornamental elk's teeth clicking against each other or the soft swish of fringe. Iron Shell had the keen senses of a warrior. But Kezawin was a daughter of the Lakota, and she knew how to move quietly.

Her fingers might have been greased with tallow, so awkward were they in untying the thong that secured the tipi door, which was a piece of rawhide stretched over a willow hoop. She waited a moment, settled her mind on the task, then loosened the knot with a now steady hand.

The autumn air was cold and thin. A shallow breath of it pinched her lungs. A full breath stabbed deep. It wasn't the air, she thought. It was the dream's piercing horns. She adjusted the robe closely around her shoulders as she cast a hasty glance at the pine-green and autumn-brown valley. The tipis rose from the ground-hugging mist in miniature imitation of the peaks of the *Paha Sapa*, which surrounded the village. The golden glow of the coming sun glistened in the mist and lent an illusion of luster to the tall, tan, sooty-tipped cones. Picketed near their owners' doors, the war ponies stood with necks drooping and hindquarters cocked to rest a leg. One camp dog was about his business early, scavenging the ashes of a dead camp fire for some forgotten scrap. The rest of the camp rested peacefully.

Kezawin hurried to the river. She found a cluster of sheltering pines and sought refuge while she dressed. The soft skin of the elk blocked out the light as she slipped it over her head, but the light and dark of the dream swirled within the confines of her dress and warred round and round her head. She stretched her arms, dove into the sleeves of the dress and popped her head through the neck, gasping for air. She sought the light. She *chose* the light.

She knelt in the tall slough grass that lined the low earthen wall that the river had cut for its bed. Lying on her belly, Kezawin dipped cupped hands into the icy flow and splashed handfuls over her face and neck. She shivered as the water trickled between her breasts, but she reached for more. It tingled and tightened her skin over prominent cheekbones like the deerhide stretched over a willow frame in the making of a drum.

She closed her eyes and shook droplets from her face as she struggled to shake the thought from her mind. She had not meant to compare her skin to that of the deer. The image had come into her head, unbidden. Perhaps she could still drive it away. The image flew in the face of the destiny she wanted for herself—the roles of mother, wife, woman respected by the people for her impeccable virtue, industry and skills. She had lived her seventeen years to that end, and she would not, *could* not see it all blow away on a dream wind.

Her father would tell her that the dream had deceived her young, inexperienced mind. Lone Bear was a holy man, a man of wisdom. Surely the daughter of such a man could not be touched by unnatural dreams. Kezawin pushed herself up from the ground and reached for her robe. Her father would interpret the dream. She would tell him every detail, omit nothing in her recounting of it. There were signs in the dream that she could not read, but Lone Bear would know them. He would tell her that it was not as she feared. She had not been touched by the deer woman.

Kezawin stood near the covered door of the tipi with the familiar geometric paintings in bright symbolic colors, which proclaimed Lone Bear's accomplishments. "Father," she said, knowing that her brother, Walks His Horse, would sleep through this disturbance if she spoke quietly enough. "Forgive me for troubling your sleep, Father, but I must speak with you."

"Now?" The voice she knew better than her own rattled with early-morning dampness.

"It's an important matter, Father. Something that frightens me."

A head of graying hair emerged from the tipi. Lone Bear hitched his striped trade blanket around his waist as he straightened to a height that surpassed his daughter's by a head. His eyes were assaulted by the sun's early rays, and he drew his face into a well-established pattern of protective folds. "Where is your husband, Kezawin? He is the one to be shaken from his blankets when something frightens you."

"My husband is not a holy man, Father." She felt her father's eyes upon her, although she did not lift her gaze from the toes of his quilled moccasins. "I have seen something *wakan*," she said quietly. "Something holy."

Lone Bear turned back toward the door. "This is not for my brother's ears," Kezawin said quickly. "And I need to feel the sun on my head."

They went to the river and sat upon Kezawin's robe in a grassy clearing, where crystal beads of dew twinkled in the morning sun. The long dry summer had diminished the river's power. It sloshed lazily in the confines of its banks while Lone Bear waited quietly.

"It was a dream," she said simply. "It came to me while I slept."

Lone Bear gave a nod, acknowledging the fact that his daughter had not sought this vision. She had not fasted and prayed for it. It had simply come to her.

"We were walking," she began. "We were searching for a certain plant, just you and I. I had never seen it, but you said it had red roots and I would know it when I saw it. We came to a river, but it was not like this." She indicated the water with a graceful gesture. "The water ran high, and we could not find a fording place. We walked. Then we saw a deer." She could feel her father's back stiffen at the word, even though he sat an arm's length away from her. She described the deer's motions with her hand. "It crossed the river, and the water only came up to its hocks. It—*he* had a beautiful mossy rack. Father, it was a buck. I was sure it was."

She looked at her father in the hope that this piece of information was significant, but she saw no change in his grave expression. She continued. "The deer began to scrape his antlers in a scraggly chokecherry tree, but the tree grew bigger, and soon he was entangled in its branches. I could see his eyes. He didn't panic. He entreated me to cross the river and free him."

"Did he speak?" Lone Bear asked.

"No. Not yet. I asked you to go with me, but you said that only a woman could use this ford. If I chose to cross, I would have to go alone. I asked you whether the red root plant might grow on the other side. You said it was very likely.

"I followed the trail the deer had taken across the river. He was deeply enmeshed, and my arms and face were soon bleeding from scratches." She held her arms out in front of her, turning them over to examine them. The dream burned so vividly in her mind that her unscathed arms puzzled her.

"I freed him," she said. "And then he spoke. His voice was that . . . of a woman." That part she knew to be significant, and she paused in the fear of that knowledge. "He said that he would give me the red root plant if I would stay with him. I refused, and he became angry and began chasing his tail like a dog. Round and round, round and round. My head was soon spinning. I heard the sound of a whirlwind, and I felt drawn into the vortex of the deer's wild dance. I had no thought of walking, but I was moving closer. Even as he spun, he watched me through flat black eyes. His lips curled back over his teeth, and the wind shrieked in my ears.

"Something white caught my eye. Another buck was grazing nearby, but this one was white. All white. I wanted to touch him. He raised his head, and I saw the red roots of the plants in his mouth. I walked away from the spinning deer. The white deer stood quietly until I reached him. He let me touch his face. He dropped the red root plants in my hands. He licked the blood from my arms and face with his cooling tongue.

"We walked to the riverbank and found an old woman with wild, tangled hair, sitting with her feet in the water. Across the river I could see the village, and I told the white deer that I would take the red root plants to my father. The woman laughed, and when she looked up, I saw the flat black eyes and the curling lips of the spinning deer. She pulled her legs out of the water and put her moccasins over cloven hooves, and then she sat cross-legged, unbefitting a woman. The village looked close, but it felt distant. I asked the woman how far it was, and she said, 'They are beyond your reach now. You are a fool if you stay within theirs.' And then she went to the chokecherry bush and began rubbing her head on it, tangling her hair in its branches. My scalp itched, and I wanted to imitate her actions."

"Did you?" Kezawin's father asked quietly.

"No. The white deer stepped into the water, and I knew that he was not a woman and could not ford the river there. He floundered in deep water. At my back I heard the woman's laughter, but I followed the white deer into the deep water. I followed him because he knew the secret of the red root plant and because he was beautiful, and I did not want him to drown."

"Did he drown?"

"I don't know," she said. "The gray light woke me."

"Did the white deer speak?"

"Not a word."

Lone Bear nodded as he looked across the river and into the trees. "And the spinning deer," he said. "What color was the tail?"

"It was a white-tailed deer."

Lone Bear nodded again. The whitetail came as no surprise. It was *can tarca winyela*, the female woods deer, a vision no woman sought. He would pray about this dream and consider the meaning of each detail, but there was no question in his heart about one thing. "You have dreamed of the deer woman."

Kezawin shivered and hugged herself against a cold that was not caused by the air.

"You are Double Woman Dreamer," Lone Bear proclaimed.

Chapter One

Near the Shayen River in Unorganized Territory, land of the Teton Lakota, west of the Missouri River
1826

James Garrett dropped to his knees in the lush curly-leafed switchgrass and plunged a handful of plant specimens into the cold creek. The water's quick flow reduced clumps of dirt to a brown cloud on the run. He swished the leafy stalks around for good measure, then sat back on his heels to study the curious bulbous red roots. The upper Missouri River was a naturalist's paradise, and this botanical specimen was an example of the kind of find that set his brain abuzz.

He sliced the flesh of the root with his thumbnail and sniffed its juicy pulp. It had a pungent scent and a woody texture. His tongue darted out for a small taste. It burned. He scooped up a handful of water to quell the sting, spat the first mouthful into the grass and leaned down for another drink.

The sweet sound of a woman's laughter drove the bitter taste from his mind. His arm froze, and the water trickled through his fingers, flowing freely like the feminine laugh that he couldn't quite believe he was hearing. It had been well over a year since he'd heard a woman laugh like that. He raised his shaggy head slowly, half hoping to find a woman of his own kind standing on the far bank and fully expecting to see nothing at all. The Sioux people, with whom he had lived over the past year, considered him to be slightly crazy, and it was just possible that he was beginning to hear things.

The woman who watched him from the opposite side of the creek was the loveliest brown-skinned creature he had ever seen. Her braided hair was as bright and black as the wing of a raven, and merriment flashed like the quick glint of a brook trout in her dark eyes. Her white elkskin dress was unadorned except for a profusion of fringe around her elbows and below her knees, but she wore elk's-tooth earrings and a dentalium shell choker. She carried a digging stick, and a buckskin pouch hung over her shoulder. James recalled the undignified way he'd just spat in her presence, and he felt the flush of embarrassment. He reminded himself that she was not, as he'd dared to hope, a white woman, but a sheepish smile crossed his face nonetheless.

"Turn your face from my shameful behavior," he said in her language. "The taste was bitter. I had to be rid of it."

"It's good that you did," she replied, lifting her voice above the water. "The red root plant may not be eaten."

"Is it poisonous?"

Ignoring his question, she turned her attention to her digging stick, using it to loosen the roots of some plant hiding in the grass. James stood up and tucked his find into his own collection pouch. Trowel in hand, he continued on his way, following the creek bank. On the opposite side the woman kept abreast of him. The watchful eye he had trained to the ground began to stray, even though he kept up the appearance of attending to his fieldwork. She moved when he moved. She paused when he paused. She dug when he dug. He was tempted to veer away from the creek and head north just to see whether she would cross over and follow him.

The fact that she was gathering roots alone was remarkable in itself. James had followed the Missouri River northward and had spent the past eighteen months with east river groups of Sioux—the Santee, the Yankton—and now the west river people, the Teton, who called themselves Lakota people. He had mastered adequate conversational skills, observed their customs and taken a particular interest in the various uses they had for the flora of this country. He had allowed the people to observe him, too, and observe him they did. He sensed their conviction that he was a bit strange but that he posed no threat to them. One by one the much-feared Lakota bands, or Council Fires—the Brûlé, Miniconju, Sans Arc, Oglala—all had permitted him to come among them.

Now, as he explored a meandering tributary, he had made his initial contact with the Hunkpapa. Their cousins had apparently sent the Lakota version of a letter of introduction in advance of his arrival, for a hunting party had passed through his camp the previous morning and had acknowledged him by name. He had offered gifts of tobacco and had told them that he had heard of their medicine man, Lone Bear, and he wished to pay a visit to one whose wisdom was widely honored. He had known from that moment to this that he was under some watchful scrutiny, but he hardly imagined they would have sent a woman to ascertain his intentions.

Their women foraged in groups for roots and berries. They traveled in small bunches to fetch wood and water, and they worked together tanning, quilling and sewing in exclusively female circles. James had observed the courting ritual in which a young woman would stand with a man beneath his robe, but always directly in front of her parents' door. He'd watched the women form their dance lines and flex their knees to the beat of the drum in the square-shouldered, sedate form of sociable dancing that was considered proper for women. They giggled readily, but always with a demure hand shielding the mouth, always subdued, at least in the presence of men.

This woman who followed him was an enigma. Moreover, she was persistent. Throughout his sojourn among these people, he had taken pains not to offend them, and he suspected that approaching a woman would be the surest way to do just that. Yet, she was attractive by any standards, even James's, and she was certainly following him.

"I am of the opinion that there's nothing edible along these banks," he said as he lifted his face to the noonday sun. "Are you finding the same?"

"Is it food you seek?" the woman asked.

"I seek that which I have not seen before." He tucked his trowel in his pouch and turned to her. "And I've not met you."

"Were you seeking me, then, James Garrett?"

Her boldness prompted boldness in him. "Had I known about you, I might have sought you, but since you have the advantage of knowing my name, it would appear that you seek me."

"It would appear that I have heard of you, James Garrett. Nothing more." She selected another plant and jabbed at its base with her digging stick. "Are you in need of food?"

He raised his hand and pointed to a grassy knoll. "My camp is just over that hill, but I'm sure you're aware of that." She looked up from her work and studied him for a moment. He knew he must look strange to her with his pale brown hair and his full beard, and he wondered if she expected him to sprout horns and a tail. But, perhaps she was flirting with him. He firmly believed that every society had its coy skirts, be they ruffled or fringed. "Have you food to share?" he asked.

"If you are in need of food, I have some." She plucked the loosened plant from the ground and cut the foliage from the roots with the quick slice of a small glinting blade.

James strained to identify the plant at a distance. It appeared to be a specimen he didn't have. "What is that?" he asked quickly.

"Feverroot," she told him as she opened her hand to let him see the tangled brown mass. "It nourishes the fevered body."

"Is there more of that over there?" He glanced upstream for signs of a place where he might cross, his interest in the new specimen suddenly displacing his interest in the woman. "I don't believe I've seen the like of it. Feverroot, you say?"

She watched him pace the bank and realized what he was about to do. "Stay where you are," she said as she bent to untie the legging that protected her calf against the brush. "I will come."

"But I want the entire plant," he muttered. "I can find—"

"Stay there, James Garrett." She dug up another plant, moved back downstream a little way, shucked both leggings and moccasins and waded into the water. It rushed past her ankles, and soon it was up to her knees. James watched her hike her skirt up an inch or two at a time to accommodate the depth of the creek. With each step she took, he hoped for slightly higher water, but between water and elkskin fringe he saw only a teasing hint of small round knees and smooth thighs.

"I could have done that," he said as he offered his hand in assistance. "Would I be unwelcome on the other side of the creek?"

Standing knee-deep in water next to the sharply eroded bank, she stared at his hand, then offered a wary glance.

"Among my people, a man assists a woman thus," he explained. "It's the proper thing. I would not harm you."

She considered the outstretched palm for a moment before switching all that she carried into her left hand and laying her right hand in his. "You speak our language well," she noted as she stepped up to the grassy bank.

"I've had good instruction." She handed him the plant she'd dug for him, and he spoke absently as he examined the small round leaves and the matted roots. "Your cousins, I believe. Interesting people. Fine people."

"My father received word that a *wašicun*, a white man named James Garrett, wished to meet him. Our Miniconju cousins say that you walk from plant to plant with your nose to the ground, exclaiming over them in your own language as though, unlike others of your kind, you know these plants to be your relations. I have seen that this is true."

He spared her a quick smile and indicated his new specimen as he moved toward the water. "This brother of mine needs a bath. You say it's effective against fever?"

"I said that it nourishes one who has fever," she said patiently.

"And who is your father?"

"My father is Lone Bear of the Hunkpapa."

James lifted his newly washed plant up and shook the water from it, mumbling his observations about the character of its roots in his own tongue. Then her answer registered in his brain. "Lone Bear? Ah, the medicine man I've heard so much about." He levered himself up on one knee. "Your father's wisdom is widely praised."

"We have heard much about you," she told him.

"What have you heard?"

She sat upon a rock and pulled one legging over her calf. "It is believed that you are *wakan*. You have been watched but never challenged, never harmed. In fact, our cousins say that you follow a trail of plants and sometimes lose your way."

"I've never lost my way," he said, his tone indignant. But he smiled on second thought and gave a careless shrug. "Once or twice, perhaps. But it really doesn't matter. Your people have been very good to me, and sooner or later I always run into someone who's willing to set me back on course."

The woman's laughter was lilting and unrestrained. "You have not met them by accident, James Garrett. They watch after you. If you are *wakan*, then you must be protected."

He laughed as he tucked the specimen into his pouch. "My own father would find it amusing to hear you describe me as 'holy.' Were you sent to watch after me today?"

"No," she said. "I was about my own work when I saw you. You found the red root plant."

"Collecting herbs for your father?" he asked. "No doubt we all have our field assistants." She looked at him curiously, then went back to putting on her moccasins. "May I know your name?" he asked.

It appeared to be a difficult question for her, almost as though she were unsure what to tell him, or whether to tell him anything at all. James had learned to wait for his answers without prodding with more questions. She stood slowly, avoiding his eyes. "My name is Kezawin," she said at last.

"Kezawin," he repeated, savoring the word. Soft and warm, it lingered sweetly on the tongue while it curled around the ear. "Will you take me to your father?"

"I would take the red root plant to my father," she said as she glanced at his collection pouch.

"The red root—oh," he said, touching the pouch. "It was the only one of its kind that I found. We can search for more."

"They are rare," she told him. "You may not see another one for a long time."

"What's it good for?" he asked as he peered into the pouch that hung against his lean hip. "You said it wasn't edible."

"It has healing power."

Carefully he separated the plant from the others in his pouch. "I would take it to your father, then, and offer it as a gift."

She held her hand out. "If you let me give it to him, he will know this as a sign."

"A good sign?"

She dipped her chin in assent, and he laid the red root plant in her hand.

"Will you take me to him?"

"I will come for you again, James Garrett. Don't cross the creek until I come for you." She walked away from him, and his feet were strangely heavy, rendering him unable to follow her. He watched her disappear into a stand of cottonwoods.

The air inside the sweat lodge was thick with steam. Kezawin breathed shallowly and indulged herself in physical self-awareness as a prelude to the awareness she sought. She was surrounded by darkness. The willow-framed dome admitted nothing from the world outside the layered walls of heavy hides. Kezawin sat naked, her chin hovering above her knees, inside Earth's warm, wet womb. Her hair made a cape over her rounded back, and a runnel of sweat slid between her breasts on its course to the puddle that had formed in her navel. Her belly rumbled, but she had no thought of food. She had the sound of her own breath to tell her that she was not an unborn spirit, but she had no thoughts now. She simply sat inside herself and became the breath and the heartbeat tucked under Earth's breast. She was a vessel into which awareness might sweep.

In the darkness the face of the white deer appeared with the red root plant in his mouth. It lingered, then went away again.

Brightness began as a small seed, opening in the dark and blossoming slowly into white daylight. The sun danced in the man's light hair. Like his brother, the deer, his face was covered with hair. He put the red root plant in his mouth, and Kezawin held her breath as she watched from across the creek and waited for the man to be transformed. But when he spat the bitter pulp into the grass, she welcomed the sign that he was human, and she laughed, as was her right. He spoke to her, and she studied him, as was her duty. His eyes were large and round, alert and curious. He acquainted himself with all that grew in the earth, and he used all of his senses, smelling, tasting and touching with his hands while he looked carefully with his eyes. He spoke to the plants as he removed them from the earth, making his peace with them in his own tongue. Kezawin watched him do these things, and she was filled with a strong sense of rightness.

He saw the feverroot and acted on impulse, incautious in his eagerness to cross the creek and learn something new. A wiser man would know the unknown thing to be *wakan*, holy in its mystery. She watched him pace the bank of the creek in his anxiety to reach her, and she warned him against crossing the creek until she came for him.

He heeded her warning, but she saw no fear in him. He invited her to touch him. Other men admired her, but they were afraid of her power, and they stayed away. This one offered his hand. Her name did not frighten him, nor did her laughter. He was a brave man. Or a foolish one. Or, if the signs were true, he was sent by her *sicun*, her guardian and helper, which had been represented in her dream by the white deer.

Awareness. In the dark womb of the earth, Kezawin made no thought. She saw what was. She accepted the red root plant from the white deer. Under the bright midday sun, she accepted James Garrett's hand.

James found his thoughts drifting to the Lakota woman as he went about his work. It had been two days since he'd seen her, and he was beginning to wonder whether she'd been a figment of his imagination. She had convinced him of her intention to return and take him to her father, and he kept catching himself watching, feeling himself waiting. He had to remind himself that he was not one to await any woman's pleasure. He hadn't the time or patience.

He hooked his fingers into his thick beard and scratched his chin as he watched the breakfast fire burn low. The water would heat quickly, and he had a razor in his pack within close reach. He had let his beard grow after giving his mirror as a gift to a Brûlé medicine man, but now he had an urge to be rid of the itching nuisance. Charles LaRoux, the old French trapper he'd traveled with for the better part of a year, had advised him to enjoy being liberated from unnecessary grooming, but James had not achieved LaRoux's unself-conscious state of unwash. He had, however, cultivated a dense growth of facial hair, and it occurred to him

now that shaving might be in order. Indian men plucked
what little facial hair they had, and a woman might well be
offended by...

Stray thoughts again. Clearly the woman had not found
him to be offensive. In his attempt to behave in a manner
that he had thought she would consider respectful, he had
refrained from approaching her. But she'd followed him.
Perhaps she was simply curious about him because he was
white. On the other hand, it was quite conceivable that she
was interested in him as a man. He had turned this notion
over in his head many times since he'd met her. Even though
he had not numbered women among his objectives for this
expedition, James had half a mind to exercise his considerable masculine charm and find out whether the latter prospect was true.

He tossed a pan of water on the fire as he came to his feet.
The sound of hoofbeats enjoined the hissing of the coals,
and James jerked his head around. She was coming. His
thoughts entertained no other possibility. She crested the hill
on a small buckskin mare, and James caught himself grinning broadly at the sight of her silhouette etched against the
morning sky. She sat astride the horse with as much grace
as any rider he had ever seen. Her only tack was a blanket
and a strip of leather looped around the horse's lower jaw
for a one-piece bridle and rein.

James quickly tucked his white lawn shirt beneath the
leather belt that held up his buckskin britches, as well as
both of the sheaths for his knife and trowel. His mouth went
dry as he watched the woman draw near. Her face was burnished by early-morning gold, and her white elkskin dress
appeared to be gilded. The yoke was heavily embroidered
with red-and-yellow porcupine quills, and the tin-wrapped
tips of fringe at the bottom of the dress jangled softly as the
pony pranced.

"Hello!" he greeted her in English as she slid down from her mount. He continued in Lakota. "It's good to see you, Kezawin. You must have heard my thoughts this morning."

"You considered coming to our camp on your own, did you not?" Her mare stood ground-tied, as though the rein were invisibly bolted into the grass.

"I thought perhaps you had forgotten about me. May I offer you breakfast? I, myself, have just eaten."

Even though she had eaten, too, she accepted the offer as a friendly gesture and knelt beside the circle of ashes that had been his camp fire. The spit-roasted rabbit he served her was still warm, and she knew she'd been given what would have been his midday meal.

James sat on his heels and stole surreptitious glances at her as she ate. Impolite as it was to watch her, he couldn't help himself. He knew she'd dressed for this occasion, and his Lakota vocabulary had become a jumble in his head. The quillwork on her dress was superlatively crafted. The brightly colored geometric designs were intricately worked into tight, perfectly ordered rows. Her dentalium shell choker and delicate shell earrings glistened as prettily as pearls. She had rouged the center part in her lustrous black braids.

"You look fine this morning," James said, fumbling for the right words. The last thing he wanted to do was embarrass her and drive her away. "Your dress is beautiful. You're a very skilled craftswoman, I see."

"My work is highly prized," she acknowledged without looking up from the food she nibbled on.

"I will know your husband before we are introduced," he said in the way of a man who fished with a baitless hook. "He will be the one who wears the finest shirt."

She held the meat still and spoke quietly. "He wore the finest shirt when I saw him last, James Garrett. If you are wise, you will not speak of him."

"He is dead?"

She nodded.

"How long?" he persisted.

"Seven winters."

"So you live with your father?"

She looked up at him. "I have my own lodge."

He knew how unusual that was, but he didn't question her further on the matter. There was a strange, lighthearted feeling that had come to him with the knowledge that she had no husband, and it was that feeling he would question later, when he had more time.

"Have you spoken to your father about me?" he asked.

"He was pleased to receive the red root plant."

"I found another," he told her. "They do seem to be rare."

Her face brightened with her smile. "It's good that you've come. You are the first white man who comes seeking medicine. My father has discussed this matter with others who have observed your kind. Some said there might not be a wise or holy man among you." He laughed, and she was glad he hadn't taken offense. "The red root plant is a good sign. We've been waiting for such a one as you."

"You knew my name."

She dismissed it with a gesture. "I knew you by the red root plant. Your name meant little to me."

It was difficult to hide his sudden flush of indignation. "Perhaps it means something to your father. You said the Miniconju spoke of me."

"Yes, they did." She finished the meat and cleaned her fingers on the grass. "We were prepared for James Garrett, whom they called a strange but harmless white man. But my father, Lone Bear, wishes to see the bearer of the red root plant." She stood, then added thoughtfully, "For that we had not expected a white man, but the signs are very clear, James Garrett. And I'm happy that you're not a true deer."

"A deer?"

She was not given to explaining herself, James realized. He accepted it as the female prerogative to be totally enigmatic. Without asking more questions, he packed up his gear, distributed it between his packhorse and his saddle horse, and followed her the four or five miles to her camp. As they approached the collection of tipis erected on the high ground above the creek, James saw one sentry standing on top of a hill. He knew there were more whom he would not see unless they wanted to be seen. He was glad he had waited for Kezawin to escort him.

As they approached, the camp came alive with curious eyes. Three young boys chasing one another and leaping over tipi stakes in a game of kick-my-tail-off stopped dead in their tracks and watched the two riders pass. Four young girls paused on their way to the creek, taking a moment to gape and giggle. One whispered to the others, but the old woman who waddled along behind shooed them toward the thicket of wild plum bushes on the creek bank. The girls hurried on, but the old woman stopped to adjust her picking apron and steal a good look at the strange sight for herself before she clucked to her dog and waddled away. James grinned at the sight of the big gray dog, who dragged the triangular travois that was lashed to his back and trotted behind the girls with his tongue lolling. He looked much like the wolf who might be counting the trusting chickens who were headed for the bushes.

Three women peeked over, under and around the willow frame of a meat-drying rack as they arranged strips of raw meat and flicked their hands at persistent flies. Nearby, a child turned for a moment from the baby she was entertaining, whose cradleboard was suspended from the branches of a cottonwood sapling. Even the infant stared.

James could only guess what aspect of his appearance might seem the most peculiar. During the past eighteen months he had traveled with other white men, but he had struck out on his own in search of Lone Bear, the renowned medicine man. He was suddenly acutely aware that he was a minority of one, and he wished he had taken the time to shave.

Kezawin stopped in front of a tipi on the southeastern side of the camp, which numbered more than thirty tipis. James followed her lead and dismounted as a tall lean man with graying braids ducked out of the tipi door. Kezawin took James's reins and introduced him to her father, Lone Bear.

"My daughter will unload your horses and turn them out with the rest, James Garrett. You will be my guest. It has been decided."

James followed Lone Bear and sat next to him on the men's side, the right-hand side of the tipi, which was richly carpeted with the hides of buffalo. Lone Bear sat against a willow backrest, and James was aware of the neat arrangement of Lone Bear's belongings, but he took care not to pointedly survey the man's home. They discussed nothing until they had shared a pipe, and finally Lone Bear said, "I have heard that there are medicine men among your people, but I have not yet seen one for myself. Are you a healer, James Garrett, an interpreter of visions, or do you have other powers?"

"I am what my people call a naturalist." He used the English word because he could think of no equivalent concept in Lakota. "My special interest is in botany—plant life. I collect all species of plants, observe where they grow, how they grow, their cycles, the animals who feed upon them."

Lone Bear nodded as he listened. "A plant-taker, then. Will you take great numbers, like the beaver-takers?"

"I will take only a few," James assured him.

Lone Bear nodded again. "You must be a healer, like my daughter."

James lifted his brow. "Your daughter is a healer? I assumed she was gathering herbs for your use."

"She does sometimes, but more for herself. Kezawin has such power as a healer. Many of the women come to her, and even some men when they have exhausted all other channels."

"But no one spoke of her," James protested. "They all say that it is Lone Bear who is the great shaman of the Hunkpapa."

"I am," Lone Bear said, eschewing false modesty as a waste of time. "But Kezawin's destiny is most unusual, and her ability to find the right leaf or root to drive harm from the body is remarkable."

"I have an interest in observing your uses of plants," James said, purposely avoiding any mention of an interest in Kezawin or her destiny. "In the time I've spent here, I've gained respect for what the shaman does, what he knows."

Lone Bear considered this for a moment and then nodded again. "It is possible that a *naturalist* might understand some things. From your description, your word *naturalist* fits any Lakota, but some, of course, are more observant than others. Have you the patience to learn from us, James Garrett?"

"I've studied for many years, but I believe that you can teach me things that our wise men in the East don't know."

"I can teach you nothing, but there is much you might learn. Do you have a vision? Will these observations you make serve your people in some way?"

James gave the question some thought. He did not doubt his own destiny for a moment, but he wasn't sure the Indian would understand it or appreciate the gravity of it. "I keep a journal," he said finally. "Much like your winter counts, except that I use words instead of pictures. When people read my journal, they can hear everything I say with their eyes. My work will be published so that many people will learn what I have discovered on this journey." He realized that Lone Bear would understand *published* only in the context of the oral tradition of the Lakota *eyápaha*, the one who broadcasts news to the village, but it was the closest word he could use.

"Then your people will all want to come here."

James smiled and shook his head. "I don't think so. Their homes are planted in the ground, like those of the Mandan, the Earth Lodge People, and they have their farms and their families. Their lives are different. They wouldn't like this place."

"Many white men of the French tongue have come to stay. They have married our women and planted their houses in the ground. We trade with them. Most of them cause no trouble."

James made no comment about the French. He owed his facility with the Lakota language to just such a Frenchman, but James was a man of science, and Charles LaRoux was not. *Joie de vivre*, had been the Frenchman's simple goal. No matter what tongue they conversed in, James and LaRoux did not speak the same language.

"I won't cause any trouble, either, Lone Bear. I shall take but a few plants with me when I leave. I've come here just to learn."

"Do you hunt for meat?"

"Only to feed myself. When my aim is bad, as it often is, I go without." James watched the old man weigh his answer, wondering whether he'd just diminished himself in Lone Bear's eyes. He knew the younger men would provide meat in return for the shaman's services, but Lone Bear appeared to be particularly fit for his age. "Do you?"

"I claim choice portions following a hunt, as is my right." Lone Bear tapped the ashes from his pipe into the fire pit, signaling the end of their discussion. "While you are here, you will improve your aim, James Garrett."

"I'll do my best," James promised as he uncrossed his legs and stood to take his leave. "But I tell you quite honestly, hunting is not my sport."

"That is as it should be. We take the life of the four-legged so that we two-legged might have life. This must be marked in your journal, James Garrett. You must teach your people that killing is not a sport." He put his pipe away in its quilled leather case. "Even the French who have lived among us for a long time are misguided in that way. Perhaps there are not enough *naturalists* among you."

James smiled. "We are a rare breed. Many people think men such as I are just a bit crazy."

"You are here because you are crazy. You are *wakan.* That which is mysterious and holy dwells within you." Lone Bear stood to hang his pipe bag on its willow stand. "Build your shelter next to my lodge, James Garrett. My daughter will cook for us both."

"I promise to contribute to her cooking pot whenever I can."

James spent much of the day selecting and trimming the poles to build his lean-to next to Lone Bear's tipi. He covered the frame with oilcloth and willow branches and built a stone fire pit in front of the structure so that he could burn sage to chase away the mosquitoes at night. While he worked, he offered a greeting or a nod at the least to each passerby who stopped to give him a curious once-over. The first man who stopped insisted that James pivot the structure a few degrees so that the entrance faced due east. Because erecting the lodge was woman's work, the man did not offer to lend a hand, but he gave a nod of approval when the change was made, then went about his business.

When the shelter was built and his gear was stashed inside, James gathered soap and shaving equipment and headed for the creek. He trimmed his hair and removed what he could from his face with a pair of scissors, stropped his razor and set about the task of shaving without benefit of a mirror. The first nick in his skin had him grumbling, but by the third he loosed an oath condemning the beard, the razor and the soul of Charles LaRoux. Down on one knee, he rinsed blood-tinged lather from his blade and took an angry swipe at the last of his beard. A sudden peal of laughter nearly caused more bloodletting from James's tender neck. He turned and found Kezawin's eyes bright with amusement.

"Ye gods, woman!" Since the expletive was lost on her in English, he sought more composure in Lakota. "You should know better than to startle a man who has a blade at his throat."

"I have never seen a man hold a knife to his own throat. It's a strange ritual." She took a step closer as she surveyed his face.

"My beard is too thick to pluck hair by hair as the men of the Lakota do." He splashed a handful of water on his face.

Kezawin extended her hand and offered him a small pouch. "When I saw that you were slashing your face a moment ago, I went back to my lodge to bring you this. It will stop the bleeding."

James stood up slowly, pointedly glancing down at his bare chest. In eighteen months he'd gone from pale-skinned scholar to the deeply tanned outdoorsman, and he was not ashamed of his physique, but his parlor etiquette was deeply ingrained, and her laughter made him uncomfortable. "Once again you've caught me off guard."

A man's bare chest was no novelty to Kezawin. She smiled. "A man should always be aware of everything around him, James Garrett. Even when he is busy mutilating his face. Take this."

He used both hands to fold his razor as he looked first a the pouch, then into Kezawin's eyes. "I might have come down here to bathe," he said.

"Not unless you wanted to bathe publicly."

He glanced down at the pouch again. "I cannot see where to apply it."

She stepped close to him and opened the pouch. "Your face must be numb after the scraping if you don't know where you've cut yourself." She took a small amount of clear salve from the pouch and dabbed it on his chin. "I will tell you when to wash your face again. The bleeding will have stopped."

A tangy scent reached his nose. He searched his brain but failed to determine the source of the salve from its smell. "What is it?"

"It is a mixture of herbs with the gum from the yellow bark tree."

"Will you show me this tree?"

"It doesn't grow here," she said. "If you stay with us long enough, I will show you. It is from the hills to the south."

She treated each cut with painstaking deliberation, and he was keenly aware of her warm breath against his neck, the closeness of her body to his bare chest, and her scent, which was a combination of wood smoke and something sweet. He dug his fingers into his palms and reminded himself that he'd asked her to do this for him. Now he didn't quite know what to do with the racy feeling she triggered in him.

"Your father has invited me to stay for a while. I've built my lodge next to his."

"I know."

He cleared his throat. "I don't wish to strain your resources, Kezawin. My hunting prowess is nothing to boast about, but I will make every effort to put fresh meat into your cooking pot."

"That is not why you're here," she told him as she daubed salve on his neck.

"Tell me what you mean," he said quietly. "You seem to have your own ideas about my purpose in being here."

"It may not yet be *your* purpose, James Garrett. I believe you have much to learn before it becomes truly yours." She lowered her hand from his neck, but she took only half a step backward. "Will you scrape the hair from your chest, as well?" she asked as she studied him boldly.

"Would that improve my appearance?"

She glanced up quickly and smiled. "Your face is much improved, James Garrett. It's a handsome face after all."

"After all the hair is scraped away?" He chuckled as he rubbed his hand over his smooth jaw. "Did you expect me to look like a plucked goose?" She laughed and shook her head. "I would have you call me James."

"I have said it wrong? James Garrett," she said carefully.

"No, just James. Garrett is my family name. James is *my* name. It's what you should call me."

"James," she repeated. "You have stopped bleeding, James. You may wash—"

With one cautious finger he touched the rows of quill work on her shoulder. "What is this purpose you have in mind for me, Kezawin? What must I learn?"

"That it is neither my purpose for you, nor yours for yourself that will—"

"You speak in riddles, when the plain truth is that you don't want to back away any more than I do." One corner of his mouth drew up in a teasing smile. "What is this purpose you speak of?"

She had not been touched by the strong hands of a man in a very long time, and this man's hands rested easily on her shoulders. He was too ignorant to have it be otherwise, and yet it felt good, and she looked into his eyes and welcomed his ignorance for the moment. To him, she was simply a woman, and he was not afraid to be close to her in the way of a man who is drawn by instinct to a woman. Kezawin banished all thoughts and let the woman in her be drawn to the man, but just for this moment.

He slid his hands over her shoulders and down her arms, touching soft elk hide, then warm woman's skin. His palms tingled with the contact. "I don't know the word, Kezawin," he said quietly, and he cupped her face in his hand as he spoke low, his voice softly persuasive. "But what I'm going to do won't hurt you. It works best if you close your eyes."

She made no move to touch him, but she did not move away. He kissed her tentatively, touching his lips to the corner of her mouth and then, lightly, the middle. She lifted her chin, and he whispered again, "Close your eyes, Kezawin." He moistened his lips and slid them over the fullness of hers, hardly moving, hardly pressing until her lips parted for him. His heart leaped in his chest, and he slanted his mouth across hers and gave in to the need to fully taste her mouth.

When he ended the kiss, he looked down at her, expecting the willingness he'd tasted on her lips to be reflected in her eyes. Her hot dark stare startled him, and although she still had not laid hands on him except to apply a healing salve, he felt as though she held him in the grip of her small hands and shook him hard. He could not have mistaken her response so completely, he told himself. He was certain she had welcomed his kiss. And then unexpectedly the heat in her eyes vanished, and she laughed.

"You find that so amusing?" he demanded. James Garrett was no inexperienced, fumbling boy, and no woman had ever sneered at his advances. "Forgive me, but I could have sworn the invitation was there."

"You are a foolish man," she said with a hint of regret in her voice. "It is I who do not wish to harm you, and yet you stand here, filling your chest like the courting grouse, daring me to strike you down."

"Strike me down?" It was his turn to laugh. "You would kill me for kissing you?"

He used the English word because he had not learned to court a woman in Lakota, but she understood him. Already they had taken a step beyond words, and the danger in that step frightened her. "I would not want to see you dead, James. You must not touch me as a man might touch a woman."

His brow drew down in his confusion. "I did not force myself on you in any way, Kezawin. Nor would I. From the first, when you came upon me by the creek, you have been—" He scowled as he mentally recounted each flirtation. "What kind of woman are you?"

"I am called Double Woman Dreamer," she told him, and she waited for him to shrink back. When he did not, she took it as another sign of his ignorance. "I have dreamed of the Double Woman, the one who is at once a woman and a deer. I have the power to heal."

"So your father told me."

"And did he tell you about the dark side of my power?" James shook his head slowly. "Two men lay dead because of me. Both my husband and my brother. The power of the Double Woman can destroy a man's medicine."

"I have no medicine, Kezawin. I'm a scientist. You'll not dream me dead." He pointed to the sheath on her belt. "Unless you plunge that knife into my heart, you'll not—"

"My dream told me that you would come, James. Our destinies are entwined. You are the bearer of the red root plant. But there are two sides, like the faces of the Double Woman, and you must take care not to touch me even . . . even if I would seem to want you to. I would need no knife to kill you."

Her dark eyes told him that she did not doubt the truth of what she said, and though he understood none of it, her conviction was unnerving to him.

Chapter Two

The crack of rifle fire shattered the peace in the piny woods. The buck's legs buckled as the sound reverberated in the hills, and a hearty "Eee-yahhh!" chased the echoing shot with ecstatic ripples. As often as not James's gunfire had signaled the flight of his prey rather than its fall, but here was a true shot and a clean kill. He wondered what kind of reception this offering would earn him from Kezawin.

Lone Bear would accept his guest's hunting success the same way he did all the failures, offering neither praise nor censure. Lone Bear's gods were credited with providing the meat whenever James made a kill, and when James returned from his occasional hunting forays empty-handed, Lone Bear found no fault with his efforts. But he was certain he had noticed a glint of pride in Kezawin's eyes whenever he'd presented her with a gutted carcass to butcher.

Gutting the carcass was far from his favorite task. He dropped to his knees beside his kill, lashed its back hooves together and prepared to hoist it over a tree limb, quietly explaining to it all the while that the job was as unpleasant for him as it was for the dead animal and that he could do just as well on a diet of dandelion greens and wood sorrel if it were not for the carnivorous appetite of his host.

Kezawin stood quietly behind a stand of pine samplings and waited for James to finish praying in his native English. Clearly he understood the need for pardon and praise when the deer's life was taken to nourish the human body. He was an unusual white man, to be sure, but then, her vision had shown her how unusual he would be. The white deer was rare, indeed. When the praying had stopped, she stepped away from her cover.

"Will you share the fresh liver from your kill with me, that we may both be made strong by it?"

Clutching his broad-bladed knife, he whirled at the sound of her voice, the surprise instantly doubling his pulse rate. "Where did you come from?" he demanded.

She lifted the strap of her collection pouch over her head. "I have some things to show you after we feast."

"Feast?" He glanced down at the carcass. Since he had always done his hunting on his own, he had made a practice of disposing of the offal, but he knew that a Lakota hunter would consume the raw liver on the spot. The idea was not an appealing one.

"Your medicine grows stronger every day, James." She took the knife from his hand and rescued the choice red organ. "As does mine. Your deer brother would share his power with us now." She sliced a portion of the liver and handed it to him before cutting some for herself.

The meat dangled from his fingers, limp and dripping with blood. He watched Kezawin eat hers, and it struck him that the process appeared no more indelicate than slipping a slithery oyster from the shell to the mouth. He thought he might manage it if he thought no more about it and did it quickly. He accomplished the haste but not the interruption of thought, and in a moment he was bolting from her sight. The sound of her laughter did nothing to quiet his rebellious stomach.

When she brought the water bag she'd taken from his saddle, she found him leaning against a tree. His face had lost its color, and she thought it a shame that he couldn't finish the succulent liver, which would restore him. She offered the bottle with a smile, and he snatched it rudely.

"I gave it a try, Kezawin. How could you laugh at me like that?"

"You ate it so quickly," she said, imitating the motion. "And it returned just as quickly. Were you offended because a woman had not waited to eat her portion until you had finished?"

"I was offended because it was raw!" He swished some water around in his mouth and spat. "You made it look better than it tastes."

"Since you never bring us the heart or the liver of your kill, naturally I assumed you were accustomed to consuming them on the hunt."

"Naturally." He tipped the water bag to his mouth again, but the taste of blood lingered. "I was actually beginning to warm up to the sport, but this leaves something of an unpleasant taste in my mouth and an unsettled feeling in my stomach." He laid a hand over his flat belly and shook his head.

"This will help."

James flinched at the sprig of wild greenery Kezawin held up to his mouth.

"But you must chew it slowly and not wolf it down," she warned as he eyed the greens uncertainly and then glanced at her.

She smiled reassuringly, and he found that the temptation to eat from her hand was irresistible. He nibbled cautiously.

Once again she was reminded of the shy animal who had foretold this man's coming, and she stood still and let him take what he would until his lips brushed against her fingers. His cool blue eyes became soft and warm when they met hers. Her heart went out to him even as she told herself it would have to a child who trusted because he was ignorant of danger.

"What am I eating?" he asked, chewing slowly as she had instructed.

"We call it bee plant. It grows in the mountains to the west, but this is something I wanted to show you. I found some nearby." She took another sprig from her pouch and handed it to him.

"Is it unusual to find this plant growing in this area?"

"It is." She produced another specimen from the bag. "I believe this one is not yet in your collection, either."

His face brightened as he examined the two botanical samples. "I must see the habitat," he said eagerly. "These hills are a veritable treasure cache, Kezawin." He flashed her a smile. "A gold mine for the likes of you and me, fellow naturalists that we are."

She questioned his use of an English phrase. "Gold mine?"

"Just an expression," he said with a shrug. "A place that yields up treasures such as these. Of course, Lewis and Clark described many new species in the journals they kept when they made their journey through here twenty years ago, but their task was more general, and they missed these wonderful mountains."

"*Paha Sapa* is a holy place. Its treasures, as you call them, are many. That's why we come here every summer."

"Show me where you found these," James insisted.

She shook her head and offered up a coy smile. "I have meat to butcher now. Tomorrow I will take you there."

James scowled at the carcass that hung by its legs from a tree. "Infernal horned beast," he grumbled. "Such a nuisance, this meat-making."

"I heard your victory cry when you hit the mark with your noisy rifle." Her dark eyes twinkled, and James saw that inkling of pride in them again. "I think there's a hunter in you, James Garrett."

Kezawin kept her promise the following afternoon and many days after that, leading James to hilltops and stream banks in a continually fruitful quest for botanical discovery. Occasionally Lone Bear joined them, but as often as not he declined his daughter's invitation, and James and Kezawin pursued their mutual interest alone. James found each new foray to be fascinating, but his guide was becoming even more so.

She had a tender regard for every plant they uprooted and an insatiable curiosity about every note he made about them in his journals. He explained the way his science called for grouping every species into classes for the purpose of study, and he showed her the characteristics by which they were deemed related. The concept that plants came in families made perfect sense to her. Her people also grouped themselves into clans, or *tiospaye*. She needed no journal to keep track of what he told her; she repeated his explanations back to him, and he noticed that she began arranging her own collection as neatly classed botanical bunches, keeping, as she said, families together. During his days as a laboratory assistant at Harvard, he'd never had a more enthusiastic pupil.

She had wandered away from him one afternoon as they foraged on foot in the pine-covered hills the people called *Paha Sapa* because they appeared, from a distance, to be black. A sudden thunderstorm took him by surprise, and by the time he ducked under a protective rocky outcropping, he was soaked. He waited, thinking surely Kezawin would return to the vicinity where she'd left him, but the moments slid past like the falling rain, and she did not come.

James began to worry. Perhaps she had stumbled into a bear's den, or perhaps she'd simply stumbled, fallen and now lay twisted and helpless on the rocks somewhere. He left his shelter and followed the path she had taken when he'd last seen her. In the pouring rain he called her name. The echo of his own voice answered. Panic seized him, and he began to run. The soles of his moccasins slipped in the muddy carpet of fallen pine needles, but he pressed on, raising his voice again and again against the thunder. *Something's happened. Something's happened.* His heart pounded with unreasoning fear, and his shouts became hoarse as his throat tightened. "Kez-ahhh-winnn!"

"James!"

He stopped, his chest heaving as he searched the rain-drenched woods and wondered whether he was hearing things. "Kezawin, where are you?"

"I'm here!" Her face appeared amid the dense boughs of a huge sheltering pine. "You're getting wet, you crazy man! Come inside."

Her laughter heated his blood, turning cold fear to hot anger as he plowed his way through knee-high saplings and dove into her shelter, a dry cocoon in which she'd managed to build a small, nearly smokeless fire. He found her crouching under the natural lean-to where there had been an attrition of a few lower branches and the higher ones swooped down to form a small den. She watched him crawl in while she hugged her knees and unleashed that free and infuriating laugh of hers. James snatched her up by her shoulders and shook her once. Her laughter died, and she gazed up at him, startled by his blazing eyes. His face was so close to hers that water dripped from his hair and fell on her nose, her cheek, into her eye. She didn't blink.

"Woman, you will never again laugh at me," he warned, his voice hoarse from shouting. "I have suffered this indignity long enough, and I will tolerate no more of it. You are willful and brazen. You fly in the face of your own conventions. Women of your kind do not conduct themselves in this unseemly fashion, and yet you—"

"Women of my kind?" she asked calmly. "What do you know about women of my kind, James? Your running around in the rain amuses me. It makes me laugh."

"My running around in the rain!" he bellowed, giving her shoulders another quick shake. "I couldn't find you. I called out time and time again, and when you didn't answer, I feared for your safety, Kezawin."

"My safety?" She resented the strong hold he had on her shoulders, but the look in his eyes did not threaten her. To her amazement, she saw that the anger had become remembered fear. "But it's only rain, James. I thought you would find shelter for yourself." Tenderly she touched his cheek and repeated, "It's only rain."

He peered at her in the dim light, and the haze in his mind began to dissipate. The tension went out of his shoulders as he relaxed his grip on hers. She was safe, after all, and untouched by the rain other than the drops he'd brought her. He thought he must look quite foolish at the moment, while Kezawin, with her dark eyes shining up at him, was a beautiful sight. He drew back and tried to push the notion of her beauty out of his mind as he leaned his back against the trunk of the tree. He was thoroughly uncomfortable.

"Are you afraid of the rain, James?"

He tried to laugh it off as he shook his head, but she touched the shirtsleeve that was plastered to his arm, and he stopped laughing. "My mother died in the rain." The words were out before he'd even thought about them, and when he heard them, he wanted to take them back. "She was quite ill, you see, and she wandered outside in the rain. There was no one looking after her." He shrugged. "She would have died anyway, as sick as she was, but someone should have been with her."

"You have not put aside your grief, and this death haunts you." She moved away slightly, as though the haunting might somehow touch her, too. "I see that you have yet to make your peace with the one whom you blame for not being with her. Is it yourself, James?"

He turned his attention to the small fire pit and the low-burning flames, and he shook his head. "I was just a boy, and I was just as sick as she was. My father left us in the care of his—the people who worked for him. Some of them became ill, too. Others fled."

"Then I see that you must make peace with your father before you can put aside your grief. Is it this bad feeling for your father that drives you so far from your people?"

"Drives me?" James scowled as he ruffled his hair with his fingers and flicked a shower of droplets in all directions. "Nothing drives me. I'm here because the Boston Society of Naturalists has agreed to publish my work, and my sponsor, Ezra Breckenridge, agreed to pay the expenses for this expedition."

The confusion he saw in her eyes gave him a sense of satisfaction. She had overstepped her bounds with all her speculation, and, of course, what did she really know? The very word *society* was difficult to translate into something she might understand. He used *akicita*, which referred to the warrior groups to which Lakota men belonged, but the concept was hardly comparable to the Society of Naturalists, a group of highly educated men. Even the concept of a fraternity did not relate to Kezawin, who was, after all, a woman. Reassured by the notion that he had elevated the conversation well above her head, James smiled and told himself there would be no more slips of the tongue unless, in these cozy quarters, they were literal.

"Boston is part of a place called Massachusetts, which is an Indian word, and it is what we call the place where I live," he explained after he had concluded it might be the one thing she would understand of all that he'd said.

"And where your father lives?"

"No. My father lives in Virginia, which is far away from Massachusetts."

"And so these others you spoke of sent you here," Kezawin said. "Why? Are the plants in Massachusetts not as good as those that grow here?"

He laughed. "Some are the very same, but many are different. The Society simply wants to know more about the West and all that grows here."

"And you are their scout?"

"No, Kezawin, I'm a scientist. I need to know, too, because I . . . I just need to know, that's all." His patient smile hinted at his conviction that few people understood that need. "I also need to publish my work, but I am a poor scholar who has no money of his own to accomplish these things, and I therefore depend on the financial backing of men like Ezra Breckenridge. But I'm sure none of this makes any sense to you."

"I understand that what you're telling me has little to do with why you are here." Her smile was equally patient. "Except that you need to know. That, I believe, is important to you. And you attend to some things very well. Much better than other white men."

The compliment warmed his smile. "You say I know nothing of Lakota women. What do you know of white men?"

"I know that most of them are poor observers, but not you." She cocked her head to one side and looked at him curiously. "Why did you fear for my safety, James?"

"I told you why. I told you more than I intended to tell you. Quite obviously it was a foolish notion I had that a man is responsible for a woman's safety. But you—" With a gesture he indicated their dry, comfortable niche in a world turned stormy. The rain fell steadily all around them, but the thick pine thatch eliminated all but an occasional trickle. "You were well able to take care of yourself. Who would have thought to find such a shelter in a tree?"

"A porcupine, perhaps." A man and a woman, Kezawin heard him say. She was a woman no man dared take responsibility for, but he spoke of them as man and woman. Unthinkable. Recklessly Kezawin savored the thought, promising herself that she would put it aside in a moment. "Tell me what you feared," she said quietly.

His shoulders quivered slightly, whether from chills or his active imagination, he was unsure. "You might have slipped and fallen, or some wild animal might have—"

She reached out slowly, and for one sweet moment, he thought she might embrace him. Her eyes suggested it, but her hands went to the buttons on his shirt. "You must let the fire dry this," she said, "and warm your skin."

Had any other woman made the suggestion, he would have had a ready response. This was a woman who kept him guessing, and that idea brought a slow smile to James's lips. Guessing could be fun, too. She unbuttoned his shirt, her small hands slow but sure, and when she reached his belt, he leaned back. His smile broadened. Undaunted, she pulled the shirt free of his pants and peeled it back from his shoulders. The dusting of light hair across his chest was a curiosity, and she rested her hands in the middle of it, testing its texture.

"Now what happens, Kezawin?" She glanced up and saw a man's look in his eyes. "If I touch you, will you laugh in my face as you so often do?" He touched her cheek with the tips of his fingers. Her lips parted as she lifted her chin, but she said nothing. He ran his fingertips over the side of her neck and continued downward, over the neckline of her elkskin dress.

"Not yet amused?" he asked in a throaty tone as he sat up slowly. "Your dress is not wet. I have no excuse to touch you as you touched me." Just the tips of his fingers. Just the slightest pressure and the slowest descent. Skin against skin against skin. His touch made her nipple tighten. "There's my excuse," he whispered, and he covered her mouth with his.

Her fingers curled in his chest hair, and she opened her mouth to drink deeply of his kiss. She responded only as a woman, wanting what a woman wanted, feeling the delicate need, like the quick flutter of a brightly colored wing. His way was different, but it had been so long since a man had touched her, and that man had been as young and inexperienced as she. Now here was warmth sparked by something different, and yet not different. It was still man and woman, just as he had said. But when he groaned in the way of a man whose needs would soon transcend his reason, Kezawin knew the moment had to be over for them.

He made no move to draw apart, but he straightened and rested against the trunk of the tree, tipped his head back and gave her a heavy-lidded stare. She put his shirt over a branch and added dry tinder to her fire. There was no room for either of them to move about and no way to distance themselves mentally from each other. The awareness of breath, flesh and heat was tangible, and the attraction between them had redoubled itself with a kiss.

"Perhaps it's time I knew more about this kind of woman you say you are, Kezawin," he said quietly. "Are you the kind who makes a man crazy with her games?"

"That would not affect you, James." Her laugh was brief and guarded. "You are crazy already."

"I believe you are one of the few people, Indian or white, who knows that isn't true."

"I know you to be *wakan*," she reminded him. "That much I know."

He waved the notion of holiness away with his hand. "Why do you tease me, Kezawin? You spend a great deal of time with me, and I know you find it pleasant to...to..." He waved his hand again, as though the words he wanted might be somewhere in the air. Finally he looked at her straight and hard. "Why do you laugh at me? No, why do you laugh the *way* you do? The other women are... different. Demure. *Feminine.* I don't know," he said, dropping his hand in exasperation. "It's as though you have a secret—a grand joke that none of the rest of us knows anything about."

Sitting with her legs tucked under her, she scooted closer, her dark eyes anxious. "Did I look different when you kissed me, James? Just before or just after, did you see anything change in my face?" Even as he shook his head slowly, she waved her hand above the part in her hair. "Perhaps on my head?"

"No. Nothing but a woman's eyes, a woman's mouth."

"Good. That's good."

A woman's eyes, he thought as he sought to plumb their depths for whatever this secret might be. They were soft and wary, like the eyes of a doe, but set in the smooth-skinned, fine-boned face of a woman. "What else could I expect to see?"

"I am Double Woman Dreamer." Her voice became hollow as she said the name. "In a dream I have seen the Double Woman, who is able to change herself from woman to deer and back again. I am not like other women. Laughter comes to me, and I do not try to control it. My quillwork is unsurpassed. I have the power to heal."

"Those are wonderful gifts, Kezawin. Laughter, creativity and a healing touch, all residing in one lovely woman." He saw that none of this comforted her, and he had a disturbing thought. "Is this why you never seem to be included when the women gather in groups for quilling or picking fruit or butchering? Are they jealous of your skills?"

Kezawin laughed freely once again. "Suspicious, perhaps. Wary, I would say. Never jealous."

"I think you're wrong. I've seen how much is offered for your quillwork. I've seen the women come to your lodge and bring their children for whatever it is you do to alleviate their aches and pains. And I've seen the way they clear a path for you when you pass by." He touched her cheek. "I think you're very lonely, Kezawin. I believe I am your only friend."

"The Double Woman Dreamer has no friends," she said, avoiding his eyes. "I dreamed that you would come and that we would help one another. You follow a road that lies next to mine."

"We are special friends, then. A society of two." He smiled at the notion that she thought she had dreamed of him before she ever saw him. It was an endearing fantasy. "The naturalist and the medicine woman. It's a poetic alliance, I think."

She smiled, her eyes brightening at the thought that she might at last belong to a group, however small. "We must have a name for our society," she decided. "What did you call the ones who sent you here? The society of the Massachusetts place."

James laughed, pleased with the fact that she'd remembered the name of his home. "The Boston Society of Naturalists, which is hardly as imaginative as your *akicita* names, the Kit Foxes, the Brave Hearts and the others."

"Ours will have a secret name so that no one can steal its power. But I have not heard you sing of this alliance. Have you done so?"

He had used the Lakota word for *song* as a close approximation for *poetic*, and her response brought more meaning to the remark. He smiled warmly. "I should sing like a bird if only you would stop leading me this merry chase."

"Chase?"

"At least give me more than one kiss at a time."

She glanced away.

"I would stand with you before your father's lodge and kiss you beneath a courting robe if that would please you more," he offered.

"Your touch brings me pleasure, James. I will not deny it. I have, for so long, taken care not to desire any man because I would not take the form of the deer woman. I will never let her use me that way—not if I can help it—and if I have led a chase, as you say, then it is possible she may have—" She clutched her breast suddenly and looked at him with dread. "She may have slipped inside me, or I may have—"

"Kezawin, that's nonsense," James insisted, half-laughing. "Were I to find myself suddenly kissing the lips of a deer, I assure you I would remove myself from the embrace."

"You would be dead," she said without emotion. "It is not a risk a wise man would take."

"But if you have dreamed of me—"

"We are to share our knowledge, James, and nothing more than that. And perhaps it is true that you are to be my only friend."

"I don't think I would mind that," James said with a smile.

It was a season of plenty for Lone Bear's people. Prairie fires the preceding fall had burned off much old grass, and after plentiful spring rains, a thick new green carpet covered the hills and plains. Great herds of buffalo grazed the land contentedly, moving at their leisure, and the people were never far behind. A campsite might serve them for a week or a fortnight by James's count, and then one morning they would be on the move again, lodges struck and travois loaded within less than an hour of the singing of the announcement that it was time to move on.

When the signal came, Garrett was caught up in the excitement of being mobile again. A wave of restless energy seemed to flow through the camp as each person tackled his assigned tasks. No discussion was necessary. The plans had been made by the *wakincuzas*, the ones who decide, and an official leader had been chosen from among the warrior societies. For the rest of the people, the destination was a matter of trust, and they enjoyed the anticipation. They might be headed for a site they had used in summers past, or maybe the scouts had found a new variation of an old theme—a place where water, grazing, firewood and windbreak were all in good supply. For the Lakota, the land traveled over was as much a part of being home as the encampment was, and James Garrett found himself absorbed with the love of changing scenery.

It had taken some adjustment. Before joining Lone Bear's band, James had traveled with LaRoux, the Frenchman, and sometimes with two or three of LaRoux's trapper

friends. They had moved from camp to camp as their fancy
and the friendliness of the Indian people permitted. Now he
followed the rules of the band, some of which he learned the
hard way. The most difficult requirement was that everyone stay within the bounds of the march. Behind the scouts
the *wakincuzas* marched at the front, and the police surrounded the people on the sides and at the rear. No one fell
behind, and no one wandered off to hunt, not even for botanical specimens. When James threatened to break the
rules, Kezawin warned him that the *akicita* would be forced
to destroy all of his belongings, including his collection and
his journals.

Once he accepted the rules, he found that there was much
individual freedom to be enjoyed. When the band was on
the move, they would make several stops during the day and
camp for the night on ground that never failed to yield
something worthy of the naturalist's inspection.

Even more interesting than the discoveries he was making about the land were his observations of Kezawin's work.
He had begun to regard it as Kezawin's calling because, although in his opinion it had no scientific basis, what she did
seemed to be effective. Her herbal medicines were used to
treat wounds, animal bites, festering cankers, internal
complaints and the infirmities of the aged. Occasionally a
woman would even bring a horse or a dog for her to treat.
Even though he was not privy to her consultations, James
kept an eye out for improvement in Kezawin's patients, and,
more often than not, what he saw amazed him. He had little faith in medical doctors, who, among other shortcom-
ings, had failed his mother, and who generally had little to
offer for a wounded limb other than the suggestion that it
be lopped off. The notion that Kezawin's healing skill was
bestowed by a dream was one he regarded as utter non-

sense, but his observations of the results of her remarkable work began filling his journals.

The journey seemed circuitous at times—west, then north, then east. It took them from the hills through stretches of prairie to the foot of a range of high mountains and back to prairie again. One landmark that James found most impressive was a rocky tower that seemed to have thrust itself from the ground in some long-past volcanic upheaval. Its steep sides were deeply grooved as though some demon in the earth had clawed at the mass as it escaped the underworld and shoved its way toward the sky. The band made camp within view of this monolith, and James could barely contain his excitement at the prospect of exploring the area.

"It has many names," Kezawin explained as they approached the wooded base of the structure. "Some call it the Bear's Lodge. We call it *Tiipaśotka Wakanśica*, The Tower of the Bad God."

"A fitting name," James said as he tipped his head back to watch a cloud sail past the soaring pillar. The ancient Greeks would have coveted its fluted symmetry, he thought. "Are you afraid of it?"

"It's a holy place," she said. "We regard it with respect. We shall take nothing from the ground here."

"But we might find something—"

"Nothing we can't find elsewhere. It is not a matter of fear, James. It is a matter of showing respect."

"Is there a way up to the top?"

"The falcon has a way," she said with a laugh.

"Perhaps something wonderful grows up there." Pebbles skittered under his moccasins as he sidestepped a scrub pine and scanned the summit. "There might be something magical up there—something that would give me power over the deer woman's curse."

"It's not a curse as long as you use the proper caution." A smile danced in Kezawin's eyes as she repeated, "It is a matter of showing the proper respect."

"I've known few women who commanded quite the level of respect from men that you do, dear Kezawin. Are you sure there isn't some small measure of fear involved?"

"Not on your part, certainly." She swept her hand in the air to dramatize the tower's height. "Go ahead, James Garrett. Scale *Tiipaśotka Wakanśica* and count your coup. Bring the magic down from the top."

"There's a way," he said as he looked up. "One could find a way with the proper tools and enough ambition."

"We will go to *Mahto Sapa*, Bear Butte, which is east of here. That one you can climb, and there, perhaps, you will seek your vision. I think this ambition of yours lives in the absence of vision."

"I think they're one and the same." He put his arm around her as they walked. It was an intimacy she had come to permit and one he had come to enjoy because of the comfortable closeness it afforded them. "In my world the men would be afraid of you, too, simply because you are too smart. I'm going to miss you."

James had often spoken of continuing his life in that distant place he called Massachusetts, but for Kezawin the idea of his future there was a distant thing, as well. His mention of leaving was another matter. In her world, the people moved when it was a good day to move, and that was the day they spoke of it.

"You are leaving now?" she asked.

"No, but soon I'll have to. I don't want to get snowed in along the way."

"You'll need meat."

"I have yet to bag a buffalo. Before I leave, I'd like to do that." He pushed a low-hanging branch clear of both their faces and smiled down at her as they walked together. "I would like to bring you a buffalo."

"Then you must hunt for one." The smile she returned was full of mischief. "And if you cut out the heart and eat it before his blood has cooled, then you will gain the strength of the—"

"Arghh!" he groaned as he bent down and scooped her off the ground. Laughing, he bounced her a couple of times, hefting her slight weight. "Do I have to pass another of your bloody tests to prove my strength? What about this?" He tossed her up again. "I think I shall scale this rock with you on my back to prove that I have all the strength of the buffalo bull. How would that be?"

Kezawin laughed along with him. "If you don't want the best parts of the carcass, bring them to me. Better yet, I shall go with you."

"What? And scare the game with that impudent laugh of yours?"

"Not at all," she protested with a toss of her head. "I shall see that you don't catch sight of some new bloom and lose the trail."

"Oh, ho," he declared with mock solemnity. "The magic lady has a practical side. Food first, flowers for the potions later. Let's try it, shall we?" He nodded toward the top of the tower. "They say we're both *wakan*, touched by the gods. Let's put ourselves to the test. Perhaps we can fly."

Her eyes followed the direction of his gaze. The strange grooves seemed to pull the spirit upward with the promise of the chance to soar. "It's a beautiful thought, but that is not to be our test," she told him.

He lowered her moccasined feet to the ground slowly. Her body slid against his, and he knew what his test would be. He breathed deeply of the scented oil she used on her braids. It was one of the many things about her that had once seemed strange, even distasteful, but now gave him pause only to think, ah, yes, the sweet smell of her hair.

She had become an exotic fantasy, the more desirable because he could touch her but he could not move her. Her will was as strong as his, and her mind—could it be?—just as quick. In a richly appointed parlor or on a polished ballroom floor his tongue was as artful as any man's, but standing there beneath the wide blue sky in the shadow of *Tiipaśotka Wakanśica*, a piece of earth that stood in stark contrast to its surroundings, he had told a woman that he would miss her when he left. He had used no art—a startling slip that left him feeling unarmed, which was no way to face a test.

They stood close. Kezawin had not taken her hands from his upper arms, and James had not moved his from her back. It was in his mind to try to steal another kiss and see how much pleasure she would allow herself before her superstitions came back to haunt her, when he noticed that something at his back had caught her eye. She raised a wide-eyed signal that he was to turn cautiously.

An albino buck returned their stares. For a moment the three were rendered motionless by a delicate balance of wonder and fear that bound them hypnotically together. The late-afternoon sun filtered through the pale green leaves of a stand of cottonwoods and created a mottling of shadows on the deer's white back. As he lifted his head and twitched his nostrils high in the air, one garnet eye glinted in the sunlight. While they could no more look away from the creature than they could draw breath, James and Kezawin linked hands and let the electricity in the air flow between their bodies until the buck turned and darted back into the trees.

Kezawin glanced down at their hands and then up at James. His eyes reflected her own awe. "You saw him, too?"

"Magnificent," he replied, his voice hoarse with wonder. "Celestial. A rare sight, truly. I have never—" He frowned at her when he caught that familiar haunted look in her eye. "That was a buck, Kezawin. It could not have been your deer woman."

"But I have dreamed of him, too," she said quickly. "It was he who first brought the red root plant. And then you came."

James looked back at the spot where the albino had disappeared into the trees. "You're saying the white deer was my harbinger, then."

She knew he didn't appreciate the power of her dream, and even though he had told her on more than one occasion that the *wakan*, the realm of mystery and holiness, was no mystery to him, she knew that he really did not understand. No matter how simply she might try to explain her *śicun*, her spiritual guardian, James was not yet open to the concept. Yet the white deer had brought him to her, and now that he spoke of leaving, the white deer showed himself to James. What was the meaning?

"I knew you when I saw you," she told him. "We shared something immediately, and there's more to be shared. Not," she added quickly, "as man and woman but as—"

"Colleagues," he supplied in English, but the only Lakota word he could use was, "*Kolas*. Friends. Friends of the plants and—" he gestured in the direction of the buck's retreat "—friends of the white deer."

Kezawin brightened. "Yes. Friends of the White Deer. That will be our secret name. I've learned much from you, James."

"There's more I would learn from you before I leave. Would you permit me to watch you administer your medicine?" He saw that the suggestion was alarming to her. "To the children, perhaps. Let me see how you use the herbs we've collected. Let me make notes. It would add a new dimension to my work. My people would learn a new respect for—"

"My medicine might not work for them. It might not even work for you. You would be required to prepare yourself."

"I'll do whatever you ask. I'll take part in the ceremonies, or whatever you say. Perhaps your father will allow me to observe his medicine if he sees that you trust me."

"If my father will perform *inipi* with you, you will be purified in the sweat lodge. Then you may learn of my medicine. As for my father...as I told you, you are more observant than most white men."

Again the compliment warmed his smile.

Chapter Three

Thunder Shield often watched Double Woman Dreamer, often admired her, but always from a safe distance. It was one thing to stand aside while her father claimed a portion of meat from his kill, as was their right, or to stand beside his wife, Red Calf Woman, when she offered a pony for Double Woman Dreamer's healing for their daughter. It was quite another to loaf in the shade and watch the way her dress hitched up a little on her hip when she reached to drape a filet of venison over the highest pole of her drying rack. Noticing the curve of her ankles and the sleek shape of her calf and taking pleasure in the way his body yearned as he watched was deliciously unsafe. Such a pastime could only be indulged from a distance, for this was Double Woman Dreamer, whose looks could kill a man.

She was his younger brother's widow, and if Thunder Shield had been foolhardy enough, he could have claimed her for his second wife. Red Calf Woman was not as industrious as some, and she would be glad for the help. She had mentioned more than once in recent months that her own sister, Walks Slow, was already nineteen winters and without a husband. She was without a husband for good reason, for her hips were as broad as a man's shoulders, and she never seemed to have her wits about her. She was far from Thunder Shield's choice for a second wife.

He scratched his bare back against the bark of a cottonwood tree and considered the woman who would have been his choice for a first wife if only he had waited a couple of years in choosing. In that time Kezawin had become such a beauty that his younger brother, Iron Shell, had competed long and hard to win her favor. Even though she bore him no children, Iron Shell was the happiest of married men for three years. And then she had become Double Woman Dreamer. Iron Shell had been advised to leave her, but he would have none of any man's warnings against his wife, and he had paid the supreme price. Her power had been too strong for the young warrior. Not long after his wife had had her vision, Iron Shell was killed on a horse raid among the Pawnee. Double Woman Dreamer's brother had fallen in the same raid. There was no mistaking the measure of her power.

Neither could a man ignore her beauty, which became a stronger lure as the years passed. More than one man had thrown caution to the wind and tried to court her. It was not uncommon for one who had dreamed of the deer woman to defy the tenets of Lakota propriety and become openly promiscuous. Although Double Woman Dreamer lived as no other woman lived, alone in her lodge, and acquired a reputation for her healing power and her unsettling laughter, there had been no gossip. No man claimed intimate knowledge of her, and no woman had seen any sign. The people were inclined to accept her friendship with the white plant-taker as part of the mystery of two who were surely *wakan*.

Thunder Shield was not. It turned his stomach sour to see her drying the meat of the white man's kill next to the darkening strips from the flank of buffalo meat that Lone Bear had claimed from Thunder Shield. The white man had brought down nothing larger than a deer, and for that he used a rifle. Thunder Shield doubted that James had the skill to hit the mark with a lance. And yet this puny offering of venison seemed to please the woman.

What was worse, Thunder Shield had, on occasion, chanced to observe the two of them foraging for all manner of plants. The white man showed no respect for himself as he groveled in the ground, even stooping to the point of gathering wild turnips and plums like a woman. When Double Woman Dreamer laughed that unsuitable laugh of hers, the white man hadn't the decency to be embarrassed for her. Often he laughed with her. Thunder Shield had never seen them touch each other, so he could not accuse them publicly, but he wasn't certain this James Garrett was truly *wakan*, and his blood grew hot when he thought of what might be between them. Thunder Shield was as brave as any man, and he dared take no more pleasure in her than he did at this moment. If James wasn't crazy, then he must have been ignorant.

Blood that was already hot began to simmer when Garrett appeared. Thunder Shield strained to hear the exchange of words as the tall white man offered Double Woman Dreamer a handful of wildflowers and some remark about finding the blooms without losing his way. Thunder Shield took her laughter as a sign that the gesture seemed as foolish to her as it looked to him, but then she praised Garrett's "tracking skills" and offered him food. Before he had given his action sufficient thought, Thunder Shield pushed away from the tree trunk and emerged from the river bottom thicket, approaching the couple.

"Ho, Garrett! One might take you for a brother to the buffalo. You do so much grazing."

James knew the stocky man as one who had an eye for Kezawin. Thunder Shield's hungry looks were hardly subtle, even when his wife was standing beside him, but given the contrast between the two women, James found the man's behavior perfectly understandable. Irritating, but understandable.

"I've learned that we are all brothers to the buffalo, and there's much to be said for our brother's fare." James gave Kezawin a conspiratorial smile. "Especially when it earns a man an invitation to supper."

"Will you be eating your own kill or mine, Garrett?"

"Whichever happens to be in the pot, I should think." Turning to Kezawin again, James added, "I had thought to do a little fishing today. If I have any luck, perhaps you would welcome a change from red meat."

"A change from antelope and venison, you mean," Thunder Shield said. He snapped a dry stalk off a tall yucca plant as he edged closer. "Some say the size of the game is the measure of a man."

"Is that so? Some say the size of a man's ears is a measure of his intelligence, but in your case the equation doesn't seem to add up." James smiled, trusting the insult would be taken tit for tat.

"Scouts have located a large buffalo herd. It's time we permitted you to hunt with us, Garrett. You've loafed around our camp long enough." Thunder Shield's smile accompanied his return volley. "Let us see whether you're any kind of a man at all."

"Stop this nonsense," Kezawin snapped. "A medicine man is not expected to hunt buffalo. He is—" She glimpsed a scruffy brown camp dog sneaking through the grass to get a jump at her drying rack. "Ssst!" The dog skulked away, and Kezawin turned her scowl directly to the two men. "I am entitled to a portion of your kill, Thunder Shield. Your wife comes to me, and so do your children. And you, James Garrett, you are my father's guest. You are not required—"

"By what right do you call yourself a shaman, Garrett?" Thunder Shield demanded.

"I call myself a scholar, a vocation that has no meaning here. But I will not be called a coward by any man. I'll join your hunt."

"It's a good day to die, Garrett." Thunder Shield snapped the twig in two and dropped it in the grass. Turning on his heel, he called back over his shoulder, "Leave your rifle. It will do you no good, anyway, and I would not have you shoot one of us by mistake."

As he watched the man disappear in the camp circle, James wondered how he'd suddenly earned himself a rival. For weeks he'd been tolerated, watched—an object of some curiosity, but considered harmless enough. "Leave my rifle?" he mused. "How am I supposed to kill anything without it?"

Kezawin grunted with disgust and disappeared into her tipi. James followed.

"I haven't had much success with a bow," he said as he let the flap fall to cover the doorway. "I've tried it once or twice, but not seriously." Kezawin turned a hard look on him, and realized he'd committed a breach of etiquette. She glanced left and right in the way of a woman checking for personal things she may have forgotten to put away. "Excuse me," James offered with half a smile. "May I come in?"

"Have you a death song, James? This may be the day you will sing it."

"I'm sorry." Palms raised in mock self-defense, he stepped back. "I know this is rude, just walking in like this, but I didn't know it was a capital offense."

"And I thought your good sense outweighed your pride, but it must not be so with any man, not even you."

"You said I should hunt for a buffalo," he reminded her.

"I did not say you should participate in a surround."

"A surround? What's that? He said they were going hunting."

With a sigh, Kezawin reached for a buckskin pouch that hung from of the ribs of her lodge. "You have no medicine, no weapons, no skill in these matters and no sense about—"

"I have a rifle," he insisted as he watched her untie the pouch. "Some of the other men have rifles. Is there some rule against using one to hunt buffalo? The beasts are so big I can hardly miss. One shot and I'll have my kill and my self-respect, and you'll have—"

"It won't be like stalking a deer, James. You must follow the orders given by the *akicita*. If you make a move before the signal is given and scare the herd, the *akicita* may destroy your property when you return. If you break ranks, they may flog you." From the pouch she pulled a rawhide thong, to which a disk-shaped amulet was attached. "Your rifle would do you no good. There would be no time for reloading it."

He ducked to allow her to put the necklace over his head. It hung in the deep V of his shirt, and he took the disk in his hand, running his thumb over the smooth surface. He lifted his gaze to Kezawin's warm brown eyes and smiled. "Does this mean I'm wearing your colors?"

"I will pray that the *šicun* of the white deer will protect you. This is made from an antler. Not from the *white* deer, of course, but he is the one who brought you here."

James dismissed her concerns with a wave of his hand. "Kezawin, I'm not going to put myself in any danger. If I don't kill anything, it won't be—"

"Men who are trained for this from boyhood anticipate danger when they ride in the surround. You are not trained for it. For you—"

"For me?" He hooked his hands low on his hips. "You think it's too dangerous for me? Too difficult, too tricky? What else? I came here alone, Kezawin—on my own—to a land I knew nothing about, inhabited by people who were strange to me. I'm not a hunter or a soldier, but I take risks to do what I do, and that . . . that . . ." He jabbed his finger in the air and thought better of using the word that came to mind. "That posturing braggart who is *so well trained* suggests that I haven't got the nerve to go out there and hunt those dumb, woolly beasts with his little sporting brotherhood. Well, I've got a piece of news for both of you. I'm—"

"You are a good horseman, James," she said evenly. "Control your mount. Guard yourself against *tatanka*'s horns. Do not ride into the center of the herd, and remember, do not disobey the *akicita*. Thunder Shield is a member, and he seems to have taken a disliking to you."

James shifted his weight from one leg to the other as he reclaimed his composure. "He's jealous," he said with a shrug.

"Jealous?"

"He wants you, and he thinks I'm in the way."

Kezawin shook her head. "Thunder Shield is my brother-in-law. He knows better than anyone what the Double Woman Dreamer does to a man's medicine."

"That doesn't stop him from wanting you. I've seen it in his eyes. He looks at you the same way I do." But he saw the fear in her eyes, and he tried to allay it with a chuckle as he laid his hand on his chest. "Since I have no medicine, there's nothing here for your power to destroy."

Kezawin took no joy in the knowledge that his cocky attitude would soon be eradicated by a test for which none of his experience had prepared him. "Come. We will go to my father. Perhaps he will give you a lance that has some power."

There was little talk among the hunters as they rode through the tall grass, following the scouts who had located the buffalo earlier in the day. Their approach was downwind, and they carried nothing, wore nothing that might jingle or clatter. James had been told to leave his saddle behind because the leather squeaked. Like the others, his upper body glistened with grease, which overpowered human scent and served as protection against the sun and biting insects.

Had it not been for his light brown hair, blue eyes and skin that had tanned to a golden hue rather than bronze, James would have looked very much like the thirty other men, who moved with the gaits of their horses as if they were all of a piece. James wore buckskin breeches, much like their leggings, and his hair, which nearly reached his shoulders, was kept in place with a deerskin headband. He carried a three-foot lance, given to him by Lone Bear, and he had a spare that he'd secured with a loop over his horse's withers. The others carried bows and quivers of arrows, but Garrett knew that for him such equipment would have been useless baggage. The hunt promised to be an adventure, and if by chance he should make a kill, that would be a bonus.

At the top of a hill, they could see the herd—not a large one by Great Plains standards, but numbering in the hundreds and grazing contentedly in the broad valley's thick grass. Instructions were given in sign, and James paid close attention. The hunters were divided into two groups, and he understood that his group would circle wide and approach the herd from the opposite side. He was watching the exchange of hand signals when his horse suddenly bolted under him, as though the animal had been stung. Within a few prancing steps the big sorrel was brought under James's firm control, and he looked around to find the entire party scowling at him—all but Thunder Shield. With a pointed glance at the amulet that hung around James's neck, the stocky warrior gave an ominous smile, and James noticed that the end of his quirt handle was carved in a sharp point.

So this was the way of it. James made up his mind to stay clear of his newfound rival as they formed a column and headed out to take up a position on the other side of the herd. Once in place, the two columns closed in slowly, and now it was the experienced hunting ponies that were hard to control, anxious to get on with it. But like James himself, who was prepared to take a few stabs at a buffalo just to make a good showing, his horse was merely along for the ride.

Then the herd began to stir. Shaggy heads were raised one or two at a time, and an undercurrent rose with them among men, mounts and prey. Complacency became awareness. Restraint became daring. For one breathless instant the inevitable was apparent, and every nerve was exposed to the tension in the air. Then one huge bull leaped into motion, and the cry came from the leader, *"Hoka hey!"*

Suddenly there was a whirlwind of galloping horses, stampeding bison and a melee of shrieking, yelping men. The lead bull was turned back into the herd by a quick rider, and the bunching buffalo began running in circles. The mounted hunters fired a volley of arrows and charged the confused beasts with their lances. James found himself surrounded by whoops and shouts, bawling and bellowing, the smells of dust and blood, horse sweat and greased men. His heart pounded as he dug his heels into his mount's flanks, raised his lance and charged into the brown thickness with his own rousing, ''Eee-yahhh!''

It was hard to find an animal without an arrow or a lance sticking out of it somewhere. Everything was part of the blur of motion. James guided his horse with his legs and took several wild stabs at fleeing prey, succeeding only in hanging on to his lance. The energy of the initial attack had surprised him as much as it had the buffalo, and he was caught up in the frenzy. But soon he realized he would do better to take aim, and he saw that the others sought to puncture a lung by driving the lance between the ribs. The task looked easier than it was.

After several near misses, James rode up beside a young bull, raised his lance aloft with both hands and drove it home. The bull bellowed, spun and charged its killer. James watched with horror as a deadly horn gouged his thigh. His horse wheeled, and the horn slipped away again, leaving only the searing pain behind. The bull went down on its knees, then flopped over on its side.

James jerked off his headband and tied it above the wound, twisting the ends around his knife to make a tourniquet. He wanted out, had to get out, but the hunters and the hunted swirled around him. He tried to make his way around one young brave's mount, but the horse suddenly reared, and James saw the cause. A bull the size of a locomotive had lowered its head for the charge. The horse came down, impaling itself on the big bison's horns, and the rider fell to the ground.

The young man scrambled to his feet and looked around him. There was only a sea of buffalo and the white man, James, who saw the cloud of uncertainty and the spark of fear in the hunter's eyes. He reached out. ''Come on! Get up behind me!'' With an agile leap, the young man took the seat James offered.

When they had ridden clear of the knotted carnage, the young man asked for the use of James's horse. "I haven't made my kill yet."

"Hell, I saw what happened to your horse," James shouted. "I got one. You're welcome to a share of it."

The young man's heated look told James what he thought of the offer as he slid over the sorrel's rump. He jerked his chin toward the spare lance. "Give me that, then."

"You're going back at it on foot?"

The brave snorted in disgust and turned on his heel to return unarmed to the fray.

"Come back here!" The young man turned, and James tossed him the lance and slid off his horse, favoring his wounded leg as he landed heavily. With an expletive for which there was no Lakota translation, he handed over the reins. "I don't want your death on my head. Go get your supper, but bring me back my horse. I'm not up to walking back to camp."

Within a short time it was over. Though some of the animals had escaped to graze other prairie flats, the grass of this one was strewn with buffalo carcasses. Sees The Enemy, the young man who had borrowed James's horse, had made his kill, and the women were coming to butcher, load up their packhorses and carry the meat and hides back to camp. The thrill of James's success had lost its edge as he sat in the grass and let Sees The Enemy help him bind his wound.

It pleased him to see Kezawin arrive leading a packhorse. He knew it was not a measure of her faith in him, for all who would eat were expected to have someone there to butcher. The elders and the shamans were entitled to claim choice portions, but the good hunters had more meat on the ground than their women could handle, and no one would deny a share for the "tail-tiers," those who were without hunters. Food-getting was a communal effort with communal benefits.

The women searched for arrows and lances marked with their hunters' signs and set to work. James knew he ought to be returning to camp to tend to his leg, but he sat in the grass on a gently sloping hillside and watched. He could see no sign of surprise when Kezawin identified her father's lance and unsheathed her knife. She hadn't looked for James at all, but he believed she knew where he was. He believed she felt him watching her. He wondered self-indulgently whether she knew he was hurt. He'd stemmed the flow of blood, but whatever damage lay beneath his buckskins ached like a son of a bitch. It pleased him, though, to watch her belly-slit the beast he'd brought down himself.

When she'd finished packing the meat and the hide, Kezawin headed for the spot where her hunter waited. His pride suddenly pricked him, and he managed to mount his horse before she reached him. They rode to camp together, but the words he wanted to hear from her never came. The story of his hunt babbled in his head, but since she said nothing, he kept it to himself.

"You must go to my father's lodge," she told him when they reached camp. "He will make medicine for your wound."

James scowled. He had given a chunk of his flesh to feed this woman, and now he was being dismissed. With his teeth clamped together over the demands he wanted to make, he wheeled his mount and trotted him in the direction of Lone Bear's tipi, punishing his injury with the jarring gait.

"Lone Bear!" The leathery face appeared in the doorway. James slid to the ground, exerting tremendous effort to keep his knees from buckling. The blood stain was spreading on his breeches again. "Can you do something about this?"

"I'm ready for you," the old man said. "Picket your horse and come inside."

Picket his horse? He was seeing black spots before his eyes, but his stubbornness kept him going until the horse was secure. Lone Bear's gesture indicated a buffalo robe pallet, which James gratefully dropped upon, grumbling all the while in his native tongue. "It isn't something a woman could appreciate, anyway, the speed, the thrill, the...the... Damn her, she could show some concern. She could pay some attention. It isn't every day that a man—"

"Kezawin tells me that you often speak to the plants in your language as you take them from the ground," Lone Bear said as he tossed a sprig of sage on the small fire that burned in the center of the tipi. "Is this part of your medicine?"

"Kezawin says I have no medicine." Through the haze of smoke and black spots, he saw the creased face. "I made a kill, didn't I? I came back alive, didn't I? I've got good medicine. I've studied. I've been no man's field assistant. I've identified...I've named..."

James was talking to the wind, talking nonsense, and he knew it. Lone Bear helped him replace his pants with a breechclout, and he lay there, his head swirling with his pain while he rubbed his burning eyes and listened to Lone Bear's chants. Lone Bear bound his leg, and the chanting continued as the smoke rolled on. Damn the smoke, he thought. Damn the beast with its stabbing horns, and damn the fickleness of women. He'd shown her he could do it, and he wanted to hear her admit it. He wasn't without courage.

He was tired of hearing about this medicine thing. She had the power. *She* had the medicine. He knew he had to get back to a civilized world where a man was respected for his work—important work—work that would go down in the annals of science, and damn her! He'd risked life and limb for a bundle of meat, and she hadn't even acknowledged his efforts.

Sometime during the course of Lone Bear's ritual, James had fallen asleep, but he awoke in the dead of night, and his leg was throbbing. The old man was asleep. The air in the lodge was heavy with smoke and ashes. The embers in the fire pit smoldered. Moonlight streaming through the smoke hole at the apex of the lodge made a sooty haze. Gingerly James touched his thigh and felt the heat and swelling. He heaved himself from the bed and stumbled out into the night. Her door was several yards away—several long, painful yards.

"Kezawin!" he whispered. "Let me in. I need your help."

The rawhide door slid away, and he ducked through the opening, grabbing at the hide as he passed through and landed on one knee. He pitched forward into her arms. "No chants," he groaned. "No smoke. It's festering. Lance it . . . drain it. Give me . . . whatever you . . ."

She lost her robe in her struggle to hold him up, and his cheek slid against her bare breast. His back was slick with sweat and grease. The second thing she would do, she decided, was bathe him. She tried to get a grip on him, and he nuzzled her and groaned. The bath might be third or fourth, she amended as she deposited him on her own bed. First, she reached for her dress. Then she added wood to the dying embers in her fire pit and filled a buffalo's stomach, or paunch, with water. When the cooking stones were hot enough, she dropped them into the water to make it boil.

The swelling in James's leg had tightened the bandaging. Now the wound was hot and angry. Kezawin would fight it with more heat. She applied a hot wet chamois compress, but James sucked his breath through his teeth and threw the first one off. Kezawin calmly reheated it, reapplied it and held it in place.

"Good God, woman!"

"Do you want my help or not?"

"Your father nearly suffocated me, and now you scald me."

"You will keep your voice down."

He dropped his head back on the pallet and sighed. "I'm sorry. It's just that it's . . . gotten worse."

"You should have taken care of it right away."

"*You* should have taken care of it right away." He wanted to bite off his tongue. He had no intention of letting her think he felt slighted by her lack of concern. "You're the medicine woman," he added.

"I don't treat men."

"You're treating this one."

She looked at him, and her eyes softened. "So I am." Taking the soft piece of deerskin up, she turned quickly to dip it into the hot water again. "Why did you wait for me to finish the butchering? The other hunters had gone. There was no need—"

"Were you surprised that I made a kill?"

Gently she laid the chamois over his ragged flesh, but she avoided his eyes. "It was a good kill. You put only one hole in the hide."

"But were you surprised?"

"You're a strong man and a good rider."

"Did you think I couldn't kill a buffalo without using a rifle?" he persisted.

"You were untested." She soaked threads of sinew and one of her precious steel needles in hot water. She wanted everything hot, hotter than the fever in his leg. Blood and pus flowed from it now, carrying the illness out of his body.

"I've been tested now," he said stubbornly. "I passed, didn't I?" He heard the adolescent swagger in his voice, and he managed a thin chuckle. "I surprised myself, and that's the truth of it. I've never liked to hunt, but I felt compelled to prove that I could do it, and once I found myself in the thick of it all—" he lifted his head to be sure he had her attention "—it was exhilarating, in a way. The surprise, the fear, and then the throwing off of fear—it was exciting until that damnable beast gored me." He saw that she listened with only one ear as she busied herself with boiling something. "What's that?"

Kezawin handed him a dry sprig, and he launched into an automatic examination by sniffing, turning it over and over to see it in the best light, sniffing again. "The tea from this will calm you," she said.

"I'm calm. Where can we find this? Can we—"

She laughed. He was talking like the plant-taker again. "It grows in dry country far to the west. I traded for it. After I stitch the wound I shall give you another tea to nourish you and help your spirit drive away the sickness in your leg."

"I'll need my journal," he said, and he lifted his hand in the direction of his lean-to. "I must take notes on everything—" She handed him the book, and he looked up at her, astonished. "You took my journal?"

"I have your plant boxes here, too."

He braced himself up on one elbow. "Why? What would you want with my—" Understanding dawned in his eyes. "You thought I would get into trouble on the hunt today, didn't you? You thought the *akicita* would come back here and destroy my belongings."

"There was that chance." She brought him the tea in a rawhide bowl. "If the man is sufficiently penitent, often the *akicita* will collect items from the people to replace what was destroyed. This work of yours could not be replaced. It was my job to protect it.''

"Thank you.'' Steam from the bowl carried a pungent odor to his nose, but when he sipped, he found the taste surprisingly pleasant. "You're right. There was that chance. Thunder Shield nearly had my horse on the run just before the surround.''

"I have no desire to explain anything to Thunder Shield, but if it will keep him from scheming against you, I will swear an oath that I am no man's woman and that I am to be no man's—''

He gripped her arm. "You'll do no such thing. What is or is not between us is not his business. I don't know what you take me for, but I'm not a coward. I'm not afraid of Thunder Shield.''

"I know you are not a coward, James. I never thought you were.'' She cupped her hand beneath his and helped him raise the bowl toward his mouth. "Drink this now. The stitching will be painful.''

Kezawin washed him while the tea did its work, making him groggy and relaxed. Not unlike a bit of fine old brandy, he thought as he gave himself over to the pleasure of her ministrations. The throbbing in his thigh had become a dull ache as the heat she applied drew out the infection. He smiled at the way she rubbed his chest in smooth circles and told himself that soon he would be throbbing elsewhere.

"You are leading me a merry chase again, Kezawin.''

"Do you prefer to smell like the buffalo?'' she asked. "I am chasing the smell from your body.''

"Mmm. Keep chasing.'' He gave her a sleepy-eyed smile and drained the bowl, then added, "I was referring to the feeling I got earlier that you hated to see me go off on this hunt for fear that I might be injured. But when I was injured you—'' He set the bowl aside and tried to make light of his complaint with a halfhearted shrug. "You chose to tend to the buffalo instead of me."

"And you chose to watch me while you sat there bleeding."

"I wasn't bleeding. I'd stopped the bleeding, and I didn't think it was too bad. But you didn't know that." He angled his head to get a look at her eyes. "I thought we were friends. A society of two, we said."

"You should have gone to my father immediately," she insisted, avoiding the eyes that would demand more of her than she could permit herself to give. "I have treated men on few occasions. Only when a man is desperate does he come to me, and then it seems that often... he loses his battle."

"That's why I came to you before I got desperate. Kezawin—" He caught her chin in his hand and turned her head toward him. "You thought enough of my work to take it under your wing for a while. What about me?"

"I would not want to embarrass you, James. A woman grieves over a man only after he is dead."

James's shoulders shook with silent laughter as his hand slid away from her face. "So you refuse to flutter over me, do you?"

"If you die, I shall cut my arms and my hair and keen most pitifully since there will be no one else to mourn you properly."

"If I die!" He nearly choked trying to contain his laughter. "You mean I have to *die* for your concern? Is there not one bit of sympathy for the wounded friend? Not one, 'Oh, poor James'?"

She laughed with him. "Shall I call you *onŝila*? Poor thing! It is what a woman says to a child."

"Ah, I see. That's why you avoided me. A woman may not show her sympathy for a man whose leg has nearly been torn off by a raging fire-eyed beast, is that it?"

"Onśila," she crooned, letting him see the mischief in her eyes as she petted the soft springy hair on his chest. "Would sucking at a woman's breast help you to heal your wound?"

"It might," he said with a slow smile. "It couldn't hurt."

"And would—" The suggestion stuck in her throat. His eyes were soft, warm and inviting. Deep in her womb, there was a slow stirring, a persistent yearning to lean closer, to touch, to entreat. The tea had produced the soft glaze in his eyes, but Kezawin reminded herself that she had had no tea. There was something else at work in her, something insidious, something she must not allow even the smallest berth within herself.

She took up her needle with a vengeance against that thing that would not let her be. She believed it to be the same thing that made pus in James's wound, and she would fight it, drive it out. She spoke coldly. "Today you have hunted the buffalo and made a kill. You are not a man to be pitied."

James was too warm to feel the chill. "I like your medicine," he said, smiling. "I shall forget my bid for sympathy if I may have more tea."

"Try not to move," she said as she poised the needle for the first stitch. "And I shall try to work quickly."

He closed his hand tightly around the edge of the curly hide upon which he lay, and, still smiling, he turned his face toward the fire. "The breast is another matter, however. I shall not forget your soft breast."

When at last he slept, Kezawin covered him with a red trade blanket and sat beside him, admiring his face. She didn't mind the shadow of his beard anymore, nor the pale color of his hair and his skin. Many times she forgot to think of him as a white man. She had tried to forget that he was a man at all, but that was impossible. Too often she saw the man's look in his eyes, and she felt an answering stir within her belly.

When the runner had brought the news of the successful hunt and recounted the hunters' injuries, her heart had thudded in her throat. Then she saw that James had bound his own wound, and she went about her business, all the while knowing he must have pain. If he had been killed, he would have been the victim of his own male pride, and his destiny would have gone unfulfilled. She did not pretend to understand the nature of that destiny, but she knew that somehow it was bound with hers. The white deer would not let her forget that.

But the deer woman would not let her forget the other side of her fate. Kezawin feared the same part of herself that was feared by others, the part that seemed to fly in the face of all decency. It was the part that mocked her femininity, the part that made her long for a man while it denied her a perma-nent place in his life. The gifts bestowed by her dream made her unique among women, and that uniqueness was its own curse, for she could never again truly be one of them. Stories were told, stories that rang with the authority of tradition. It was said that this one's grandmother or that one's uncle had actually seen the metamorphosis take place—deer to woman, woman to deer. A man must never lie with the Double Woman Dreamer, for who could trust such a woman? After the dream, one never knew.

Kezawin knew. She had experienced the urgings of the deer woman in visions of herself and this man that made her dewy, as though she had been touched, and left her craving in the knowledge that she had not, could not, would not be touched. Her laughter was a signal to all others to beware of her power. Beside it, a man's medicine might crumble. It was said that she might use it to charm him, seduce him, lure him to his death.

Not this man, she told herself. When she had heard the news of his injury, her heart had cried out, *not this man*. She would fight those awful, wondering stirrings even as the care she felt for him continued to deepen.

And it had deepened. With tentative fingers she touched his warm face and saw that the contrast between her skin and his was pleasing to the eye, like a soft piece of buckskin dyed with a berry stain and decorated with white quillwork. She brushed his hair back from his face and saw its contrasts, too, in the thick hair the color of a pronghorn's back, tumbling in soft disarray over a high forehead, and the strong stubborn chin, stubbled and square. No longer the face of the strange white man, it was a face that brought her sunshine in the morning, a promise of a day filled with good things to be shared. It was the face of her friend.

Yes, she thought enough of him to take him under her wing for a while. And he would buoy her up with the warm smile of a man who saw her as Kezawin, not Double Woman Dreamer. But because she knew who she was, they could never be lovers.

Through the open side of James's lean-to, the morning sun touched his aching leg. When he found that the leg would not support his weight, he fashioned a crutch from the limb of an ash tree and tried to carry on with his business. By midday he was back in Kezawin's tipi, his leg swollen and infected again. She repeated her treatment, offering him more herbs to fight the infection from the inside. Lone Bear stuck his head in a couple of times to inquire about his guest, but he offered no advice. Some men did not respond to a shaman's medicine, but few chose the alternative the medicine woman might offer them. Because this man was both white and *wakan*, no one could predict his actions.

By nightfall James's body was plagued by high fever. Kezawin worked over him, draining his leg, bathing him, forcing him to take what concoctions she could offer and praying all the while that her medicine would not overwhelm his own.

"Don't take my leg," he croaked with a dry tongue. Kezawin slipped her hand beneath his head, and he lifted heavy eyelids. She smiled at him as she brought a bowl to his lips, but he blocked it with his hand. "I want to come out of this with two legs, Kezawin. Do you understand? *Two* legs."

"I understand."

"That's not part of the treatment, huh? Hacking off limbs?"

She shook her head. "Not for a friend. If you were one of the Crow people, or one of the Pawnee, I might consider it."

"Doctors back home do it to friend and foe alike."

"I would never offend you that way," she promised. He let his hand drop away from the bowl and accepted the drink. "The healing happens inside you, James. I can nourish you and try to draw the illness out, but you must call on the powers that give you life. You must pray."

He heard her earnest plea, and it shook him to the core. It reminded him of a small frail woman whose prayers had been uttered between desperate gasps for breath, and of a man who spoke of prayer, then closed the door, leaving the room dark, his footsteps echoing in the hallway. James swallowed the bitter potion and pushed the bowl away.

"I have no faith, Kezawin. I have only will. My own stubborn will. That's my power. That's my *śicun*."

"Your will does not give you life, James."

"I *have* life. Where it came from, what power made it, what it is I am not certain. I only know I have life now, and I shall not give it up." He took the bowl back and drained the contents. "Neither am I willing to relinquish my leg. Your medicine works. I know it. I've seen it." He gestured toward the foot of the pallet. "Hand me my journal so I may make notes on this treatment of yours."

But as soon as she put the book in his hands, he fell asleep again.

James recovered gradually from his leg wound, and as he did, he kept his journal close at hand. Kezawin showed him the medicine she made, not only for him, but for others, and he filled page after page with notes. This much they shared, but whenever he tried to touch her, she drew back. Whenever their laughter settled into smiles, then into soft hungry looks, she turned from him and went her own way. Their days were filled with each other, but she refused to speak of nights. When he spoke of a man's loneliness, she asked him to speak of something else. Her medicine had cured him, but her mythology was driving him crazy.

Lone Bear performed the *inipi* for James, but it proved to be an empty experience. Kezawin tended the fire outside and rolled hot stones under the buffalo-hide walls as they were needed inside the dome-shaped lodge. The small lodge filled with steam, and James sweated until he was light-headed and impatient with the smoke that made his eyes burn in the dark and the old man's monotonous singing. The two men went from the steam-filled lodge to the cold river, after which James dressed and went looking for Kezawin to tell her that he felt clean but uninspired.

As the days passed, they spoke less and less. It was the time for grass to turn from green to lifeless dun and for the hot wind to fill up the ears and isolate the mind, but the changes were more than seasonal for the society of two. One morning Kezawin emerged from her tipi to find that James's shelter had been dismantled and that he was gone.

Chapter Four

Ezra Breckenridge was a man of wealth and power. His grandfather had secured the Breckenridge fortune as a merchant in colonial Boston. His father had established political influence as a member of the Provincial Congress, and his mother had, by virtue of the fact that she was one of the Boston Dexters, contributed social standing to the family's list of credits. Ezra had successfully continued those traditions. Money crowded its way into his pockets along with politicians and highly-placed friends. Those aspects of his life were well in hand when he sought to add his own chevron to the Breckenridge family crest by pursuing loftier interests. He became a "man of science."

At the age of fifty he was not about to take up the study himself, and his son, Orson, failed in the vicarious achievement of Ezra's personal goal by getting himself booted out of Harvard in his freshman year. The alternative, then, was to become a patron of science. Financing a promising young naturalist's expedition into the continent's interior promised to affix the name of Ezra Breckenridge to a piece of work that would survive him in a way that no brick monument could. It would bring him the respect of learned men.

At last the wandering protégé had returned, which meant that a celebration was in order. The Breckenridge home in Cambridge was ablaze with light, and carriages lined the driveway as the rich, the influential and, indeed, the scholarly alighted upon the cobblestones and mounted the steps to the white-columned porch of the huge square frame house. Immediately upon his return to Boston, James Garrett had delivered a vast collection of neatly pressed and mounted botanical specimens, which were displayed on every table, sideboard, shelf and mantel in the several rooms in which guests would be entertained. They would, as well, meet the man of the hour, the man who had followed Breckenridge's instructions so admirably.

Breckenridge listened with one ear to the polite conversation being traded at his elbow while his other ear attended to the voices that filled the foyer after each knock at the front door. James was late, and Ezra Breckenridge did not appreciate being kept waiting. One could not be expected to discuss the collection with the more erudite of the guests assembled in the drawing room without some commentary from one's field assistant.

"We're anxious to have Garrett back in the lecture hall," one of the men was saying. "He's a fine teacher."

"It must have been a splendid adventure," the other man said. "If I were twenty years younger, even ten, I think I'd have a look at those great Western mountains and deserts myself. Have you seen the journals, Breckenridge?"

"What? Oh, no, not yet. I believe he means to turn them over tonight. I do hope he doesn't make too much of a production of it, considering the work we have left to do before anything is committed to the printed page."

"Yes, I daresay you'll spend much time consulting."

"Any piece of work bearing my name—"

"Any piece of work that boasts the auspices of Harvard University—"

"Certainly must be—"

"Above the pale."

"Yes, yes, above the pale."

"Indeed, fine young man."

"Extraordinary scholar."

"Excellent mind. Courageous mind."

"Indeed."

Breckenridge's smile was thin and lifeless. It would not have served his ego to reveal his anxiety over the tardy appearance of a field assistant. He cocked his ear toward the foyer. "Ah. I believe our adventuring colleague has found his way to our door."

James Garrett squared his shoulders and stepped across the Breckenridge threshold, telling himself that one hour of parlor chitchat would be his limit. After one hour, he would select from the long list of places he'd rather be and excuse himself to attend to a pressing matter of some sort. He handed his top hat and his velvet-collared black cloak to Breckenridge's butler and ran his hands quickly through his hair. He still hadn't adjusted to the shorter style.

He had provided Breckenridge with a duplicate of his Western collection, which should have been sufficient entertainment for the evening. James resented the summons to appear as part of the display, but it was one of the unwritten rules that one humored the wealthy man who exhibited a hobbyist's interest in science. Let the man dabble as he would. Give him the vehicle he had chosen to impress his equally wealthy friends, and he would do his part to further the cause by investing in another project. The academic community depended upon the endowments of the rich. Pure science, which was but a source of passing curiosity for most people, was widely financed by the dabbler. James knew his duty, and he had come to perform it with as much charm as he could muster, after which he would welcome a tankard of ale at the Green Dragon.

"Welcome! Welcome, my boy." Ezra Breckenridge's hand fell heavily on James's shoulder as he turned to his guests and gestured with a flourish. "Ladies and gentlemen, welcome the man who spent two long years in that unsettled territory west of the Mississippi River, gathered the specimens you see and brought them back for our edification and enlightenment. Mr. James Garrett."

James dipped his head in response to polite applause. "Ezra Breckenridge is a great friend of science," he told the gathering. "His sponsorship made the venture possible, and I thank him for that."

In the midst of the obligatory applause, Breckenridge leaned closer to ask, "Where are the journals? Did Hector stash them aside with your hat?"

"The journals?" James glanced around the crowded drawing room. "I saw no reason to bring them to this event."

Breckenridge's scowl came too quickly. It took him a moment to recover his bland smile and give James's padded shoulder a patronizing pat. "We'll talk later. Everyone is anxious to meet you. Of course—" his signet ring flashed in his solicitous gesture to include a third party in their conversation "—you know Professor Harding better than I do."

James offered a handshake to the plump white-haired man who stood near Breckenridge's elbow. "Good evening, sir."

"Quite a good evening for you, Garrett."

"For all of us," Breckenridge added.

"Would that we could all have made the journey with you," the professor said. "But you've brought us the far horizon, Garrett, and we're anxious to hear the stories that must accompany this remarkable collection."

James had carefully selected the stories with which to regale Breckenridge's guests. They wanted to hear about the bear and the bison, the splendor of the mountains and the strange ways of the Indians. He spoke of the Lakota, even offered a taste of the language, but he said nothing of Lone Bear or Thunder Shield or Sees The Enemy. He jealously guarded Kezawin's name.

After he had given James time to mingle with the guests, Breckenridge ushered him into his study and shut the door. The party became a distant buzz while the host took his seat in a commanding high-backed upholstered chair behind a polished inlaid desk and produced a neatly penned document from one of its drawers.

"This is our agreement, my boy. In return for my financial backing, I am to receive a complete collection of labeled specimens *with* commentary."

By nature the scene was one to tie James's stomach into a knot. The words "my boy" were unpleasantly reminiscent of "young man," and the man behind the desk gave him a familiarly accusing stare. Reminders of his father brought out James's icy reserve. He reached inside his coat and drew out a cheroot.

"Care to join me?" The invitation was merely perfunctory. When Breckenridge waved the offer away, James stepped over to the fireplace and took his time lighting the cigar with a bit of kindling. He puffed, then drew the cigar from his mouth and studied the burning tip for a moment as though he were observing something of greater import than Breckenridge's statement. Finally he took a chair.

"I expected you to turn the journals over to me tonight," Breckenridge said.

"You seemed anxious to display the specimens. I had those prepared first. My commentary on the collections, which includes a representative of everything I collected, will be delivered shortly."

"I want your journals just as they are. There's no need for refinement of any kind at this point, Garrett. Knowing your reputation, I'm sure you were quite thorough. I am anxious to publish the findings of the Breckenridge expedition as soon as possible, and I have already arranged for—"

"My journals are my property," James reported flatly. "I assumed that you would donate the specimens and the commentary I shall provide to one of the institutions you endow, but you may do with them as you please. The journals are personal, and they are mine."

"I beg to differ, Mr. Garrett. We both know that the journals contain the meat of the work."

"That's true." James drew slowly on his cigar and created a blue veil around his face. "I set out to assemble a botanical collection, to classify it and to describe it, and that I have done. Beyond that, I met with a world we know nothing about, and my journals contain observations from that world. That, sir, is a piece of work that is not mentioned in our agreement and to which you have no claim."

"I have a claim to anything resulting from the Breckenridge expedition. I paid for it, and I own it."

James eyed the man through a lazy haze of smoke. His journals were filled with wonders that were beyond Breckenridge's poor power to imagine. He could never own them. Some of what James had written would not be published, not by himself or anyone else. His memories were not for sale. What would be published by James Garrett and no other person was a work that had taken a direction he had not foreseen. While the earlier part of the work was thorough, enlightening and definitive in its field, it was the journalizing of the past few months that made the work unique.

"I assure you that I will fulfill my contract with you, Breckenridge. You won't be disappointed with my commentary, which will be carefully written in layman's terms. It will be pleasant reading. You can have it printed, claiming your sponsorship on the title page. I'm sure your friends will find it amusing." James stood up and took one last puff on his cigar before tossing it into the flames that licked the firebox inside the classically constructed fireplace. He had lost the taste for strong cigars. An open camp fire and a long-stemmed pipe filled with the soothing taste of *kiniknik* would have appealed to him more. Shared in the ritual of the Lakota, the pipe might have tempered the growing anger of both men.

"You'll regret resisting me on this, Garrett. The journals are mine. You would be hard-pressed to find an attorney in this town who would be willing to represent you should this matter land in court."

"Then I shall represent myself."

There was a soft rapping at the door. "Are you in there, Father?"

"Yes, yes, come in," was the impatient reply. Flat brown eyes set in a round rubicund face peered around the door. "What is it, Orson?" Ezra asked.

"I thought you might be having some sort of trouble, sir. Our friend isn't holding out on us, is he?"

"Come in and close the door, Orson." Ezra pushed his chair back abruptly and circled the desk. "I believe Mr. Garrett realizes how foolish it would be for him to offend me. Isn't that right, Mr. Garrett?"

James glanced at the blotchy-skinned son, who stood in front of the door with his arms folded over his chest, then returned his attention to the ample-bellied sire. In another few years he thought they would make a fine pair of bookends. "It was not my intention to offend you," he said. "But neither do I intend to give you my journals. If you take offense, then so be it."

"I'll see that no one else finances your work," Ezra blustered as the color began to rise in his face. "I'll see that no one else gives you a penny. I can do that, you know. Do you realize that with a few well-placed words I can make certain no one will ever hear of the brilliant young naturalist, James Garrett? Peddle your journals where you will, young man, you will be outmaneuvered in this."

James's humorless smile gave his blue eyes a cold glint. "Do you intend to outlive me, too? Your present apoplectic state bodes ill for you, Breckenridge."

Orson stepped away from the door. "Are you threatening my father, Garrett?"

"I've had enough of this," James said matter-of-factly as he headed for the door. "This little soiree has ceased to entertain me. You will get the commentary we agreed upon, but the journals are mine." Orson stood his ground two feet in front of the door as James paused to drill him with his eyes. "Excuse me." James gave Orson a moment to size him up. The shifting of the eyes assured James of Orson's self-doubt, and he swept the junior Breckenridge aside with a brush of an arm.

"Your work will never see print," Ezra warned, his voice quavering with anger. "Your expeditions are finished, your career, your reputation—"

"I bid you good night, sir."

* * *

James headed directly for the Green Dragon, where the Medford rum and the friendly company soon improved his mood. Having reacquainted himself with friends and fellows from the university, he traded tales and raised his glass for toast after toast. The yellow light from the tavern's oil lamps threw tall shadows on the wall—winsome serving girls in silhouette and the shapes of brawny dock workers rubbed shadowy shoulders with scholars, merchants and politicians. No story was too farfetched nor overly ribald, and the only weight thrown around was that which bellied up to the bar.

"Say on about the woolly-headed buffalo, Garrett. How much spearing did you have to do to bring him down?"

"Puts me in mind of the time I sailed to Africa. Saw the most amazing creatures. Rhinoceroses. Elephants."

"Did you bag an elephant, Cap'n?"

"Almost. Had him in my sights."

"But this buffalo. How big did you say he was?"

"Big enough," James told the crowd. "Big enough to feed your family for an entire winter."

"Not ol' Charlie's pack o' brats. Fourteen last count, right, Charlie?"

"How 'bout the women, Garrett? How much spearin' did you do with them wild redskin wenches?"

James set his glass down carefully and studied the grain of wood in the table.

"Puts me in mind of the native women I saw in Africa. They wore very little, of course, and when you're trading, you learn to pick and choose. The young ones—"

"Lakota women do not have red skin, nor do they—" James glanced up. He was surrounded by expectant leers.

"What color skin do they have?"

"What color is it under their—"

"Enough!" His chair clattered to the floor as he came to his feet. He saw their surprise and realized he'd surprised himself. Truly he knew only one Lakota woman, and he'd risen to her defense. He sought to regain his customary self-control. "The, uh . . . the Lakota women are quite modest. Quite reserved, actually."

"You mean they wouldn't give you a tumble, Garrett?"

There was a round of chuckles. "Handsome specimen like yourself?"

"Or maybe they was all hags."

"Maybe he didn't know the right words."

"Or the right price. Did you offer them a bit of—"

"No!" Anger flared in his eyes, even though its source was elusive. James had always been a sporting sort when it came to a little harmless ribbing among friends. He took up his glass and tossed down the last swallow of the potent rum. It gave him a warm feeling and put a smile back on his face as he sat down again. "I had nothing to offer but clumps of weeds, my friends. The ladies were not impressed."

"The next time you go on one o' these trips of yours, take along a few trinkets," someone suggested. "A man can use a little diversion no matter where he wanders."

"Beads and weeds, beads and weeds. I've got a length of somethin'll give 'em what for."

James joined in the laughter. Everyone knew Charlie had all he could handle at home. The faster the rum flowed, the fewer boasts any of them could hope to make good. But when a peal of light female laughter rose above the bass tones, the image of a woman half a continent away appeared to James. Her hair was black and glossy, and her face was covered with rain. Mink eyes flashed as she laughed, and his heart quickened. He jerked his head around.

The woman had red hair and berry-colored lips set in a pallid face. She laughed good-naturedly as she served tankards of ale to the men at a nearby table.

"Betty's as wild as any red savage," a voice at James's elbow confided. James turned, and his old friend, John Glover, gave him a knowing smile. "She's given you the eye several times tonight."

"Has she, now."

"Quite blatant about it, she's been. I think your hunting story caught her fancy."

A slow smile spread across James's face. His hunting prowess had finally garnered its due respect. He raised his voice across the room. "Mistress...Betty, is it? Would you be good enough to refill my glass?"

Betty hovered over James's table, leaning over to top off tankards, and treated James to an unobstructed view of her ample bosom. He pushed his chair back from the table and offered his lap when she said she was anxious to get off her feet. She smelled of ale and kitchen grease, and he wished for wood smoke and sweet grass. He pushed that wish aside, admonishing himself to wish realistically. Betty was real.

She ran her hands over his shoulders, assessing his physique beneath the padding of his coat. "Lusty one, ain't you? Strong enough to bring an elephant down with a spear."

"Buffalo," he corrected, and squeezed her waist. She laughed lustily and wiggled her bottom against his lap. He closed his eyes, nestled his chin in the ruffle of her scoop-necked blouse and nuzzled the valley between her breasts. He pushed the din of the tavern to the edge of his brain. There in the corner of his mind he found a soothing memory of brushing his hot face against cool firm breasts.

"I can get us a room upstairs," Betty whispered.

James lifted his head and looked at the woman. He was half-surprised to find curly red hair instead of sleek, black, beautiful... God in heaven, reality could be such a disappointment.

She misread his dark expression. "You'd have to pay for the room, but I wouldn't charge you nothin'."

"You're very generous."

"I like you." She smiled, and he saw that she had green eyes.

"Why?" he asked. "Have you had a vision of me? A bolt from the blue promising that I would come?" She looked puzzled. He gave her the kind of pat on her hip he knew she could understand. "I like you, too, Betty. There's nothing complicated about you or your offer." The look he gave her was blatantly sexual. "And I shall come. That much I can promise."

"No hurry," she said, then whispered in his ear, "Just take your time and enjoy your friends. I'll make the arrangements." She sat up and made every effort to dazzle him with a smile.

The smile did nothing for him. There was no mystery in her eyes, nothing to engage his imagination. But she engaged his sex, and that was all he needed. "I have a room," he whispered back. "It isn't far."

Ingersoll's was one of the more reputable lodging houses in Cambridge, and it was for that reason that James chose to usher Betty through the back entrance and up the dark narrow twist of a stairway to his room. He warned her to avoid the fifth step, and each of them bypassed the creaky tread. The hour was late, and James knew he risked eviction if the other boarders were disturbed. In the cold night air he had lost his initial enthusiasm for the plan he had conceived in response to Betty's squirming on his lap. The sooner he could tend to the needs he'd long neglected and send the woman off with a heavier purse, the better he'd like it. Her glassy-eyed smile and her hiccupy giggle were beginning to irritate him.

He intended to whisk Betty in ahead of him as he opened the door, but the shadowy figure standing in the middle of his room stopped him cold.

"What are you—"

The hulking figure tossed his cloak back over his shoulder, briefly blotting out the moonlight coming through the small window behind him. James stepped over the threshold as he pushed Betty behind him.

"What do you want?" James demanded as he loosened the fastenings on his own voluminous cloak, shoved it to the floor and tossed his hat aside. The intruder edged away from the writing table. A bit of steel glinted in his hand.

"He's got a knife!" Betty whispered at James's back.

"I've got nothing worth stealing, man. Be gone and we shall forget we ever—"

The dark shadow lunged across the room, but James was ready with a shoulder block. They crashed to the floor together as James grabbed for the arm that brandished the weapon. The intruder's cloak became a third party in the grappling. They rolled together and became entangled, struggling for control over the deadly blade.

James realized the man's superior strength and inferior agility as he sought to gain the cloak as an ally. If the heavier man managed to reverse their positions and land on top, James would be lost. Betty's cry for help filled his ears, and the intruder's hot, sour-milk breath assailed his nostrils. In one quick move he tossed the cloak over the man's head, rolled him over on his stomach and pushed his face against the floor. The man grunted and convulsed as though he dangled from a noose. Then he was still.

A single taper bathed the room in shadowy unreality. With his chest still heaving from his efforts, James pulled himself off the cloaked hulk on the floor and rose on one knee. A second taper joined forces with the first, and there was a gathering of voices. James looked up. Mrs. Ingersoll held her candleholder aloft and stared with wide eyes. Her flannel nightgown flowed to the floor like cream. Mr. Lorry from down the hall crept closer with his taper, and Betty hovered behind them. There was a buzzing of curious voices in the darkness beyond the door.

"Who is this?" Mrs. Ingersoll demanded. Her face fell into a scowl, and her eyes darted to indicate the cowering woman behind her. "You know we do not permit this, Mr. Garrett."

James glanced down at the cocooned intruder, up at Betty's huge glassy eyes and finally at Mrs. Ingersoll's outraged face. His shoulders shook as he gained control of his breathing. Relief combined with a feeling that he was surrounded by absurdity, and laughter bubbled in his throat.

"What is the meaning of this, Mr. Garrett? What have you done here? This is a respectable house. I won't permit such goings-on in my—"

"Look! There's blood!"

Mr. Lorry pointed to a dark pool seeping, gathering, growing beside the bundled attacker. James rolled the man over and peeled the cloak back while Betty's tongue suddenly sprang to life. "He was waitin' in here, just waitin'. He had a knife. When Mr. Garrett told him to just go on out peaceable, the bloody thief went for him, just like—"

The knife was buried to the hilt in the man's belly. James felt for a pulse in his neck and found none, but he detected something tucked beneath the man's coat. He pushed one lifeless arm aside and found two leather-bound books. He motioned for more light, and Mr. Lorry stepped closer, curiosity and candle both ablaze. James turned the dead man's face toward the light.

"Damn you, Orson. If you weren't so fat you could have stuck the journals in the front of your trousers. They might have saved your worthless life."

At the inquest, Betty and the witnesses from Ingersoll's Lodging House helped James clear his name, but he was not allowed to reclaim his journals. Upon his return to Ingersoll's, he received notice of his eviction and a summons to a meeting with Barkleigh Harding, who was the chairman of the Botany Department at Harvard. Harding met him in a tiny cubicle at the back of a dusty storage room near the laboratory. James interpreted the arrangement as a sign that the level of his acceptability had slipped a notch.

"I'm sure you realize that this Breckenridge affair has become a sticky business for us here," Harding said as he took a seat on one of the tall wooden stools that stood near a bank of oak cabinets.

James planted his foot on a lower stool and braced one hand on his knee. "The man broke into my room," he said evenly. "I was forced to defend myself."

"We know that, James. Breckenridge is a pompous man, and his son was a fool."

"There were no charges."

"Good," Harding said, nodding. "That's good, James. I would hate to see you rotting in prison over a thing like this."

"The authorities are holding my journals."

"No." Harding glanced away. "No, they're not. Breckenridge demanded them with his son's personal effects."

"He has them, then?"

"I have them." Harding leaned forward, bracing himself on his thighs. "He wanted me to sort through them. He plans to publish the findings of the Breckenridge expedition, but, of course, the findings are over his head."

James offered a humorless smile. "The mourning for his son seems to have gotten short shrift."

"I suspect that vengeance will take precedence over mourning, James, and I suggest you look to your own safety."

"What's to be done with my journals?"

Harding pondered the question for a moment. "I'm not quite sure what to make of your journals. Whether they be fact or fiction, they are certainly fascinating. I was unable to set them aside until I had read every word."

"Fact or fiction?" James fairly exploded at the suggestion. "Sir, you know my work. I have studied your own work, Nuttall's, Say's. I know my predecessors by heart, but I daresay the depth of my work, *my* journals surpassed anything accomplished thus far in the territory west of—"

"You daresay so, do you? Just what was all the hocus-pocus with the Indian woman, James? You seem to have gone beyond the bounds of simply observing primitive culture. In fact, I would say you gave some credence to her heathen practices, coming dangerously close to crediting her with medical knowledge, or, worse yet, some God-given power to heal."

James's pulse pounded in his ears. The man spoke of Kezawin, and James felt like a traitor. He had never intended to expose her to this kind of unsympathetic scrutiny. He wanted to write about the things he'd learned from her, but he had planned to edit the journals so that she would not be labeled sorceress or witch by those who knew nothing of her life and her traditions. Not that their labels would ever touch her in her world, but they would touch him, and how would he respond?

"I said nothing of God or supernatural power," James pointed out. "I took note of her herbal prescriptions, and I observed their effect insofar as I was allowed. She treated an injury of mine with amazing success."

"Yes," Harding acknowledged with a thoughtful nod. "That was interesting. I should tell you that your...shall we say, sentiments toward the woman are apparent in your writing."

"I came to respect her. I learned a great deal from her."

"As much as you learned from me or from Thomas Nuttall or Thomas Say?"

There was an undeniable challenge in Harding's hard look. His white hair and the soft folds of aging skin only served to add weight to his authority. "Of course not," James acquiesced quietly. "She is uneducated and...and untutored in scientific or philosophical thought." In his mind he saw a clear picture of her face, and it was as though she had heard him denounce her. His heart ached, and he groped for some way to redeem himself. "You must understand that she is—"

"A savage, James. Their brains are smaller than ours, you know. They are simply incapable of participating in a higher level of—" He waved his hand in a gesture of dismissal. "Of course, you know all that. You were out there for two years, and you have a man's needs. I trust the woman was attractive in her own way, and you—"

"Sir, I beg you to return my journals."

Harding stood slowly, his joints protesting the weight they were required to carry in their advanced years. "I sympathize with your dilemma, James. It is a piece of work that contains moments of genius. On the other hand, there are certain aspects, certain elements, certain implications—" He waved a hand in a dramatic lecture-hall gesture. "It could ruin you, and you know it. Fascinating as they may be, pagan superstitions must be termed 'nonsense' by the scientific mind. One must not seem to portray such rites as anything but—"

"Their rites had no part in my study. I described the use of herbs in treating injury and disease."

"By a woman who thinks she can turn herself into a deer. Good God, man, you'll be the laughingstock of the scientific community!"

"I had no intention of mentioning that aspect of her life. It has no bearing—"

"No bearing! It's hocus-pocus, I tell you. It's one thing to observe the primitive and describe them from the viewpoint of a civilized, intelligent, English-speaking, God-fearing white man, but it's another thing—" Harding was displeased with the emotionalism he'd begun to display, and he reined in and tempered it with scholarly reason. "Much of your work is, as I said, valuable, enlightening, deserving of attention. I intend to placate Breckenridge by publishing it as his work, with you as his field assistant."

"His field assistant!"

"And James," Harding cautioned, "I suggest you disappear for a time. Visit your family in Virginia. Perhaps in two or three years, when Breckenridge's furor over his son dies down a bit, you can come back and be reinstated with the university."

"I am relieved of my teaching post, then?"

"I'm afraid so. We cannot risk losing Breckenridge's generous endowment."

The stagecoach left Scollay Square at three o'clock in the morning. At that hour the huge conveyance lumbered over the cobblestone streets of the sleeping city without interference from other traffic. It rumbled over the ruts of the Boston Post Road and headed south. Covering about six miles to the hour, it would take at least two days to reach New York—two days for the traveler to mull over his plans.

James had no plans. He had given considerable thought to putting the elder Breckenridge in a grave beside the younger one, but some measure of reason had intervened. Professor Barkleigh Harding, a man James had once admired, had sacrificed one man's career for the good of the university. Perhaps he'd been prudent, but James wondered how many others might be cast adrift in deference to the same cause.

Harding's parting warning that James must now look to his own safety was a concern that James had all but set aside, until he had tried to engage an attorney's services to help him recover the journals. No one had been willing to take his case. He heard several conflict-of-interest excuses, and one particularly cool-mannered lawyer told him that he might want to be as far from Boston as possible should new evidence surrounding the circumstances of Orson Breckenridge's death come to light.

Once he'd exhausted the legal channels, James considered what was left. The journals had been stolen from him through legal channels. In order to get them back, he had to play the game. He had gone to Harding's office late in the day to return his keys, say his farewells, play the role of the gentleman who understood the old professor's position and would be grateful to see his name listed as an assistant on the Breckenridge project. The recognition would help him establish himself elsewhere, perhaps in New Haven. They had laughed, agreeing that Harvard's loss might be Yale's gain. James returned his keys. Harding tossed them in a drawer, locked his office and went on chatting as they strolled together for the last time down the deserted corridor.

When they reached the foyer, they shook hands and went separate ways. Harding was off to a dinner engagement.

James circled the building, readmitted himself with a duplicate key and returned to Harding's office, where his
master key made burglary an effortless operation. He knew
that in Harding's mind the journals belonged to the university, and logic dictated that Harding would have kept them
there. James found them in the drawer with his keys.

The coach bumped along in the early-morning darkness,
and James thought about Harding's suggestion that he return to home ground to lick his wounds. Home ground. He
had left his boyhood home near Falmouth on the Rappa-
hannock River with his father's threats ringing in his ears.
Eternal damnation awaited the son who refused to honor the
wishes of his father. His father wanted James to be a tobacco farmer, but James had no interest in farming, and he
took pleasure in defying the wish of the father who had left
a gravely sick child and a fragile wife to die in the rain. With
an inheritance from his maternal grandfather, James had
paid for his "Yankee" education. He had not been home in
more than ten years, and he had no wish to return now.

Word of James's hand in Orson Breckenridge's death had
undoubtedly reached Falmouth and Ridge View, the Garrett farm. His father would insist that James had killed a
man in defense of some intellectual nonsense and that his
place in hell was assured. Then he would offer James a
chance to redeem himself. He'd need only tuck his tail between his legs and do his father's bidding. And how that old
man would relish playing the role of magnanimous father to
his prodigal son!

James had no taste for farce. He had no apologies to
make to anyone. His life was still his own, and he had his
journals. There were also the pages of new journals to fill.
James Garrett's life's work would carry *his* name, not his

father's and not Ezra Breckenridge's. What had seemed like a dead end was clearly a fork in the road. He would ride the coach to the end of the line, then head west again.

Chapter Five

Paha Sapa, The Black Hills
Summer, 1827

The Moon of Ripening Chokecherries was a time when the sun made the days long and warm and invited the men of the Lakota to fulfill their vows by offering the Gaze at the Sun sacrifice. The bands of Teton Sioux gathered on the banks of Spearfish Creek in the bosom of *Paha Sapa* for the twelve-day Sun Dance ceremony. They came to hallowed ground where, since the beginning of the old ones' collective memory, the men had pierced their flesh and sacrificed their own blood for the good of the people. It was a sacred time, when mothers brought their babies forward for ear piercing, when young men sought their first visions and mature men reached for higher levels of visionary experience, and when women sought signs portentous of love, a fertile womb, a successful birthing.

In her search along the creek bank for the thick-stalked bulrush, Kezawin had found such a sign—a spear of gama grass with four heads—a promise of love. Her discovery had brought forth a burst of laughter. Surely *Tunkašila*, the Grandfather Above, intended this for her amusement, that she should find it and not the others who searched together in their groups. She had thought of leaving it for a more likely candidate, but, no, this was her find, and she tucked it carefully into her leather pouch. In the privacy of her lodge, she took it out again and rubbed the stem between her thumb and forefinger, making the heads dance.

"Daughter, I have news to tell you."

Kezawin put the stalk of grass under her sleeping robe and added a sprig of sage and a piece of dry cottonwood to her fire. "You are welcome here, Father," she announced.

Lone Bear ducked inside and took a man's place at the back of the tipi, where a willow backrest provided him with comfortable seating. He accepted Kezawin's offer of fruit and jerked meat, but he took only small portions. He was anxious to tell her what he knew.

At last, when he had eaten, Lone Bear launched his news. "Our friend Garrett is a captive of the Skidi." He watched Kezawin's eyes widen.

"James?" she whispered, then summoned a stronger voice. "Was he taken after he left us last summer?"

Lone Bear shook his head. "Two white men were riding with a Yankton scout. The Skidi took only the whites and left our cousin for dead. His relatives found him and brought him here for healing."

"How long ago?"

"Two days."

Kezawin knew what that meant. Three more days. The summer solstice was a time for ceremony there in the hills, but in the flat country not far to the south, the hated Pawnee, to which the Skidi band belonged, honored their gods in this season, as well. The Lakota Sun Dance lasted twelve days, but the Pawnee ritual took only five. Kezawin's brain buzzed with an invasion of images—a party of three, a whirlwind of dust and horses, yelping riders with hair roaches bristling like quills over the crests of their shaven red-painted heads. And in the midst of it all was the face she had not forgotten. She heard the pounding of the horses' hooves and the racing heartbeats, first his, then hers.

"Our cousin is safe," Lone Bear went on.

The sound of her father's voice drifted in the periphery. Wise words meant nothing now. Only one truth was clear to her. "He cannot be left to the Skidi."

"They may have killed him," Lone Bear said quietly.

"No. If he were dead, I would know it."

"How?"

Kezawin looked at her father, and he saw that she had an understanding beyond explanation. In that moment, James Garrett lived. His heart beat as surely as hers did. "The Skidi might know of me," she said. "Many people have heard of the Double Woman Dreamer from Lone Bear's band."

"If word has reached them of your beauty, they will be ready to take you, and Garrett will still die."

"I must prepare a sweat," she decided. "I must be clean, and my head must be clear enough to receive a good plan."

Kezawin traveled alone. She knew that no weapons would protect her once she reached the land of the Pawnee, and she carried only her skinning knife. She recognized, too, that it was her own will that led her on her southward journey, but she had conceived her plan in the steam of the sweat lodge, and when she had worked it all out in her mind, the air in the lodge had seemed to lighten.

The Pawnee were earth-lodge people, and they had long been enemies of the Lakota. The horse Kezawin rode and the one she led would be tempting prizes, as would the bundles she had lashed to the packhorse. She, herself, would be of value, as well. A woman was a potential child bearer first and a laborer second. Either way, she would be valuable property. By now they had spotted her, and they knew she was theirs for the taking. They were simply watching to see what this lone Lakota woman was about.

Flat sunbaked plains stretched endlessly before her, but she had seen the signs of a village nearby. There had been horse dung, and the grass had been grazed. The Pawnee were not rich in horses like the Lakota, but they had a few. Kezawin knew that the sentries would show themselves before she would ride close enough to see corn patches or the earthen mounds that she had heard about but had never seen.

They appeared all at once at the top of a rise. Four of them approached on horseback at an easy gait. Kezawin's buckskin mare pricked her ears, but Kezawin held her gait steady, matching the riders'. Her heart pounded, but she stared straight ahead and gave no sign of fear. Her only advantage was the sheer audacity of her action, and she counted on impressing them with nothing but that. Only when they put themselves in her path did she slow her pace. She came to a halt and gave the sign that she had come to talk.

The four men scowled beneath heavy brows. Their smooth scalps glistened in the sun, and their war clubs were handy. A fleeting picture of her skull being bashed open like a ripe squash ran through Kezawin's mind, but she squared her shoulders and suffered their perusal of her. They would know the meaning of the deer hooves that dangled from her belt, and even if they had no respect for Lakota medicine, they would see that only a woman with strong power would ride alone into the land of her enemy. She was obviously not lost, and by this time they had assured themselves that she was, indeed, unescorted.

The four men exchanged a few words and then wheeled their horses as if on signal. One brave took the lead while the others dropped back to surround Kezawin. They rode together in tight formation until they crested a ridge. On the sprawling flat below, Kezawin saw the bright green leaves of young cornstalks flickering in the midst of tawny grass, and beyond that were the Pawnee lodges, popping from the ground and sprigged with grass like the round bald heads of the men who dwelled in them.

Kezawin hid her thoughts behind an expressionless face as the four men led her into the village. Some of the people climbed onto their earthen roofs to get a good look at the Lakota woman who came to their village unbound and leading a packhorse. One child lost ground in his effort to scramble up the side of the house behind his older brother, and as his feet skidded in the clods of dirt he'd set rolling, he let the backward motion take him while he craned his neck for a sliding peek at the strange woman. On the rooftop above him, a little girl tugged at her mother's skirt, and Kezawin could hear the foreign words spoken in a familiar tone, putting off the child's demands for just a moment.

Her Skidi escorts led her to the bread-loaf-shaped entrance to one of the larger lodges. One of the men spoke to another and sent him on his way. Then the remaining three dismounted and signaled to Kezawin to do the same. An older man emerged from the lodge, and the three spoke to him in deferential tones. The full curve of each of his ears was pierced and adorned with looped strings of beads and fine bits of bone, which rattled softly as he nodded, listening. He spared Kezawin a glance, and she made the sign that she wanted to trade. He looked surprised.

The man who had been sent away appeared again, followed by a young woman. He barked a command, and she stepped closer to Kezawin. "I am Sweet Grass Woman, once Yankton, now second wife to Sky Runner of the Skidi."

The young woman spoke haltingly in the Nakota dialect, which bore enough similarity to Lakota that Kezawin had little trouble understanding. "I am Kezawin, daughter of Lone Bear of the Hunkpapa. I am also called Double Woman Dreamer."

Sweet Grass Woman took a single step backward. Kezawin lifted her chin and waited calmly. When the older man questioned her, Sweet Grass Woman had much to say, but Kezawin was more interested in the men's reaction than in the gist of Sweet Grass Woman's introductions. The wariness in their eyes was a good sign.

Sweet Grass Woman realized her own value when all attention turned to her as she translated. She threw her shoulders back and relayed the message of the men who had taken little notice of her until this moment. "Mark Of The Badger, chief of the Skidi, says that Double Woman Dreamer does not appear to be a fool. He wishes to know why a daughter of the Hunkpapa would come here to trade with the Pawnee."

"I am told that the Skidi took a white captive several days ago. I believe I know this man. If he is the one, then I wish to buy him from you."

This news prompted some discussion between Mark Of The Badger and the leader of the scouting party. Sweet Grass Woman waited patiently to relay his reply. "The Skidi have two white captives. The strongest of the two is being prepared for Tirawa. Mark Of The Badger has not yet decided about the other one."

James was as strong and healthy as any man. Kezawin shuddered inwardly, thinking no other white man would please the Pawnee god more than he would. "The man I seek is *wakan*," she said through her interpreter. "I, who have dreamed of the deer woman, have also dreamed of this man. He is a holy man and must be protected. He has medicine that will make mine stronger. That is why I have come to you without fear. My *sicun*, the white deer, has brought me to buy this man."

After more discussion among the men, Mark Of The Badger gave the matter some thought and finally relayed his offer. "Let us see what you have to trade."

Kezawin unloaded her packhorse and displayed four buffalo robes decorated with quilled borders. The vivid colors and superb work were, Sweet Grass Woman noted, signs of the work of one who had dreamed of the deer woman and could therefore call herself Double Woman Dreamer. Kezawin offered a pipe bag, a pair of saddlebags and a saddle blanket, all decorated with the same uniquely designed quillwork. Although Mark Of The Badger was not visibly impressed, the offer was clearly more than any white captive was worth.

"Mark Of The Badger accepts these gifts and the two horses," Sweet Grass Woman translated. "You may take your captive and return to your people unharmed."

"It must be the man I seek," Kezawin said.

"Mark Of The Badger says that one has already been chosen for Tirawa. You have traded for the other one."

James's arms ached like the devil, and his right foot had gone to sleep again. Since his capture he'd spent much of his time trussed up and braided like a knot of fancy bread. He wondered how soon these people planned to bake him. He found his situation particularly frustrating because he wanted nothing more than a chance to move about freely and observe Pawnee customs and habits, even partake insofar as he might be permitted. Instead, he was permitted almost no movement at all.

For a time they had kept him in the same lodge with Red Girard, the hulking young trapper who had broken several Pawnee bones before they'd taken him down. James had spent an entire day bound back-to-back with Girard, long enough for each to become thoroughly sick of the smell of the other. From the first, the Pawnee had taken an interest in Red's strapping physique and his flaming hair, and Red had worried aloud that he'd probably broken some chief's son's nose and would pay dearly for the transgression. He assumed that they were trying to decide where to hang his hair when it was all over.

Neither of them knew much about the Pawnee beyond the fact that they were enemies of the Sioux, which meant that James's proficiency in Lakota would not earn him any friends among his captors. After a time Red had been taken away, and James had been left in the corner of the huge earth-walled lodge with the chief's horse. Each morning he and the horse were taken outside. The animal was permitted to graze, while James was allowed only a few moments to tend to his needs before he was herded back inside and tied up again. At night he was taken to water, and then he and the horse were returned to the corner and secured there with leather thongs.

James fastened his mind on the shaft of light that shot through the center smoke hole. Everything else bore down on him and threatened to bury him alive. The air smelled dank and earthy, and he struggled with the oppressive darkness. The inside of his nostrils were coated with dust, and a gash he'd received on his neck in the initial scuffle with his captors was festering. Without his hands he could do nothing to help himself.

He anticipated the origin of every sound outside the lodge. The dwelling housed a dozen people, the members of what appeared to be three related families. James didn't blame them for spending most of the daylight hours outside, but he was glad when a woman or a pair of children would spend a few moments within the lodge. Even though they ignored him, he welcomed their company and some relief from the boredom.

There was something going on outside the lodge even now. With his cheek pressed against the packed-dirt floor, James strained to listen. The deep rumble of men's voices was too distant to allow him to discern anything other than the fact that a conversation was in progress, but it was a form of distraction. It was something living, something human, and James felt dangerously out of touch with both elements.

The old man, his "host," entered the lodge with a buffalo robe over each arm. James peered across the room, and when the shaft of light struck one of the robes, he noticed the quillwork. The intricate designs were Sioux. The sight touched his heart the way a piece of his mother's needlework might have. He thought of the airy tipi with its opaque walls, the floor carpeted with buffalo robes and the smell of meat boiling in the cooking pouch. A woman entered, carrying more decorated goods. A second woman followed. The entryway was like a tunnel, which echoed the sounds made by those who approached and made for a moment of wild anticipation. James knew before she came through the door that it was another woman, because he could hear the soft click of elk's teeth and the music the tin-wrapped ends of the fringe on her dress made. She entered as a shadow and moved toward the light.

He knew the days and nights in this hole had broken him at last. He had lost touch with reality, and his mind saw only what it wanted to see. Kezawin.

And Kezawin saw that James was the man she had purchased. Relief poured through her like the first hot soup after a long fast. She moved quickly to kneel beside him and slip her hand between his face and the dirt floor. He uttered her name, and she felt the warmth of his breath on the inside of her wrist. He closed his eyes and turned dry, cracked lips against the same spot. Her stomach tightened, and she longed to examine him thoroughly as would the mother of a newborn, but she turned instead and said over her shoulder, "Ask Mark Of The Badger if I may cut the slave's bonds. I have paid dearly for him, and I want him whole and healthy."

"Slave?" James croaked while the translation was made on the far side of the room.

"I have purchased you, James Garrett. You belong to me now."

"Better you than him."

Permission was granted through Sweet Grass Woman, and Kezawin unsheathed her skinning knife and sliced through the rawhide that bound James's hands behind him and fastened his wrists to his ankles. He groaned as his blood rushed to his extremities while Kezawin helped him to sit up. He looked at her, blinking several times as if to clear his vision. He reached out to touch her braided hair, then her cheek. His fingers trembled against her skin.

"You must not touch me, James," she whispered. Her voice was as unsteady as his hand. "You are my slave."

"How did you find me?" he asked. "How did you know I was here?"

She peeled back the collar of the shirt that had become a filthy rag and examined his neck. It was too dark to see, so she leaned close and sniffed for signs of flesh rot. "What else have they done to you, James? Is there anything—"

He grabbed her shoulders. "Are you here alone? You didn't come here alone, did you?"

"You must not touch me," she repeated as she shrugged his hands off. "You *are* my slave. I would see to your wounds if you would tell me what damage has been done."

"Just what you see," he said impatiently. "Kezawin, who's with you? Who brought you? Who's looking out for your safety here?"

"No one came with me. The Pawnee is our—"

"I know," he said, cutting off the word as though it might be a curse. "I know that. Woman, you've lost your mind. You are as crazy as your people think I am. These people have had me tied up here for days—God knows what they have in mind. What made you think one woman, one crazy little woman—"

Laughter threatened to ruin her staid demeanor as she sealed his lips with two fingers. She couldn't hold back the soft smile that had blossomed in her heart when she heard his words of concern for her.

When she took her fingers away, he added, "One very beautiful, very brave woman."

"We will not be permitted to leave until tomorrow, and we will have to walk."

"Walk?"

"The two horses were part of the price."

He digested the news with a quiet sigh. "There was another man taken prisoner with me, a trapper named Girard. Somehow we have to secure his—"

"We will talk of that later," she said as she stood up and offered him a hand. "Are you able to stand?"

He got to his feet on his own, but his legs wobbled, and he finally steadied himself with an arm around Kezawin's shoulders. "I'm not touching you. I'm leaning on you."

"You are like a newborn calf."

"I felt as though I'd been crammed back into the womb these past days." He glanced up at Mark Of The Badger and

Sweet Grass Woman, who had become a half-interested audience. "Is he going to let us walk out of here?"

Kezawin nodded to Sweet Grass Woman, who relayed the question. "Mark Of The Badger will permit you to go as far as the river. Your slave should be washed. One might mistake him for a horse."

Mark Of The Badger pinched his nose as he told his joke and laughed all the harder when he heard the Lakota translation.

"One did, in fact, mistake me for a horse—one nearsighted old—" James grumbled. "I would not be apt to commend Pawnee hospitality to my friends, but I can think of a few enemies I might like to see—"

"Hold your tongue, James," Kezawin warned as she helped him to the door. "We are still guests here."

They bathed separately, and when Kezawin returned to the spot James had chosen for his bath, she found him dressed only in a pair of wet knee-length drawers. His buckskin trousers and ragged shirt and socks were flapping in the breeze on a nearby bush while he sat on a fallen cottonwood and struggled to pull his boots over bare feet. Kezawin laughed merrily, and she wondered what kind of white man could have been chosen over James, who looked as healthy and appealing as any man she had known. He looked up and delighted her with a boyish grin.

"One of these times you will catch me without a stitch, and then we'll see who has the last laugh."

"*Tuki*, white man," she teased in a way of a woman challenging a man's boast. She set a pouch and several other items down beside the fallen tree where James sat. "Remember that the Double Woman Dreamer laughs at anything that amuses her."

"And if you find that you have paid dearly for a joke, Double Woman Dreamer, who should laugh then?"

"The deer woman," she said as she tugged at a dead branch and pulled it free of a thatch of silver-leafed buffalo berry bushes. "I am never more than one step ahead of that wily trickster. I cannot forget that she has two faces."

"None more beautiful than the one that came for me today. When you came into that dark pit and stepped into the light, you looked so like—"

He wanted to say *an angel*, but it occurred to him that in his world he'd seen no dark-skinned likenesses of angels and that he could think of no Lakota word for the concept. Yet if ever an angel had interceded in his life, it had happened today. His mother had spoken of angels when they had both been gravely ill, and he had imagined bright-faced, golden-haired creatures in filmy white frocks. But the one who had stepped into that hellhole's single shaft of light wore the skin of the elk decorated in earth's warm hues. She had hair as black as the raven's wing and eyes that mirrored his pain the moment she saw him. She was at once the essence of heaven and earth, and when she had knelt beside him and lifted his face out of the dirt, she'd lifted his heart, as well.

Even now he was a little stunned and slow to act. She paused in her efforts and looked at him, waiting for him to complete the comparison. What had she looked like?

"Something *wakan*," he said as he realized his tardiness in lending a hand. He jumped up from his seat and pulled the dead branch clear of the living ones. He tossed it to the ground and turned to her. "You were a ray of hope that shattered my despair."

"You were a pitiful wretch," she said, avoiding his eyes. She broke a dry limb off the branch, remembering how relieved she had felt the instant her eyes had adjusted to the lodge's murky interior and she could see that the man on the floor was truly James. "I must tend to those wounds lest you become wolf bait."

"*You* wound me, Kezawin, even as I sing your praises."
He broke off two stout sticks, measured one against the
other and searched for a third.

"I hear no singing. I doubt that your people can make a
good song, for I have never heard you—"

The third stick snapped between his hands as he raised his
voice in close approximation of a traditional Lakota song.
He composed the lyric on the spot and fashioned a tripod as
he sang softly to her.

"She comes to me
Happily am I delivered
She takes me from darkness to light
Woman whose eyes soften with mercy
She comes, she comes."

He looked up at her only after he had finished his song,
and he saw his own surprise reflected in her eyes. He wasn't
sure where the song had come from, and now that the notes
had taken flight and there was only the sound of the lazy
river and the look of surprise in Kezawin's eyes, he felt like
an awkward youth. "You were . . . quite a sight."

"Because you needed someone."

"Because it was you who came."

They built a fire pit together in silence. Kezawin soaked
James's tripod and set it in place, and when she had water
boiling in the paunch she had borrowed from Sweet Grass
Woman, she took bits of bark and dried buds and prepared
an infusion to treat James's wounds. He watched her without asking questions. The fire crackled and hissed, while at
his back his shirt and pants flapped in the breeze. The warm
afternoon air smelled like freedom.

She bathed his neck in the hot liquid. He jumped reflex-
ively at the first application, but his skin made its adjust-

ment, and the heat became a source of comfort. For the time being he gave little thought to what ingredients might have gone into the concoction as he leaned back against the fallen cottonwood and gave himself over to Kezawin's care.

It was good just to look at her, to admire the details that had lodged themselves unstintingly in his memory and to take fond note of those that he must have overlooked months ago. Her eyelashes were long, dark and absolutely straight. He had not remembered that spiky straightness. But he had not forgotten the way her eyes crinkled at the corners when she laughed, nor the way light and shadow accented her angular bone structure. There was nothing cool or hazy about her. She had a summer face. Her skin enjoyed a love affair with the sun.

"The woman who translated for you must have been with the Pawnee for some time," James said finally.

"She is Yankton, but she has a Pawnee husband. She was probably taken captive long ago."

"Why didn't they take you?" he asked. She glanced up at him, then continued to bathe a scrape she had located on his side. "Are they afraid of you, too?"

"The Yankton woman told them of my medicine. They saw that I dared to come among them and that I came alone."

"Why did you do it, Kezawin?" When she didn't answer, he caught her hand. "Why?"

"Why did you come back?"

"My work was not finished." He couldn't tell her he had no place else to go.

As a courtesy she accepted his answer, but she pulled her hand from his and continued to bathe him.

"You could not have known they wouldn't kill you," he persisted.

"Death is always a possibility. They may kill me yet, James. They may kill you." She gave him an enigmatic look, one that could almost have been a challenge if it had not hinted at fear.

"I'll give you my word, I'll say nothing to offend them. I'll not do anything foolish. You've risked enough."

"I have traded valuable goods for you," she reminded him as she swabbed his neck with a viscous potion that smelled of mint. "You are mine until I say otherwise."

He nodded once and lifted his gaze to the river's far bank. He smiled. "I understand."

When they returned to the village, a voice hailed them in French, and they turned to find Red Girard enjoying a meal in the shade of one of the smaller lodges. One woman hovered nearby while a second offered him more food.

"This is the life, *n'est-ce pas, mon ami*? I see they've given you a woman, too." Red laughed. "There's been quite a procession of them bringing me food and whatnot. I think I'm supposed to take my pick, but each one seems prettier than the last."

James opened his mouth to reply, but Kezawin grasped his elbow and murmured, "You must say nothing."

James turned his answer into a hesitant smile and waved to the man.

"Ask them for some clothes, Garrett," Red suggestion jovially. "You look like the very devil. Look at me!"

James took note of Red's new white trade-cloth shirt and the strings of hair pipe and beads that hung around his neck. He nodded, still smiling broadly as he muttered aside to Kezawin, "They've certainly taken a liking to him. It must be that French charm."

"Come away, James," Kezawin insisted with an urgency that puzzled him.

While they were sharing the evening meal with Mark Of The Badger's family, they heard men chanting at either end of the village. James thought it a pleasant custom, this lifting of voices at the end of the day, though this was the first time he had heard it during the week he'd spent in captivity. Associating the word *pleasant* with any part of the Skidi had not occurred to him, but now that he was free—almost free—he noticed that the men were ready to perform their version of retiring to the drawing room for a smoke while the women gathered up their wood and clay bowls and the kettles they had acquired in trade.

Not unlike children of any race, the boys were intent on plying some craft with their fathers, for they had brought forth bundles of sturdy cherry wood shoots and laid them at the elders' feet. There was much discussion as Mark Of The Badger and his older sons or sons-in-law broke open the bundles and apparently instructed the youngsters in making their selections. James concluded that it was time for arrow making.

"We must sleep," Kezawin announced abruptly. "We have a long journey ahead of us."

"I don't know whether there's room in my stall for the three of us," James grumbled as he uncrossed his legs.

"Mark Of The Badger's daughter provided a robe and showed me where we are to sleep." She caught his smile. "Remember your place, James. Remember our situation."

He tried to remember. He tried to keep their precarious relations with the Skidi in the forefront of his mind as he lay inches from Kezawin's warm body beneath their borrowed sleeping robe. He wondered what she had on her mind as she lay there next to him, stiff and still as a corpse and trying to make herself breathe evenly. She wasn't fooling him. Two of the women had come to bed. One snored, and the other wheezed. But Kezawin was wide awake.

"Kezawin?" he whispered.

No answer.

"I hate this pile of dirt. I don't want to sleep in a lean-to, either. When we get back, I want to sleep in a tipi."

Silence.

"We must speak to Red before we leave tomorrow. If he chooses to come with us, I don't think they would stop him. Do you?"

One long, deep breath. No answer.

"On the other hand, he seems to be having a pretty good time of it. They must prefer the beefy sort."

Silence.

"They took my journals. I'm having the devil's own time keeping people from—"

"They gave me your books," Kezawin whispered harshly. "They kept what they could use, but they have no use for your precious books."

"Ah, good, then I—"

"Stop this, James. I have no wish to face tomorrow's sunrise after a sleepless night."

"Good night, then," he clipped, and turned his back on her. He closed his eyes and counted backward from a thousand, and his critical awareness of her finally melted like paraffin. He drifted on the muffled rhythm of a distant drum.

But Kezawin's thoughts were full of the smiling white man with hair the color of blood, and she could not sleep.

Mark Of The Badger roused them before daylight. Kezawin clutched the sleeping robe to her breast while the Pawnee elder bound James's hands and feet once again. She could see that others stood in the shadows of firelight, waiting. James offered groggy protests, but he did not fight.

"You cannot take him," Kezawin demanded, hoping the desperation that spun in her head did not sound in her voice. "I have paid for him. We have an agreement, Mark Of The Badger. No man of your stature would break his—"

"Mark Of The Badger does not claim your slave." Sweet Grass Woman stepped closer. "The white man must not leave the lodge now. You must see to it, Double Woman Dreamer. Later, when Tirawa has been satisfied with our petition for good crops and good health, you will both be permitted to stay or go, as you wish."

Mark Of The Badger gave Kezawin a hard searching look. He carried more lengths of rawhide. He glanced at James, then back at Kezawin. She nodded dumbly, and he turned and strode out the opening. In the far corner she heard the clatter of wood. It was the gathering of weapons, a sound all women dreaded.

"What the hell is going on here?" James demanded in English. His hands were tied behind him, and his feet were bound together, but he managed to roll over and sit up. He turned to Kezawin, who huddled behind the buffalo robe, and he continued in Lakota. "What are they doing? Why did they tie me up like this? Did they think I would interfere with their morning prayers?"

"I have never witnessed this practice of the Skidi, but I have heard stories."

"Stories of what? What are they doing?"

"It is not the way of the Lakota. These people have strange ways, just as your people do." She reached for her dress and slipped it over her head. He thought her eyes seemed markedly wilder when her head popped through the neck opening. "When it's over, we can return to the Lakota. We will sleep in a tipi, and there will be no—"

"What are they doing, Kezawin?"

She said nothing. He resumed his practice of listening for whatever muffled sounds might be heard through the thick earthen walls and trying to guess what they meant. The village seemed to be mobilizing.

"Are they being attacked?" he asked. "Is that it? Cut me loose, Kezawin. Trust me. Let me—"

He heard an anguished shout. Someone called his name. Red Girard? James concentrated on the sound. He heard it again. "What are they doing to Red?" He peered at her through the dim light, searching for answers. "Kezawin?" His heart pounded as the shout came again. "Kezawin! What are they doing to Red!"

"You cannot help him, James. You must not try."

"My God, they're going to kill him. Kezawin, they're going to kill the man!"

Kezawin hugged her knees. She closed her eyes and gripped her own forearms, digging her nails into her skin. Morning light eased its way through the smoke hole and into the lodge.

"You must . . . you *must* cut me loose."

"I must take you back to the Lakota," she said quietly.

The voice had moved to the west end of the village, and Red's cries were desperate and angry. "Garrett, you son of a bitch, help me! They're going to burn me alive. Do you hear me? Where the hell are you, you coward? Damn you, you've got to help me!"

"Kezawin, please," James whispered. "We can't just sit here."

"They would kill you, too, James."

"Garrett!"

"Kezawin, we have to do something." His struggle against his bonds was useless.

"I must take you back to the Lakota," she repeated. "That's all I know."

"Kezawin, I know that man. I traveled with that man. Cut these off. Cut them now!"

His shout was enjoined by a distant agonized cry.

"He will feel no more pain," Kezawin whispered. "They have made a quick, clean kill, and the rest will not matter."

"Oh, God."

"You could not have stopped it, James. Had they chosen you, I could not have stopped it."

Outside, the morning was pierced with thunderous cries. James's shoulders slumped as he lowered his forehead to his knees. Kezawin touched his hair, and he shuddered. "You knew," he groaned.

"I knew."

"You could have told me." He lifted his head and stared at her as he realized the import of what he'd said. "If you had told me last night, I could have done something."

"You are not a warrior," she said. "You are a medicine man. You are *wakan* and must be protected."

"Protected! What kind of woman are you? How could you save one and let another—"

"I paid the price for the captive who had not been chosen. Until I saw you, I did not know which man I had bought."

They stared at each other as they listened to the frenzied cries outside the walls. "You should have told me," he said, controlling his voice. "A man decides for himself, and you think me less than a man."

"I think you are meant to be more than just a man. The Pawnee did not choose you, because the white deer chose you first."

"So *you* say."

"You cannot know your destiny when you are puffed up with pride, James Garrett. Your friend is dead."

The crazed shouts were dying in the distance now as a different voice claimed James's ear. A single male voice, a mournful cry, plaintive and hollow with sorrow.

"He's dead, you say? Then what can that be?"

"I believe that is the grief of the man who took him captive," she told him. "He was required to make the kill. Now he grieves, for he has taken a life."

James shook his head in disbelief.

"Your friend is dead, James. You had no power to prevent his death. Put aside your male pride and mourn for him."

Chapter Six

Mark Of The Badger's parting gift to Double Woman Dreamer was a horse. It was not as fine an animal as the two she had traded, but it would serve her well on her journey. He hastened to add that she was welcome to remain among the Pawnee, for it was clear that her medicine was strong, and her courage was unique among the Lakota. If she stayed, he said, she could keep her slave and no man would interfere with her. Kezawin graciously declined his offer, explaining that she had a strong vision of where she must be and what she must do, and she dared not ignore those requirements.

James said nothing. By the time Sweet Grass Woman had ducked into the lodge to tell Kezawin that Mark Of The Badger wished to see them, he had ceased to struggle. He wasn't even sure he wanted his bonds cut, for they had become the only reality in the midst of a nightmare. His hands and feet were tied. He was incapacitated. Everything else was too absurd to be real. He said nothing when Kezawin cut him loose, but he rubbed the soreness out of his wrists, gathered his journals and emerged from the lodge like a man who walked in his sleep. Someone handed him a bundle, which he dutifully lashed to the gift horse's back. He might have suggested that Kezawin ride, but he said nothing to her.

When the time came, he led the horse, and Kezawin walked behind.

As they passed through the village, James peered at the solemn faces of the people. He didn't care that his actions might be considered rude. He didn't think about it. He thought about the young boys bringing bundles of sticks to their fathers for arrow making. They had worked side by side, old instructing young. How had they used the arrows that morning? Who had used them? Each face he passed was suspect. Was it you? he thought. What part did you play? Dark eyes, all of them, dark and inscrutable, full of terrible secrets. There were traces of soot on their faces and bits of white ash in their hair.

James had seen nothing. He was there, but he was not there. He was not to blame. He had heard the cries, but he was bound, tightly bound, hand and foot. Is there blood on your hands, young fellow? Don't show me. I don't want to see. I was not there. There stood the woman who had brought food to a man she knew she would kill. How could you do it? his eyes accused. How could you call it anything but murder? How can I call you anything but savage?

They were headed west and then north. At the west end of the village on a barren knoll stood two charred poles and the smoldering ashes of a fire. Nothing stirred. The mid-morning sun made the moist summer air heavy with heat, and the smell of burnt blood hung in the air. James stared in hot judgment at the place as he passed. Kezawin attended to the earth, as was her custom. She stopped to dig a few plants, then caught up with James, who set a steadfast pace and did not vary it. They walked without exchanging a word until late afternoon, when the need for water drew the packhorse to a spring-fed pond and a shady resting place.

"Sweet Grass Woman gave us dried meat," Kezawin said as she pulled the bundle off the horse's back and took a rawhide pouch, a parfleche, from the rolled trade blanket. "I found roots to boil with it if you wish to make camp here."

"I want none of their meat."

She let the dictum stand in silence for a moment. "I hope the roots will be to your liking," she said finally. "It is a bit early in the season, but they don't look bad. I will cook them first and add meat to my portion after you have eaten."

He watered the horse and brooded while she cooked. He ate in silence, then brooded while he watched her eat. He told himself the smell of the Pawnee meat turned his stomach, but in truth it did not. The wild roots had not satisfied him, and he brooded over that, too. It irritated him that Kezawin had cooked just what she knew she would eat, and when she was finished, there was not a morsel left in case he had changed his mind. He brooded while she cleaned up from the meal.

"Do you realize what they did to him?" he asked, breaking the silence.

The cottonwood leaves rustled overhead. "I have heard many stories," she said quietly.

"They didn't burn him alive, did they?"

"No. They shot him with an arrow first, from side to side, under the arms. Death came quickly."

"Why did they keep yelping and screaming, then, and why—"

"It is the Skidi way. It is not the Lakota way. I cannot explain it."

"But you prevented me from doing anything about it."

"I was not the one who tied your hands."

"No, but you wouldn't *untie* them."

"Is this the way the white man grieves? It seems a strange way to ease your loss, this counting the things you might have done. Death hears none of this."

James sighed and tipped his head back. He watched a cloud roll by. "They were all in on it, weren't they. I could see it in their eyes. Even the children."

"What did you see?"

It took him a moment to put the words together. "Blood lust."

Kezawin puzzled for a moment, and then she realized that he had used Lakota words for an idea that was not Lakota. Blood and sexual desire did not belong together. A woman's menstrual blood was taboo for a man. She could only guess what he might have meant by the paradoxical term he had contrived, but she decided not to question him about it. Instead she said, "You have taken life yourself, James."

He stared at her. It unnerved him to hear the words. How had she known? His fingertips felt cold, and his palms became clammy as the blood rushed to his face and pounded in his temples. Her eyes were dark and inscrutable, like the eyes of the Pawnee villagers. He had filled his ears with his own protests and consigned the blood to them, but now the eyes were Kezawin's. And she knew him.

"That wasn't murder," he said more desperately than he'd intended.

"No. Not when you need the animal's flesh to nourish your own. Not when your family is hungry. But life is never taken without regret." She looked at him anxiously. "When you take a plant, do you not express that regret in your own language? Usually you say something for each one."

James's mind reeled with confusion. What was she thinking? Then relief settled over him. She didn't know about the man he'd killed. That was good. It didn't matter what she was talking about, because she didn't know, and he had just realized that he didn't want her to know. One moment she was intuitive beyond what was humanly possible, and the next she was utterly naive. If she imagined him saying some kind of prayer when he dug up a plant, she was mistaken, of course. As often as not he muttered his observations to himself, but there was never any regret. He was a scientist, for God's sake. And he hadn't committed murder, either. He had defended himself. There was no point in trying to explain that to her and no earthly reason for him to be so ill at ease.

"As you say, hunting and plant collecting do not constitute murder," he said in a calmer voice.

Since he had chosen not to hear what she said, she set her thoughts aside and asked, "Have you had much success with stealing?"

James was shocked. "What kind of a question is—"

"We need another horse."

"Oh, yes. A horse." He had stolen nothing but what was rightfully his, which couldn't be considered stealing, could it? Perhaps the Lakota would consider it stealing, in which case they would honor him for his single success. "Who could I steal a horse from?"

Kezawin smiled. "Anyone who turns his back for a moment."

He had already tried it once. They had come across a small band of people camped in a draw. Kezawin had identified them as Ponca, and she'd said that they would be an easy mark. When he asked why, she said proudly that the Lakota people with their cousins the Yankton and the Yanktonais had "moved those Ponca people aside long ago." James had sized up the little family band and decided he might be able to move the four women and the several youngsters aside—one or two at a time—but there

were three men with them who might not be so easily
budged. Besides, they only had four horses. He told himself that the Ponca must be close to their village, so they
didn't need the horse he wanted as badly as he and Kezawin
did.

Gauging the distance between the grazing horses and the
breakfast camp fire, James had decided that he had the advantage of surprise. But stealth was not his strong suit. He
had rushed his move and stampeded the horses in four
directions, making his escape only because he was mounted.

After four more days of doing more walking than riding,
he had decided to try it again. They had seen signs of a small
party of horsemen in the area, and after they had made
camp, James told Kezawin that he was taking a short ride.
She had said nothing, and now as he crouched in grass that
stood as tall as a horse's back and downwind of a five-man
hunting party, he wondered at the trust she had shown him.
He was loathe to have her witness another failure, but if he
was killed, she would be left alone and horseless there on the
prairie. He wondered whether it had occurred to her that he
could decide simply to ride away.

But, then, she didn't know that he had run once before.
She couldn't know the taste that running left in a man's
mouth, the bitter taste of his own bile.

He had located the hunters' camp at dusk, then doubled
back to the river and returned, having covered himself almost completely with mud. Night had fallen, and he smelled
the fat dripping from the meat on their spit into their camp
fire. The aroma brought out the claws within James's belly.
He decided that when he got back to his own camp, he
would break his fast. He'd eaten enough roots. He wouldn't
make any explanations; he would simply take jerky from the
parfleche and tear into it with his teeth. It had been an ar-

duous march with only one horse and no time for hunting forays. Principles were fine, but a man had to eat.

But first he had to get the job done, and this time he wouldn't rush it. His own horse was staked just beyond the rise, out of sight of the camp. He was going in on foot this time. He felt a mosquito pierce the skin on the back of his neck. Mud offered some protection—although an occasional pest managed to penetrate—and also interfered with his scent. He covered the insect with his palm and silently pressed the life out of it. This time he would wait until the men slept. *This time* he would come away with a horse.

He closed in inch by agonizing inch, pulling himself on his belly across the last several yards. He used Kezawin's skinning knife to cut the first horse's tether. The animal went on grazing. The second horse took a few unhurried steps and found better grass. As James sliced the third tether, he thought of Kezawin again. When he'd asked for the knife, she had given it to him. She had not questioned him. She'd extracted no promises, nor had she offered words of caution or advice. Had she forgotten that he'd failed once? One more tether, he told himself. The fifth horse, the stout buckskin—that one had his name on it.

His heart leaped in his chest as he sprang onto the buckskin's back and let loose with a brash, irrepressible "Eee-yahhh!" The other four horses scattered as James bent close to the buckskin's neck and dug his moccasined heels into its flanks. The horse leaped and shot after them as though his hindquarters were tightly coiled springs. James heard the hiss of an arrow as it whizzed past his ear, but he fastened his mind on the rise. The buckskin's powerful hindquarters catapulted them over the top. On the downhill slope he stretched his gait, and James leaned off the left side and concentrated on the staked horse. He reached out, caught the rawhide tether and gave it a jerk as the buckskin careened past the docile old mare.

The tether became a firebrand as it slid through James's fist. "Eee-yahhh!" he yelled again, pouring the pain into his fury. The small wooden stake tied to the end of the rope smacked the curled edge of his hand, jerking the docile mare to life. Four horses galloped into the night, and two streaked after them.

Kezawin had their meager provisions packed and ready. They rode to put some distance between themselves and the victims of James's coup. Beneath a star-sprayed predawn sky they made camp, sheltered within a valley of stark, eroded clay mounds. A silty creek provided water for the horses. Kezawin examined the stolen buckskin as she picketed both animals where they might reach what tufts of grass were available. The stout gelding was painted with black streaks of lightning and signs of hail. His tail was bound with red deerskin, and a swatch of the same dyed leather was attached to his bit. It was evident that James had counted coup on a Lakota war party, perhaps a group of her Brûlé cousins.

Kezawin smiled secretly. His success was not to be underrated simply because he had raided an ally. They would have killed him if he had been less cunning, careful or quick. She would not make him feel foolish by telling him that he had counted coup on a party that would have helped them. James had earned his victory. She thought it would be fun to see those five warriors return to their village on foot and hear what stories they would tell their women.

"Boil enough meat for both of us," James hailed as Kezawin brought what scrub wood she had found. He clutched a strip of his shirt in his rope-burned hand. With his good hand he had dug a fire pit and surrounded it with stones, and his voice was full of exuberance. "I feel as though I haven't eaten in days."

"You know, James—" The firewood clattered to the ground, and Kezawin straightened with hands on hips. "I traded a great deal for you. I think I may generously permit you to boil the meat to suit us both."

James laughed and reached for the parfleche. "The world's best chefs are men, dear Kezawin, as you shall soon learn."

"I said *I may*." She gave him a bright smile, and he saw her pride in him couched in her teasing manner. "It is more likely that I will decide to cook for us myself."

"I'm well on the way to purchasing myself back from you," he told her. He squatted beside the pile of wood and began breaking it into shorter lengths. "The buckskin is yours, and he is twice the horse your mare was."

"Yes, he is. Geldings are best for endurance, and the buckskin is as swift as the wind. That's why I can never ride him."

"But he's even tempered," James protested as she knelt beside him. He braced his hands on his thighs and looked at her with earnest concern. "You can't be afraid to ride him, Kezawin. Not you. I hid in the grass, waiting for the right moment, moving so carefully, all the while considering my choice. Of the five, I picked the buckskin, and I chose him for you because he was the best. You traded a buckskin away for me, and I brought you a buckskin."

"I traded a mare. She was dependable and pretty, but she was not a fast horse. A woman may not ride a fast horse."

"Why not?"

"A woman will make a fast horse slow."

He drew one eyebrow down and hiked the other. "How?"

"By riding it. If a woman is allowed to ruin a good horse, it is well-known that her family will suffer."

Her expression left no room for doubt. She did not question the validity of this time-honored discretionary measure. James considered the idea for a moment. It seemed a convenient way for a man to keep his wife's hands off his best horse, but for a man who had anticipated the light he might bring to a woman's eyes with the best gift he had to offer, this bit of folklore was annoying.

"I stole the horse for you," he insisted. "I thought you would be pleased."

"It was a bold, brave move. I will honor you with a robe painted with your story."

"*I* wanted to honor *you*." He gestured dramatically with his wounded hand. "You saved my life."

"Is this horse a gift, or is it payment for your freedom?"

"It's a gift!" he bellowed. He clamped his jaw shut and took a deep breath, searching for his rational self. "It's a gift, even if I do owe you my life. Right now the horse is all I have, and I want you to—" He extended his hand in supplication, and he saw the blood-soaked bandage. "I *stole* that horse," he reminded himself. He glanced up at Kezawin. "I'm offering you a stolen horse as though it were my own to give."

"It was a fine coup," Kezawin said enthusiastically. "One against five, and you had no weapon."

"In truth, I have nothing of my own to give you. Nothing that would express my—"

"You have your books."

He gaped at her. "My journals?"

She nodded.

"What would you want with my journals?"

The look on James's face reminded her of the proud man who had once offered the Double Woman Dreamer anything he owned if she would cure his wife's fever. She had named his Appaloosa brood mare, and his eyes and his mouth had become pinched. "What do you want with my spotted mare?" he'd asked. Kezawin had glanced at the man's wife, whose eyes were downcast, and she had agreed to accept one mare of any color.

She leveled her gaze at James. "What would I want with your swift gelding?"

"What would you want with a man?" he challenged. "Why would you buy a man, Kezawin?"

The question hung in the air between them.

"I can accept the gift," Kezawin said quietly, then added with a shrug, "but you will have to be the one to ride him."

"Fine." He snapped another dry stick and tossed it into the pile they'd made together, then struck the flint angrily and made sparks fly. "It's probably true," he grumbled. "You probably would make him slow."

James belonged to Kezawin now. The story of how Double Woman Dreamer had come away from the Skidi camp unharmed, bringing the plant-taker with her, gave strong testimony to the power of her medicine. The white man was hers to do with as she pleased, and the old ones noted that she seemed to put him to good use. Her medicine was clearly stronger than his, but he had something he called *science*, and along with that he used the white man's books. The wise ones speculated that if the white man was cautious enough, the deer woman might not kill him and Double Woman Dreamer's medicine might be stronger than ever. To that end, James the plant-taker spent long days with the medicine woman, but he spent his nights in Lone Bear's lodge.

He chafed under the invisible yoke. At first he made light of his indentured condition, but it was clear that he was expected to do Kezawin's bidding as long as he stayed with the Hunkpapa. He was free to move about the camp without any physical restraints, but he was not his own man. He

owed Kezawin his time and his labor, and he was constantly
aware that it was *her* work that he was doing. No matter that
her work was exactly the object of his interest, it bothered
him that she chose the time, the place and the means for it
to be done. On more than one occasion it occurred to him
that he might just walk away, and then he remembered the
ways of the Skidi and decided he could serve a little longer
as field assistant to Double Woman Dreamer.

James did his share of hunting and fishing, even tanning, but every task became more arduous as summer
pressed on. The days grew hot, and no rain fell. Game
ranged far in search of better grass. For those who gathered roots and berries, the harvest was meager, and those
who gathered medicine needed a sharp eye and great patience. Stream beds shriveled and cracked like old skin as the
river's network of arteries hardened for lack of rain. Men of
vision sought high places, stretched their arms and cried to
the sky. The grassy hillsides turned tan, and only the dust
grew more plentiful.

The band had moved westward into the rugged Missouri
breaks, encroaching upon Crow territory. Doggedly they
followed the foraging game. Hunters went out in small parties—brothers, friends, fathers and sons—and James
formed a new bond with Lone Bear, who showed him that
squirrels and magpies made good meat on a day when there
was nothing larger available. James came to enjoy fishing.
Impatient with pole fishing, Lone Bear recalled younger
days when he could wield a pronged spear with as much
agility as a bear using its own paw.

"The river is slow this summer, and the fish are sleepy,"
Lone Bear observed one afternoon as he studied the activ-
ity in the shallows. "They're not interested in your grass-
hopper, Garrett. There are too many grasshoppers around
this summer."

James flexed his shoulders and scratched his back against the furrowed bark of his oak backrest. Lone Bear had set out enough snares to trap anything that dared to scamper among the trees that shaded the meandering riverbank. One way or another they'd have something to eat before the day was over, and James was content to have it the lazy way. He watched Lone Bear poke around a deadfall, and he assumed the old man was searching for better bait. "Grasshoppers are as good as grubs," James said, but he really had no preference.

Lone Bear found the long forked pole he'd been looking for, and he set about sharpening the prongs and carving barbed notches in the crotch. James ignored the project until Lone Bear handed him the finished fishing spear. "The best time to learn to fish is when the fish are lazier than you."

James sat up slowly. "Lazier than—"

"You can learn, Garrett. You're quicker than you used to be." The folds in his face rearranged themselves as he smiled. "And I've slowed down some."

James knew his scowl was wasted on the old man. He set his pole down and accepted the spear. "What am I supposed to do with it?"

"Take off your pants. It's too hot for them anyway."

James had not worn a shirt since Kezawin had brought him back from the Pawnee, but he clung to his buckskin breeches simply because he dreaded the final indignity of baring his legs. He'd taken to wearing a breechclout under his britches, and he was relieved when the sight of his pale legs elicited no audible snickers. Lone Bear motioned for James to wade into the water.

"Like so, Garrett," Lone Bear instructed, going through the motions. James saw the enthusiasm of youth hampered by an old man's body, and he was drawn into the sport by an urge to imitate, to do what the mentor had once done. He crouched the way Lone Bear crouched, and they waited together. When a fish approached, James lunged, splashed, speared, and the fish swam away.

"Is that how you made your coup on five hunters, Garrett? The fish are no less wary than they were. Try again."

Each try was a closer approximation of success. "Patience," Lone Bear repeated quietly. "Let him come to you. Welcome him. Welcome him. He will come."

James waited. When the water from the last splash stopped dripping, it was replaced by the sweat from his brow. He took a quick swipe at it and assumed his frozen stance once again. Out of the corner of his eye, James could see his trainer holding the same position, waiting. The sun pulsated on James's back, and a bead of sweat gathered at the tip of his nose. Between the pillars of his legs, into the shadow of the colossus shimmied a silver-finned fish. Silence, stillness, waiting, waiting...thunk! Lone Bear became the imitator as James wielded the spear to its mark, and both men whooped victoriously.

They shared a meal on the riverbank, neither complaining of the meat's silty taste. Lone Bear spoke of other summers without rain and the lean winters that followed. The notion troubled James as he imagined snow on the ground and hunger in Kezawin's eyes. It seemed incumbent upon him to provide for the three of them. His skills were sharpening, he told himself. He had proved that again today.

"Why did you let Kezawin ride into Pawnee country alone?" James asked without preliminaries.

"You were her friend. I told her of your capture because I knew she would mourn your death."

"But she came after me alone."

"Who else would go?"

It was a candid question, all the more chilling because the answer was, truly, no one. No one from this world, no one from the world he'd left behind. It took James a moment to find the will to press on quietly. "You should not have allowed her to go there at all. There was every chance they would have ignored the valor of her act and murdered her in some terrible way."

"How could I have prevented her from going? It was within her to do what she did."

"She's a woman, Lone Bear. She should be protected."

Lone Bear shrugged. "She is Double Woman Dreamer." He paused, considering the white man's challenge before turning it back on him. "Who dares threaten her?"

"She risks her own safety thinking this medicine will protect her. It's all she has." He chuckled humorlessly. "She has an aging father and a so-called slave, but everyone else is either fearful or disdainful of this deer woman thing, and she has no friends. Surely her father—"

"Who dares protect her, Garrett? You?"

"Certainly." Lone Bear's hard stare made James shift uncomfortably. "While I'm...as long as I'm..." He floundered, then added hastily, "I have no fear of Kezawin's dream. I respect her. I respect her as a healer, as effective as any I've seen, but I don't believe her dream can kill me. And I have learned that she is not a woman who permits—" No matter what James had learned, he could see that Lone Bear knew more, both about Kezawin and about himself. "She's a good woman," James said. "A daughter to take pride in. A woman to be respected."

"So you have offered more than protection, and she has left you alone in your blankets." Lone Bear nodded solemnly. "I have wondered how much there was between you."

"No more than she has allowed." James's very scalp was growing hot. He had never spoken thus with a woman's father, and he felt the man's eyes boring into him in search of his private thoughts. He tried to erase his favorite imaginings by clearing his throat. "We have a friendship, Kezawin and I."

"I rode against four Crow warriors to save a friend once," Lone Bear recalled. "But I don't know any man who would walk into a Skidi village alone to free a friend." He pondered for a moment. "Kezawin seeks to protect you from the deer woman, but perhaps the deer woman has no power over a white man." He smiled. "Or perhaps she has no taste for white meat."

James might have suggested that perhaps Kezawin herself had no desire for him, but even in his worst moments of frustration, he knew better.

Whether he rejected the concept of the deer woman, James could not deny that he saw two distinctly different Kezawins. Within the perimeter of the village, she stood apart from him even as they worked together. He had learned his part in each regular task and needed little instruction. They consulted over the medicine she made, took food in the traditional way with the men served first and stood together at the edge of the community's activities like marginal members. But when they were away from the village, foraging for medicine or food, Kezawin showed James a different face. Her private smile was spontaneous and unrestrained. A flash of that smile could make James feel like a different man.

One day they came upon a huge prairie dog town. As Kezawin and James reached the top of a grassy rise, the town below leaped into action. A rodent lookout yipped his warning, and all of his relations dove for the nearest burrow. Kezawin laughed and flopped on her belly in the grass, motioning for James to follow suit. Grateful for the protection of the buckskin shirt she had given him, he knelt beside her, then extended himself with all the indulgence of a weary elder. They had been walking all morning, and he could use the rest.

Stretched out side by side, they parted the grass and spied on the sprawling village of small earth mounds. Within a few moments, furry little heads began to appear. By twos and threes the creatures tested the air and nosed their way above ground. James glanced askance and saw the first inklings of Kezawin's smile in her dark wistful eyes.

"Your father would have his snares out if he were here," he suggested quietly.

"Not until the prairie dogs have put on a good layer of winter fat." The smile bloomed as she cast him a glance before scooting ahead for a better view. "Look, James. See how they tear their food with their hands and put it into their mouths like little people? They are one with us, and we would not take them without asking."

"And do they grant you permission to boil them up for supper?"

"The spirit of all living things grants us permission. *Sometimes.* Sometimes they get away, and we go hungry. But when we take them for our food, we ask them to nourish us, and they do. And we grieve for having taken their lives."

He rolled over on his back and folded his hands on his stomach. "If I'm going to eat them, I'd prefer not to become friends with them first."

"They are one with us," she repeated as though she were instructing a child. "Like the buffalo and the deer. Only a friend would give his life to nourish you."

"They don't ask to die."

"No, and neither do we. Some days are theirs, and some days are ours. We nourish them, too."

He thought of the proverbial fattened corpse fattening the worm, and he chuckled. "Do they thank you for it?"

"Yes. By feeding us. We are part of the circle."

He lifted his head and stared at her. He saw the rouged part in her hair, the white elk's-tooth earring lying against her brown skin and the light of universal insight in her eyes. *Only a friend would give his life to nourish you.* He rolled over again and propped himself on one elbow while he laid the grass aside with a careful hand.

The busy little animals had forgotten the intruders and returned to their activities. Some of the older ones had jobs to do—earth-moving, grass-cutting, nest-shredding—but others, especially the smaller ones, wrestled, chased one another, petted and played. Everyone found time to socialize.

"Do you see how they are?" Kezawin said excitedly. "They kiss, just the way you do. See that one? He reaches up with his hand and caresses the other's cheek, and they kiss and kiss." She giggled. "Such a funny thing to do."

"Look how they enjoy it," James said, grinning now. "Look, that one combs the other one's hair. She's smiling. She likes having her hair combed. See? She kisses him back."

"Ah, but he turns to that other one now and kisses her."

"And the first one will have none of it," James exclaimed softly. "She pulls him around by his shoulder, and there he goes, down on his rump. And the tussle is on!"

"The second one is no longer interested."

"She's too fat anyway. It's the first one he wants. Spirited little wench. She'll give him a run for his—" James looked at Kezawin and laughed silently. He had no Lakota word to finish the phrase.

"She'll lead him a merry chase?"

He rolled on his back again, grinning up at her, and lifted her thick jet braid from her shoulder. "As you do me. Let me comb your hair," he said as he untied the bit of leather that held it at the end. "Like the prairie dog, with my paw." She stifled a giggle. "Just between friends," he added as he loosened the plaiting from the bottom. "You have beautiful hair. I see that now."

"What did you see before?"

"I saw...black hair, thicker and blacker than any I'd ever seen." He undid the second braid and separated the three hanks before lifting his hands and plunging his fingers into her hair, lifting it away from her head. She smiled as he stretched his arms slowly, letting the rippled hair slide through his fingers. "You see how good that feels? Your friend unbinds you and sets you free."

"My hair."

"Your hair." He smiled. "It's longer than my arm."

She touched the wisps of sun-bleached hair that fell across his forehead. "Yours grows longer, too."

"Shall I let it grow?" he asked as he returned his fingers to their starting point to run them through her hair again. "Shall I braid it and wear a band around my head to keep it out of my eyes?"

"If it gets in your way."

"Comb it for me," he urged. "With your fingers."

Her fingers were shy at first, but they took more and more until she had a handful of thick fine hair. "It's softer than mine—like the back of a horse's ear. Or like beaver, close to the skin."

"And yours shines like the blackbird's wing. I thought of it so many times after I left."

She trailed a finger along his cheek. "You have a handsome face. I see that now."

"What did you see before?"

"I saw light-colored skin such as I had never seen, and I thought this would be fine for winter skin, to blend in with the snow, but in summer—" She shook her head. "Then I decided it was not so unattractive."

"Not so unattractive, hmm?"

Her eyes brightened. "And now I see the face of my friend, James, and it is a good face—a face that makes my own skin feel warm when I see it."

He smoothed her hair behind her shoulder and basked in the light of her eyes. "Does your skin feel warm now?" he asked.

She nodded.

"Mine does, too. See how we are?" He curved his hand around the back of her neck and drew her closer. "'He reaches up and touches the other's cheek, and they kiss—'" her lips touched his hesitantly "'—and kiss.'" Her hair fell to one side and made a curtain as his lips touched her hungrily. He took her in his arms and rolled over her, the look in his eyes no longer teasing. She saw the entreaty in them, and she lifted her chin and met his open kiss eagerly. He prodded her lips apart with his tongue, then flickered and flirted, coaxing her tongue to play with his.

"Such a funny thing to do," she whispered when he gave her the chance.

"If you laugh, I won't be able to do it." He brushed his lips against her cheek and inhaled the scent of dry grass and dewy skin.

"I won't laugh."

This time she parted her lips of her own accord, and he slid his body against hers as he rose on his elbows to approach her from another angle. It was as though his flint had struck steel. The spark that flashed between them set them both aflame in that nest of grass under the hot sun.

They exchanged deep, probing kisses and writhed against each other, stoking the fire. They were melting together, blending breaths, tasting the salt from each other and harmonizing in urgent, elemental tones.

He wanted her. He'd never wanted anyone this much, so much that the deep physical ache made it impossible to remember how her clothes worked. He pressed his face against her breast and rubbed his forehead over the ridges of quillwork that edged her dress. He needed her. He slid his hands over her hips, letting the soft chamois skirt caress his palms and allowing the need to build. He lifted his thigh against the hardness of her mound and made her moan. He needed to feel her skin next to his. He needed to bury himself inside her, and she needed him to touch the deepest part of her.

"Help me, Kezawin."

His voice cut through the thick mist of desire. *Help me.* She heard his pain, and an image of blood gushed forth inside her head. She had pierced him somehow. She closed her eyes tightly and fought to control her erratic breathing. She would not let it be. She would *not* let it happen.

She gripped his shoulder. "She will not have you, James. I swear to you, she will not . . . I will not . . . *we* will not . . ."

He raised his head. His pulse pounded throughout his body, and his chest heaved against her. "Kezawin, I want to make love to you."

"Don't look at me, James," she begged. "Please don't."

It took a moment to get his bearings and steady himself. The woman in his arms was steeled for an assault, and he could have sworn moments ago that they were storming a castle together. He took her chin in his hand. "Open your eyes," he ordered quietly. "Look at me." When she complied, and he saw her fear, he smoothed the hair back from her face and whispered. "I would never hurt you, Keza-win."

"I know that," she said quickly. He pushed himself away from her, and she sat up, brushing the grass from her hair. "Are you in any pain?" she asked.

"Pain?" He felt damnably uncomfortable as he got to his feet and watched the prairie dogs scurry into their holes.

While his back was turned, she looked at her hands—yes, they were still hands—and quickly touched the top of her head. She straightened her dress as she stood up. "You were not . . . there was no injury, then."

He turned to her and let her see how it was with him. "You were once a married woman. I assume you've known the extent of a man's passion." She parted her lips to answer, but he spoke again. "No, there is no injury. No apparition maimed me in any way for daring to kiss the dreaded Double Woman Dreamer."

"You must not take her lightly, James."

"And you must not take me lightly! I am made of flesh and blood, Kezawin, not drowsy illusion. I walk on two legs, not four, and I have no twigs growing out of my head. I don't apologize for being a man rather than a rodent, and I *am* a man! Those poor dumb creatures are no brothers of mine. I am a man!"

He gestured as he spoke, but the creatures had been smart enough to take to their tunnels when he'd started shouting, so he had no one to point at but himself. He swung around, coming face-to-face with Kezawin once more. Her eyes were wide, and a sudden breeze riffled her hair, just as he had done with his hands. He reached out to touch it, and he lowered his voice.

"I am a man, and you are a woman, Kezawin. That's the way it is. For all your wisdom, you cannot find a way to change that basic fact."

Chapter Seven

As a toddler, Mouse Face Boy had been coaxed into a tree by his brother, Blue Heels. He had fallen and broken his hip, and the small bones had not mended properly. Blue Heels, who at the age of thirteen winters should have been spending all of his energies preparing himself for manhood, now devoted himself to his younger brother. It was Blue Heels who made certain that Mouse Face Boy seldom wanted for amusement or ample portions of his favorite foods, and who often carried the lame child about the camp on his strong young back. With so much attention from his older brother, Mouse Face Boy hardly complained, but the pain was ever-present in his hip.

Their mother, Many Plums, had tried to find ways to relieve the boy's pain. Her efforts to protect him had kept him closer to her than the Lakota believed was healthy for a boy of eight winters. Finally she took the risk of requesting the medicine of the Double Woman Dreamer. Mouse Face Boy happily reported that his hip didn't hurt as much after he saw the medicine woman, and he demanded her treatments regularly.

At first Many Plums forbade Blue Heels to take Mouse Face Boy to Double Woman Dreamer's lodge, but both boys objected to the separation. Like all Lakota mothers,

Many Plums indulged her boys. And since the medicine woman had gone to the Skidi village and brought back the white man, her medicine had been widely praised. A boy might be safely treated by the white man under the powerful auspices of the Double Woman Dreamer. Many Plums instructed Blue Heels not to look the beautiful medicine woman in the face, always to stand near the door of her lodge and to see that when she came near Mouse Face Boy she did not touch his male parts.

Blue Heels watched from his post beside the door. The white man applied a warm poultice to his brother's hip, followed with a cooling compress, then repeated the process. The older boy saw nothing improper in the way the Double Woman Dreamer stood to the side and prepared the medicines to be administered to Mouse Face Boy, who remarked many times about how good the treatment felt. The white man gently wrapped and unwrapped the boy's hip while Mouse Face Boy told stories about the crow he kept for a pet.

Satisfied that his brother was not in any danger, Blue Heels began playing a game with himself. He dared himself to get a look at the Double Woman Dreamer without actually looking her in the face. He would stare at the floor for a long time, then let his gaze sneak up to her quilled moccasins, the fringed bottom of her dress, up the tail of her belt to her waist, to the yoke of her dress, and then he would try to decide which way her face was turned. She was beautiful from the neck down, but the beauty he saw each time he risked a glance at her face made him swallow and swallow, and still his mouth was dry. He had to give himself a moment before he started the game again.

James knew exactly what Blue Heels was doing, and on the one hand he sympathized with the boy. He remembered being thirteen and having sumptuous thoughts about his friend Raleigh Brown's older sister. Then, in the next moment, it galled him to watch the young man making snake eyes at Kezawin and thinking about her that way. He said as much after the boys left, although he tried to slide his remark off his tongue without looking up from his journal.

"Young Blue Heels has a case of what my mother used to call puppy love."

"What did your mother mean by that?" Kezawin asked as she hung her medicine bag on its peg. "You've told me that your people have some foolish taboo about eating puppies."

"Not like that," James said with a laugh. "Puppy love has nothing to do with puppies. It has to do with young boys. Blue Heels has lost his heart, and to an older woman, as most of us do the first time. The boy has excellent taste."

"He loves a woman?"

"He has the distressed look of a boy whose skin has gotten too tight on him. If he had gathered the nerve to lift his chin, he would have devoured you with his eyes."

Kezawin turned away from the bag slowly and scowled at James, who sat against her willow backrest scribbling in his journal. "I didn't look at him, James. You saw that. I said nothing to him."

"You didn't have to. He was completely smitten by your presence." He heard the tightness in his voice, and this time his chuckle came more naturally. "I had the urge to throttle him for his insolent thoughts, because I knew them so well. I would not relive those days for all the—" He saw the worry in her eyes. "Yes, I confess to having experienced the male urge to mark territory a moment ago. One male urge recognizes another. The young pup had thoughts of sniffing around, but fortunately for him he lacked the nerve."

"I did nothing unseemly," Kezawin said as if reassuring herself that she actually knew what had taken place. "Not once did I laugh or tease either of the—"

"Kezawin, when a thirteen-year-old boy sees a beautiful woman, he wants to gawk, and he wants to run and hide, both at the same moment. His impulses embarrass him. You did nothing unseemly, I promise you."

"It's good that you were here to see that it was so. I want no harm to come to those children." She sat down beside him on the curly buffalo carpet, tucking her legs to one side in the manner that was proper for a woman. As though she might be swearing an oath on the contents of his journal, she spread her hand on the page that lay open between his knees. "We can help Mouse Face Boy, you and I, but we must be cautious. He's young, and the medicine is strong. When he broke his hip, some bad spirit settled into the joint, and it gives him pain when he moves."

"We call it arthritis," he told her.

"A bad spirit with a name is still a bad spirit," she said with a shrug. "How do the white shamans treat this arthritis?"

"With no more success than you're having—in most cases, maybe even less. But I was thinking. In one of your pouches you have a root that you must have gathered east of here, one that I think we might try. We call it pokeroot."

"You must show me the one," she said, her interest piqued. "I have stored some of my medicine in families, the way you explained last summer."

He smiled. "I noticed that you had. And I've been noting your names for plants in my journal." He thumbed through several pages and read, "*Pannunpala*. 'Two-little-workbags-of-women.' I like that better than *Asclepias speciosa*, or even 'snowy milkweed.'"

"It is good food," she said, returning his smile. "It is used when a woman's milk is slow in coming, but you also had it in your soup last night."

A voice outside the door interrupted them. "My daughter, I have news to tell you."

Quickly Kezawin made more space between herself and James. "I have tea ready."

Lone Bear sat on the man's side of the lodge and accepted the steaming bowl of herbal tea. Kezawin served James tea also, then took her place on the left side.

Lone Bear drank deeply and grunted his satisfaction. "*Ohan*. It warms an old man's throat."

"It has a touch of the food-of-the-elk," James reported, referring to the plant he had once thought of as bee balm. He knew that the tea's principle ingredient was lavender hyssop, which the Lakota called "leaf-that-is-chewed," but, according to Kezawin, it was the food-of-the-elk that soothed the throat.

"You are learning, my friend." Lone Bear sipped his tea several times more before he gave his news in the same tone he might have used to speak of the flavor of the drink. "Your brother-in-law waits for you in my lodge. He has spoken to me of marriage."

James's grip on his bowl faltered, and he scalded his tongue.

"Thunder Shield seeks marriage with me?" Kezawin asked, surprised.

"His medicine is strong, he says. He sees that your glances do not wither the white man, and he doubts that you would endanger such a one as himself." Lone Bear sipped again, then added, "He is obligated to bring his brother's widow to his lodge, he says. In a vision he was told that he must set this matter aright or things will not go well for him."

"Tuki!" James blurted out, and when he looked from Lone Bear's eyes to Kezawin's, he realized he had used a woman's expression instead of a man's. "Is that so?" he said, correcting the slip with an expression reserved for a man's use. He sought a tone as unruffled as Lone Bear's. "Did his vision forget to mention the deer woman?"

"No man dreams of the deer woman," Lone Bear said, dismissing the remark. "Thunder Shield's offer must be given careful consideration. You must speak with him." Kezawin nodded. She waited until her father had finished his tea, and then they left the tipi together, leaving James behind.

He plucked at a coarse curl on the buffalo rug and stared at the door. She had agreed to speak with the man, James thought. Nothing more. He took up his journal and his pen and reached for ink, jamming the point toward the target. He missed and tipped the bottle.

"Miserable damnation!" he muttered as he mopped at the spreading black stain. "Fortunately, the lady of the house has a slave to take care of such mishaps." Furiously he blotted and rubbed, blotted and rubbed. "She wouldn't marry that insufferable peacock," he told the mess he'd made. "That's what she went over there to tell him. One wife is more than enough for that popinjay. Obligation, my ass."

He took up the pen again and tried to remember the process they had used to treat Mouse Face Boy. There was the desert chaparral Kezawin had gotten in trade, the chickweed and the bee balm. No, the bee balm was in the tea. There was birch bark. Yes, and milkweed. Two-little-workbags-of-women. Milkweed was in the soup she had made, not the poultice. A fine soup. He had brought home nothing but rabbit, but she had looked at him in that glowing way she had, and she had turned his catch into something quite delicious. In his thoughts he heard the word "home," home to Kezawin, and he found it a curious concept. He slept in Lone Bear's lodge, took his meals at a camp fire and helped pull up stakes and move at intervals he had not begun to be able to predict, and yet the thought had come to him naturally—home to Kezawin.

"Things won't go well for him," he muttered. "Miserable bigamist. I'll say, things won't go well for him."

What was that puffed-up prairie chicken saying to her now? Was he spreading his feathers and doing his courtship dance? Was he telling her that the size of the game was the measure of a man? What kind of medicine did Thunder Shield have, anyway? When was the last time he eased a crippled boy's pain? But here was Lone Bear with the news that Thunder Shield had proposed marriage, and off the woman went.

It's not important, James told himself, and he read the last word he'd written in his journal. "Weed." What weed? A weed is a weed. He barked a mean laugh and printed boldly. " 'Frailty, thy name is *Woman*.' "

James had worn a path in the buffalo robe carpet by the time Kezawin returned. "Red Calf Woman told me about a place where I might find buffalo berries," she said as she reached for her picking apron. "It's a place near the river, and she says that it offers the shade from a western bluff in the late afternoon."

"Who is Red Calf Woman?" He'd aimed for an easy tone and missed the mark.

"Thunder Shield's first wife."

"His *first* wife," he acknowledged with a raised eyebrow. "How generous of her to share her personal berry patch with you."

Kezawin kept her head down as she tied the doeskin apron at her waist. If she looked up, she knew she would laugh.

"We were friends when we were girls. I had no sisters, and she and I were like sisters then."

"I should think if you were wives to the same man, you would again become as close as sisters."

"Thunder Shield said that I would keep my own lodge because I have dreamed of the deer woman, and he would not wish to have me touch his weapons, his food or the place where he sleeps."

James slammed his journal shut and tossed it aside. "Interesting notion of marriage, this man has. Would he consummate it without having you touch his precious person?"

Kezawin took a deep breath and kept a tight rein on the threat of an outburst of laughter. "We did not discuss his precious person," she managed to say, still without looking up. "I suggested that he see to the needs of his wife's sister, Walks Slow."

"Walks Slow, too? Does that make you number three?"

"Thunder Shield spoke unkindly of Walks Slow. I'm sorry I made the suggestion, for I think he would treat her badly if he took her to his lodge. I pity Red Calf Woman for having such a one as Thunder Shield for a husband." She held a buckskin pouch out to him. "Will you pick buffalo berries with me, now?"

His heart felt lighter, but she had yet to tell him what he wanted to hear. "Will I? Does the slave have a choice?"

"The friend has a choice." With a woman's knowing smile she stepped closer to him. "Thunder Shield came to my father's lodge to get a second wife. He left with no more than he had when he came."

"You refused him?"

"If I could have another husband, it would not be Thunder Shield. He is without honor. He has a greater duty to marry Walks Slow than he does to marry me. Walks Slow does not learn quickly or in the same way other people do.

She is *wakan* and must be protected, but Thunder Shield has no sense of his duty."

"And so you refused him," he prompted stubbornly.

She took his hand and pressed the pouch against his palm. "I refused him. A man without honor would be an easy mark for the deer woman."

"It is an outrage." James took the pouch, then caught her hand. He waited until she looked up at him. His quiet voice trembled now with indignation. "How dare he suggest such a demeaning arrangement to you? It is he who is unfit to share your bed, and I am personally insulted by his insolent proposition."

"It is Thunder Shield's right to propose marriage to his brother's widow, even though it is a foolish—"

"It is *not* his right to degrade you this way. If there were such a thing as a deer woman, she would curse him—"

Kezawin covered his mouth with a quick hand. The boldness of her action surprised her, but his words had to be stopped. "I refused him, James," she whispered as she slid her hand away. "Let that be an end to it."

"He should be horsewhipped, Kezawin. He should be challenged. I should—"

"Why? Marriage is easily offered, easily refused." She felt his desperation in the way he gripped her hand.

"The man has a wife!"

Kezawin lifted one shoulder. "He wants another one."

"That greedy, prideful—"

"I think Thunder Shield behaved exactly as he always does. I don't believe he was possessed when he made his offer." She frowned as she tried to recall every nuance of the proposal. "Still, it may have been so. Why else would a man propose marriage to the Double Woman Dreamer?"

James glanced through the cone above his head and took a deep, cleansing breath. "Men have been bewitched by beautiful women since the beginning of time. Thunder Shield is just like the rest of us, but he hasn't the decency to acknowledge the true source of your magic."

James's hand felt sure and strong on Kezawin's shoulder. She saw the fervor in his eyes, and she wanted to tell him that it didn't matter what Thunder Shield was like. James was a man whose strength matched her own. No other man made her see herself as a woman before she could remind herself that she was the Double Woman Dreamer. He refused to allow her to deny her womanhood, and there were times when she hated him for that. There were times when her femininity was an aching thorn in her flesh. But she knew that even as she hated him for keeping her birthright alive in her, she loved him more.

"There's magic in your eyes, Kezawin," James said. She looked up at him as if to verify the words, and he let the magic calm him. "And sorcery in your smile. If a man makes a fool of himself over that, it's his own fault, not yours."

"The deer woman does not visit your people?" she asked.

He shook his head slowly.

"No white woman has ever destroyed a man's medicine, taken his power and made him do her bidding?"

In his mind he saw an apple and a serpent instead of a deer, and some primal part of his male self instinctively avowed the guilt of women. But the deer woman was different, he told himself. Kezawin had to bear the burden of the deer woman alone because it was her dream. Yet she refused to be the noxious or even the capricious woman her dream gave her license to be.

"I don't think you can take my power," he told her. "I have given it much thought. It seems to me that the deer woman has no influence over a man who has no fear of her, and I have none. Why should I? The woman others know as Double Woman Dreamer saved my life."

"It was my destiny to bring you safely here, just as I led the white deer safely across the river," she told him.

"Why?"

"Why is a question that burns inside you like a hot brand, James. You know so many things, and still the question burns. Just know that it had to be."

He wanted no philosophy now. He caressed her shoulders, expressing his desire for physical answers. "I know you had your own reasons for snatching me from the jaws of your enemy."

I wanted to see the way the sky lives in your eyes, she thought. "It is true that I could not let you die at the hands of the Pawnee."

"Then you could not harm me yourself, could you?"

"I don't know." It was warm, and the skin of the lodge seemed to envelop her with him. "I have two faces, and I cannot tell—"

"You have one face," he insisted as he cupped his hand under her chin. "One lovely face, and, yes, it haunts me. You haunt me as no other woman ever has, but it's you, Kezawin. Not some evil spirit."

"You would tell me if you saw her in me?" she asked in a small voice.

"I would tell you." He stroked the cap her braided hair made. "Remember when I unbraided your hair?" A wistful smile was her answer. "I could free you the same way. I could teach you not to fear the woman who laughs without hiding behind her hand."

"It is not proper for a woman to laugh that way," she whispered as she watched his lips come closer.

"It seems proper to me." He kissed her softly, then brushed her lips with a plea. "Put your arms around me,

Kezawin." When she did as he asked, he kissed her again. He touched her tongue with his, and she lifted her heels off the floor as she tightened her arms around his waist. Their kiss was hot and moist, like the air in the tipi, and he loved the heat. He wanted more of it. He peppered her face with the spice of his kisses and nudged her heavy braid aside to taste her neck.

"I feel this way whenever you kiss me," she confessed.

"What way?"

"The way a woman feels when her man is close." She slid her hands along the ridges of his muscled back and pressed herself against him, giving the molten feeling inside her leave to intensify. "If you were surely safe from her, I would be what you ask—proper or not."

He put his arms around her and held her close. "Not for him," he muttered fiercely. "For me."

"Only for you," she whispered into the pocket of his neck.

"Ah, Kezawin, I'm no better than he to tempt you thus." He rubbed his hands over the soft elkskin that covered her back and pressed his lips against her hair. "I have no bed to offer, and I live from day to day. Tomorrow is a dark and murky place. I cannot face it until sun chases the shadows away and it becomes today."

It was an emptiness within him that troubled her, but one from which she could not deliver him as she had from the Pawnee. A man without a vision lived exactly as he had described. He was as vulnerable as a man who stood naked in the buffeting wind. All day long he sought knowledge, and he knew much about the world around him. But he did not know his place in it.

"It will come to you," she said. "You will wait, and you will listen. It will come to you."

What *it* was he could not imagine. Likely an ignoble end to a life that had once shown promise, which was nothing he would offer to share with a woman. He leaned back and offered an apologetic smile instead. "But the berry bushes won't come to us. It's cooler there, you say?"

"So I'm told."

As they emerged from Kezawin's tipi, the hot breeze felt good against sweat-damp skin. They walked among the gray-peaked tipis, headed for the opposite side of the camp and the river beyond. The village was quiet and lazy in the afternoon heat. They saw that Mouse Face Boy and Blue Heels had found a spot on the shady side of their mother's lodge, where they were turning dirt and water into a herd of miniature clay horses. James stopped to admire their work and to inquire about Mouse Face Boy's hip, which he learned was "not so bad today." Mouse Face Boy showed James his crow, whom he was trying to teach to say "Sapa," the name he had given the bird. Kezawin stood several paces back and enjoyed watching James with the boys.

Farther on, a breeze funneled itself between two tipis and made a little dust whorl dance across their path. James thought he might wash the dust off his body after they had gathered berries. Maybe before, he amended as he glanced back at Kezawin and smiled. Cool water would tamp a lot of things down.

"Where are you going in such a hurry with this slave of yours?"

Kezawin's step only hesitated, but she kept walking even as James stopped. Thunder Shield was best ignored, and such an impertinent question was not deserving of an answer. But James whirled to face him, and she knew that a woman's forbearance would not keep the peace this afternoon. She turned slowly and saw the telling stiffness in James's neck.

Thunder Shield was not alone. The stocky warrior stood near an empty meat-drying rack with two of his friends. The sun glistened on three levels of bronze shoulders, and their bare calves were coated with dun-colored dust.

"He waited for you in your lodge," Thunder Shield accused, jerking his chin at James. "I offered to make you a wife, but you prefer to take this white man to the riverbank and wallow with him in the mud. You are—"

"*You* are out of line," James growled. "And you *will* apologize."

"Stay out of my way, root-digger." Thunder Shield edged closer, while his friends stayed where they were. "This woman disgraces my brother's memory. Let us have an end to this pretense of virtue, Double Woman Dreamer."

James made certain that Kezawin stood behind him, where this foulmouthed lout could not touch her. He flexed his knees, ready to spring if the man should try. Thunder Shield squared his shoulders and puffed up his chest, approaching at a cocky angle. James watched and waited. The creature would slither. The creature would slide. *Welcome him. Welcome him.*

"I accuse you of many men," Thunder Shield shouted. Suddenly there was more life in the village than had been evident all afternoon. Heads appeared. Necks craned. Thunder Shield glanced this way and that, assuring himself that he had been heard.

"You have no proof, Thunder Shield," Kezawin said quietly. "I will bite the snake."

"Then you will be struck down for a liar, and I will be the one to—" Thunder Shield slid his hot gaze in James's direction. "You would dispute me, root-digger?"

"I would cut out your lying tongue."

Thunder Shield drew his knife from its scabbard and sidled like a preening cock. "You might try," he taunted, smiling, "if only your clout were not empty, like a woman's."

The two lunged, clashed and detonated the hot afternoon. They struggled within a circle of paralyzed fascination, no eye missing a trick, but only the combatants moved. They grunted with the strain of total exertion, muscle pushing against muscle for control of the blade, which glinted high against the neutral blue sky. A bare leg kicked up, and James tumbled, then rolled in time to avoid certain death. Instantly he was on his feet, and they circled each other, both sucking deep gulps of air and fine dust. Thunder Shield brandished the knife.

Kezawin watched in silent horror. She would permit no distracting cries of protest. In the heat of the sun, she felt the chill of death pass through her, and she dared not speculate. She dared not look away or even draw breath. She knew that James carried no weapon.

Thunder Shield darted, and James dodged the deadly blade. Another swipe left the brave open for an instant. James plunged headlong for his opponent's midsection. They grappled again, rolling and writhing in a tangle of limbs. The dust nearly blinded them both. Each reversal was met by an exertion of more will than wit. The knife was knocked loose and snatched up again. There was a thrust, a grunt and a sickening gurgle. Thunder Shield stared unseeing at the neutral sky while blood poured from the side of his neck and puddled in the dust.

Wretched, high-pitched keening split the sultry air. James stumbled backward, and Red Calf Woman took his place, flinging herself on her husband's body. With each heaving gasp, James welcomed piercing air into his lungs. Thunder Shield's chest was still.

James raised his arm and turned the bloodied knife over in his hand, staring at it as though it were something for which his brain had no name. Hoarse words came from his throat in English, and the name he uttered was one he had not called upon in years.

"My God." He looked around him, searching for something real, and he found Kezawin. Her eyes met his for just a moment, and then she lowered them and stared at her feet. He dropped the knife and stumbled toward the river.

A cloud of blood surrounded his right hand as he plunged it into the sluggish water. He ripped a handful of grass from the bank and used it to scrub both hands. He rubbed the wad of roots, dirt, spiky blades and bristly seed heads over his skin until it turned red and burned. His mind was as cloudy as the water, and all he could think about was cleaning death off his hands.

He knew she was there beside him, not because he heard her unhurried approach, but because he felt her beside him. He wiped his hands on his buckskin-clad thighs and turned slowly to face her. She knelt there, Madonna-like, her eyes glazed with shock and sorrow. Sick with shame, he turned his face away again.

"It happened so quickly," he said.

"Like lightning, a flash of anger unleashes its fury, and a life is over."

"I did not intend his death." Devoid of emotion, his voice was only a thin slice of its former self. "It was his knife."

"Your threat was empty," she said. "You carried no knife."

"It wasn't completely empty." He lifted his gaze to hers. A spark of heat returned to his eyes. "I wanted to rip out his tongue with my bare hands to stop him from lying about you."

"Then you *did* intend his death."

"No!" He dropped his forehead into his hand and tried to rub the throbbing away. "No, I didn't. I intended to beat him until he stopped taunting you."

"He was taunting you, James."

"He insulted us both." He sat back on his heels and studied her face. He burned inside with shame, and the look on her face somehow made it worse. He had done it for her. Didn't she realize that? Where was her gratitude? Where was her relief? Perhaps she'd not had time to realize either. "He insulted *you*. You are the finest woman I know, and I could not stand by and listen to that and count myself a man."

"Yes," Kezawin said quietly. "That is what he told you."

"What would you have me do? I was fighting for my life, woman. The man had a knife, and he was trying to kill me with it."

"I know. It was his pride against your pride, and yours was the stronger."

"The hell, you say! Since his pride got him killed, I dare say it was *his*—" He smashed his fists against his thighs, and his eyes flashed with his rage. "His stupidity! You said marriage was easily proposed and easily refused. How easy is it to kill a man! A man stands his ground, refuses to let another take what he values most, and before he can utter 'peace' and be on his way—"

"'Peace' was never uttered," she said. "But there was time for other words."

"I did not intend his death," James insisted. "It was he who sought mine. It was he who called you a whore."

"Which I am not. It is for me to defend my virtue, and I will do that in the proper way." She covered his fists with her hands and stroked them until they relaxed. "If he had killed you, I would have died, too."

"Then why do you judge me?"

"I don't judge you. A man is dead by your hand. Even though he would have killed you, now your own spirit grieves."

"I grieve for his widow," James insisted. "Not for him."

"Then I grieve for all of us."

Thunder Shield's family built his scaffold and mourned his death for four days. The men pushed small pegs into their arms and legs, the women slashed their limbs, and all of the relatives cut their hair. At the end of four days, the body was raised to the scaffold, and Thunder Shield's favorite horse was told to follow his owner happily. Amid terrible wailing, the horse was shot at close range so that it would die instantly, and its tail was attached to the scaffold. The wailing continued until friends led family members away from the bier.

James watched and waited for his punishment to be meted out by Thunder Shield's friends. No one spoke to him. No one seemed to realize he was there. Kezawin mourned, but as always she participated on the fringe of the community. She kept herself apart from him, and he thought it fitting that even the ostracized should have someone to ostracize. Surely they would punish him when all of this was over.

Perhaps they would both be punished. He began to imagine that he and Kezawin must be equally despised and that they would share some dreadful castigation once the funeral ritual was completed. He brooded as he watched the final proceedings from a lonely vantage point on a hill. The wailing had filled his head for four days, and he would welcome an end to the torment. He anticipated the moment when the community would turn to him and give him whatever they felt was due him.

Nothing was due him. No one came to demand an eye for an eye. No one spoke of the fight; no one called him a murderer. Finally, in the privacy of her lodge he admitted to Kezawin that he had fully expected punishment.

"You punish yourself," she said. "There were witnesses, and no one denies that you defended yourself."

Relief eluded him. He turned the news over in his mind, and he could not make sense of it. It wasn't finished. There was a knot in his gut that told him it wasn't finished. Perhaps the knot would be there until he was punished somehow.

"The trouble will pass," Kezawin promised.

James glanced up in surprise.

"At the river you said that you stood your ground when he tried to take what you valued most. What did he try to take from you?"

The dead man's name was not to be spoken. James's face became cloudy as he recalled that hot afternoon. "You," he said at last. He raised his brow and admitted, "But then, you don't belong to me."

She touched his shoulder. "The trouble will pass when you know what you value most."

Chapter Eight

❦

The man who had questioned Kezawin's virtue was dead, and James contended that the question was settled. Kezawin's honor had been defended because Thunder Shield's lying tongue had been stopped. But Kezawin knew that the death of her accuser proved nothing. Her people honored virtuous women, and Kezawin wanted it known that she was virtuous. Most people pointedly avoided her because they feared her power, but no one had cause to accuse her of the kind of sexual promiscuity that tradition ascribed to the deer woman. She had waged a continual war with that part of herself, and she had never seduced a man. No one could claim that she had. Ten days after Thunder Shield's funeral she had announced that she would give a feast and make the ritual known as Biting the Snake.

"But this is madness," James insisted as he dropped wild turnips, one by one, into a pouch. "You are inviting them to humiliate you publicly and then dine at your expense."

Kezawin knelt beside a large rawhide bowl. The elk's teeth that were stitched to the yoke of her dress clicked softly as she worked her granite pestle over the dried meat in the bowl. "I have been accused of lying with many men," she reminded him without looking up from her work. "There will be much gossip and speculation until I hold the ceremony and put an end to it." .

"Let them talk among themselves." He tossed another turnip with the reluctance of a boy who had to put his marbles away. "No ceremony in the world will put an end to gossip. People thrive on it." Plop went another turnip. "To stand up in front of these people and let them tell their fanciful tales as you propose to do is ludicrous. Who knows what—"

Kezawin lifted her chin and eyed him in challenge. "Do you believe that I have lain with men other than my husband?"

"Of course not." He loaded up the rest of the roots in one handful, then tossed the pouch aside with a sigh. "You have not lain with me. That much I know."

"And that is what each man knows." Snapping her attention back to her work, she mashed harder, twisted the stone and pulverized the meat and the words with studied intensity. *That much you know. That much you know.*

"But there will be lies told, Kezawin."

"Who would lie?" she asked tonelessly.

"Thunder Shield."

"The one you speak of is dead," she told the deepest part of her bowl.

"He lied about you, and two of his cohorts were standing by. They're still standing by to take up his cause, and each one will have a tale to tell, mark my words."

Kezawin sat back on her heels and balanced the rock against her knee. "If a man claims to have lain with me, he will pay the price for his lie when he bites the knife. The one you speak of did not bite the knife, and if he were here, he would not repeat his claim this day."

"Who holds the knife while the liar bites it?" James asked. He sat cross-legged, and he leaned in her direction with his forearms braced against his knees. "Perhaps I should have waited. All I ever wanted to do was cut out his tongue."

"A man who feels the knife blade against his tongue knows how close is calamity to the tongue of one who lies. One who speaks the truth has nothing to fear."

"And what about this biting the snake?"

She turned the mottled gray rock over in her hand as if she were inspecting it. The grinding end had been worn smooth. Her mother had used it, and her mother's mother before her. Honest women. Good-natured and industrious women, all, and their honor was never questioned. But the deer woman had not disturbed their dreams. Kezawin squared her shoulders and looked up at James. "I will swear that I am virtuous, and I will bite the snake."

"Good Lord, woman, I will not stand by while you put a snake in your mouth. There must be another—"

"It is important that you be present. You were mentioned. You must tell them that I have not come to your blanket." She reached for a stick and held it up for him to see. "This is the snake I will bite."

"Kezawin..." He shook his head, bracing his hands against his knees. His chest was bare, and he felt a rivulet of sweat trickle down his breastbone. "People lie. People who have something to gain will make all manner of claims. I have seen the way some of them go to great lengths to avoid you. You cannot believe that a piece of wood or the blade of a knife will mean anything to the people who treat you this way."

"Will you take the oath?"

"Yes. I count myself as honest as any man, and more so than most. But if I had taken you under my blanket and made love to you, as I've wanted to so many times, I cannot say that I wouldn't deny it if a small lie would spare you humiliation.''

She watched a drop of sweat slip into the smattering of light curly hair on his chest. Last summer she had thought the hair on his body was unattractive. Now she had to pull her eyes away from his golden tanned skin and her thoughts from his reference to lovemaking. They must talk about lies and truth now, for his uncles had apparently neglected his education.

''What is a *small* lie?'' she asked.

''One that harms no one. In a case like this, the lie would protect, and the truth would bring harm. What is between us is a private matter. It concerns no one else.''

''But if you lied about it, *I* would know. I would see that your oath could not be trusted. And *you* would know,'' she emphasized, extending the hand that held the rock. ''You would say to yourself, 'This small lie is not important,' and the next lie would come more easily. Soon neither of us would value your word, and truth would hold no meaning for you. You would be easy prey for those spirits that do mischief. And, of course, if we had joined—'' she added with a shrug, ''if we *had* made love as you say it, there would be no ceremony today.''

''All right,'' he said, holding his hands up in defeat. ''I see your point. But I'm not the one we have to worry about, am I? I'll gladly bite the knife and say the truth. But what about Thunder Shield's friends? What about his family? Some of them may have their stories already prepared, Kezawin. How can you be sure that everyone who attends this gathering will tell the truth?''

''Almost everyone I know will attend the ceremony.''

''Exactly. And how do you know that every one of these neighbors and relatives of yours has the same high regard for truth that you have?''

"Because it is what they taught me."

He watched her add dried chokecherries to her bowl and grind them into the meat. After a few quiet moments, she lifted her soft woman's voice in a wordless tune that struck him as too cheerful for the occasion. He didn't really have a clear picture of what was to take place later that day, but he had been helping her gather food since yesterday, and he knew she planned to feed a crowd. He had seen her donate food to many a feast, but never had she hosted one herself. She was always included, yet never truly a participant in the festivities. Even though most of the people were cordial to her, there was always a mutually honored distance.

Now it was her chance to give a party, and she hummed a tune as she prepared for it. James thought his heart would burst as he watched her. In a few hours she would put herself on trial. Whatever the trappings, whatever the tradition, Kezawin's honor was at stake. She would tell the people what she had done and what she had not done, and she would ask them to believe her. If they shunned her, he swore to himself that he would rage at them for their blindness. He imagined her spreading the table before them. He imagined them eating her food, then walking away without a word of kindness for her. His lips parted on the thought of another plea, but instead he watched her spoon thick tallow into the mixture. She stirred it, and the scraping of the rock against the bottom of the bowl added an element of percussion to her song.

His thoughts drifted on as she sang, and he saw her, dressed in her beautifully quilled elkskin dress, submitting to the humiliation of a pillory in a New England town square. Next he imagined her sitting in a dunking stool of old, protesting her innocence while the townspeople jeered. And then he saw himself lurking nearby. He wasn't raging. He was mute. A proper Bostonian gentleman collared him.

"Do you know this savage?" the man demanded. "She is a heathen, is she not? Has she been your whore?"

This woman a whore? This woman whose healing infusions make small miracles every day? This woman whose bright-eyed laughter is as musical as the song she hums while she works? I would sell my soul to spend one night in her arms, but she refuses me. Not one night. Not one sweet tryst by the river, not one gentle coupling.

Not one night, the top-hatted Bostonian said with a laugh. But what about a thousand, or a thousand times a thousand? What do you want from her, and what are you willing to give? And for how long, and at what price? Think, Garrett. Would you make her your whore or your wife?

"I have not slept with her," was easily said. It would cost him nothing. For a man of little faith, "I would sell my soul" was easily said, as well. In his own way he denied her, and perhaps his way was the most dishonest of all. Would he take his empty oath and walk away?

Kezawin took up a handful of the ground mixture she'd made, and she studied James's face as she pressed the ball into a patty. "The ceremony troubles you," she reflected, "but it will show that I may still be honored as a virtuous woman. No one dares to lie and bite the knife or the snake, lest something hideous befall him." She looked at him curiously. "Your people have no such ritual?"

He slid closer and reached into the bowl. She thought he wanted a taste of the *wasna*, but she smiled when he made a patty and laid it in the parfleche next to hers. Many times she had told him there were things that, as a man, he need not trouble himself to do, but he seemed to enjoy busying his hands in her matters while they talked. Perhaps he had had no uncles to teach him the things that a man might do.

The slick texture of the mixture reminded him of his mother. He remembered thrusting his hands into her bowl when she made sweet cookies, and he remembered the stories she told that often ended with a trust-in-God moral. She, too, had been an honest woman. He concentrated on forming the perfect ball as he explained, "When a white person goes on trial, he must lay his hand on a Bible and swear that he will tell the truth. The Bible is a book made of stories about the white man's God."

"Tos," she said with a nod. "Yes, that makes sense. That person would not dare to lie after making a vow on such a book."

"If he does, he is charged with perjury, which is another crime."

"Haho, you see? A lie is not overlooked."

"Maybe not in court, but in other matters..." He squashed the ball flat between his hands. "People lie to get what they want. That has been my experience. That's why I came back." Her puzzled expression prompted him to continue. "I had intended to publish my work of last summer, but the man who put up the—who provided the supplies and the equipment, the horses, the..." He had words for everything but *capital*. "That man wanted to say that the work was his, which was a lie. It was my work, and it must be published as mine."

"Then you must offer a gift to the *eyápaha* and send him around to tell about this work. You will tell him to announce your name and not the other man's."

He smiled. "It must be published in books," he explained. "Many books, so that people will know what I have learned about the plants that grow here and how they are used."

"But this is your medicine."

"I would tell others about it, but I would have them know that these are *my* findings. Mine and . . . and yours."

She watched his face color, the way it always did when he learned something the hard way, and it was her turn to smile. "You will announce my name, too?"

"Your name appears on every page," he confessed. "But lately I've wondered just how much I should tell."

"I've shared secrets with you because I believe these are things you were meant to know. And you have shared your secrets with me."

"They weren't secrets, Kezawin. Any naturalist could tell you—"

"Our medicine will not work for other shamans. I have my vision, and yours is yet to come, but who else can know these things? Surely not this other man. He cannot have our medicine. He lives in that faraway place you call Massachusetts."

"Yes, but he has a piece of my work, and he tried to steal more."

"If he makes this claim for himself, he will suffer some terrible loss. These things happen to those who make a public lie." She rubbed a greasy forefinger over the back of his hand as a gesture of reassurance. "You need not worry about this man. If he has no honor, there is no medicine strong enough to protect him."

Indeed, James thought, Breckenridge had suffered the loss of his son, and the memory brought with it another stab of guilt. Another life that he had taken. Another secret kept.

"You *do* worry," Kezawin said. "It's only because you do not understand. After the ceremony, you will."

It was the craggy voice of old Whirling Water that called the women to the center of the camp first. After they had gathered, she circled the camp once again, calling the men.

Chosen for the herald's duty because she had lived a long life, ever faithful to her husband, Whirling Water walked among the tipis slowly and with great dignity as she invited every man to come forth and let it be known whether he had had sexual relations with any woman at the gathering who was not his wife.

James dragged his feet as though he were headed for a wake. The old woman's ominous intonations gave him a sick feeling in the pit of his stomach. Witch hunts were no longer a threat in the civilized world, he told himself, yet this ceremony suggested the makings of one. If the Pawnee sacrificed captives to their gods, what might the Lakota do to a woman accused of adultery?

The feast they had spent two days preparing together was spread on blankets in the center of the women's circle. James scanned the circle and found Kezawin sitting solemnly with the others. Her beauty struck him as a curse, for he could not doubt that every other woman in the circle must be jealous of her and every man covetous.

The men gathered outside the circle of women and waited until Whirling Water charged them with the duty to point out from among those women who were gathered any with whom they had been familiar. No one rushed forward. Agonizing moments passed, and James wondered how long it was necessary to wait. Surely they could all see that she was innocent. Lay it to rest now, his mind shouted, but he kept his peace and waited with his hands clenched together behind his back.

Then a man stepped forward. James drew a deep breath. Runs His Horses, a young man, tall, handsome—why this man? James had not noticed that he was a friend of Thunder Shield's. What was he trying to do? James scowled, and the pulse in his neck throbbed as he watched Runs His Horses slowly make his way around the inside of the women's circle. He walked past Kezawin, then reluctantly stopped, shuffling his moccasins in the fine dust.

"I met this woman, White Otter's Tail, at a wooded place in the hills. I have known her intimately."

James exhaled slowly.

Whirling Water handed Runs His Horses a knife, which he placed between his teeth. He repeated his accusations. All eyes turned to White Otter's Tail, the second wife of Four Strikes. The young woman sat with her hands folded in her lap and her eyes downcast. Whirling Water offered her a stick, but White Otter's Tail shook her head.

"Aiieee!"

James jumped at the sudden outraged cry. He turned just as Four Strikes shoved his way past the men who were standing behind James. The older man, who had counted coup many times and was well respected, stalked around the perimeter of the circle. White Otter's Tail's eyes grew big and bright with terror as she leaped to her feet and stumbled several steps backward. The crowd leaned in her direction as though she were suddenly possessed of a magnetic attraction.

Four Strikes snatched up handfuls of dried buffalo dung from a pile at the edge of the human circles, and others followed suit. Stunned, White Otter's Tail stood like the doe who was cornered by the hunting party and paralyzed with fright. They pelted her with filth until she came to her senses, turned and ran. A few men and women chased her briefly, hurling their odorous parting insults. That settled, they returned, and the circle formed again. Runs His Horses, who had simply stood aside while the crowd dealt with his former lover, returned to his place unchastised.

Whirling Water repeated her charge to the men, and once again silence followed. Have they had enough? James wondered. Or would one spectacle whet the crowd's appetite for more? If someone accused Kezawin, he would be unable to hold his tongue. He would take her from this place. They needed her; they came to her for healing, and what did she get in return? He would take her from here, and they would go...somewhere else.

Kezawin waited. She sat with her back straight and her head held high. The serenity on her face bespoke a woman who understood her values and had not compromised them. She would wait until they were satisfied. If no one spoke in her behalf until the moon rose, she would wait.

At last Many Plums came forward and bit the knife. She said that Double Woman Dreamer had made good medicine for her son, and she had neither seen nor heard that the medicine woman behaved improperly. Parched Mouth, sister to Many Plums, testified similarly. One by one the women at the gathering bit the knife and upheld Kezawin's respectability. The fact that none of them had been accused served as a commendation for them, too, and each woman came forward proudly to bite the knife, for it was because of her unchallenged reputation that her own opinion was held in high esteem.

When Kezawin's gaze finally fell on him, James knew that it was his turn to speak. He stepped into the center of the circle and took the knife.

"It was suggested that I have known Double Woman Dreamer in a sexual way." He surveyed the crowd, paying special attention to the faces of the two men who had been with Thunder Shield when he made the accusation. The dead man's name could not be mentioned, but he wanted them to know that he remembered. "I bite the knife and tell you that the suggestion is a lie. Although we have spent much time together, Double Woman Dreamer has never lain with me."

He looked back at Kezawin and saw that she held his journal on her lap and a hopeful look in her eyes. He understood. He took the journal from her, held it out and spread his hand over the cover.

"Among my people, such an oath is sworn on a sacred book, and Double Woman Dreamer knows that this book is sacred to me. Before all of you I swear that I have not been intimate with this woman." He looked at Kezawin now, and saw that her eyes were downcast. "I *have* known her, however." She looked up quickly. "I have known her to be a woman of amazing courage, for she faced her enemy alone to set me free. I have known her kindness, for she has fed me and tended my wounds, and I have known her wisdom, for she has instructed me." He scanned the crowd again as he lowered the book to his side. "I have lived among you for only a short time, and my words may not be worth much to you, but know this: Double Woman Dreamer is a good woman. In my experience, I have never met her equal."

When James had returned to his place outside the women's circle, Whirling Water handed Kezawin a stick to represent the snake, which she bit and made her vow. The people heeded her oath carefully, for if she swore that she would be faithful to her husband, she could not marry again. Instead, she swore that she had been faithful to her husband, and the people nodded and said *wašte*. They were satisfied. The men went on their way, and the gathering of virtuous women was left to share their feast.

The lavish feast had depleted Kezawin's stores and made it necessary for James to step up his hunting efforts. He decided to conserve his supply of powder and shot for winter and improve his skill with the bow and arrow. Lone Bear, his hunting mentor, was willing to accompany him on occasion, but more often he hunted alone. In the quiet hours of early morning or the time of purple twilight, he stalked the pronghorn and the whitetail deer, all the while sorting through his thoughts.

In the days since she had held her feast, Kezawin had not spoken of the ritual. James had wanted to broach the subject many times, but each time he held back, thinking that he would let her bring it up, and then he would question the sense of the whole procedure. No, he would question nothing, for he was prepared to lay down his civilized judgment regarding the behavior he had observed. Again, no, he would not judge, but he would present her with a scholar's objective views. As he repeatedly turned the event over in his mind, he began to realize that nothing was as clear to him as the fact of his own confusion. Kezawin had been exonerated. White Otter's Tail had been humiliated. Had he witnessed something sacred, or profane?

He had not seen White Otter's Tail around the camp, and he dreaded hearing any news of her fate. She was a *second* wife. If her life was similar to the one Thunder Shield offered Kezawin, was White Otter's Tail so wrong to do what she did? The memory of the onslaught of buffalo dung haunted him, and he knew it was not simply a result of his concern for White Otter's Tail, but the knowledge that it might have been Kezawin.

What if she had been accused, and the man had bitten the knife? She would have bitten the snake, most certainly, but whom would they have believed? The one who had counted coup in battle, or the one who had dreamed of the deer woman? When the scene flashed through James's mind, often he saw bits of filth strike Kezawin's white dress, lodge itself in her hair or break open on the side of her face. At the thought, he might clench his fists or his jaw and let an arrow fly, generally missing the target.

In the time they spent together, James and Kezawin spoke of the properties of various plants or the scarcity of ripe fruit. He suggested new ways she might use the flour she would grind from the root she called the Cheyenne turnip, and he talked of experimenting with seeding edible wild plants and returning the following season to see whether they had multiplied. Kezawin knew he had other things on his mind. He would speak of them when he was ready.

Then he saw White Otter's Tail, and what he saw sickened him. She was scraping a hide that was staked to the ground, and her hair hung about her face, unbound and swaying with the motion of her work. He *thought* it was she. He wasn't certain, because her hair hid her face, but he was curious enough to pause in his tracks and wait. Later he realized that she didn't know she was being watched, and then he felt like an intruder of the worst kind. But that feeling came when it was too late to withdraw, too late to spare her yet another moment of shame.

She sat back on her heels and wiped her brow with the back of her wrist. With a flick of her hand she tossed her hair behind her shoulder, paused, and then, as if she dreaded it but could not resist, White Otter's Tail turned her head slowly and looked at James.

Her eyes were bleak and cavernous, and the place where her nose had been not long ago was now a third empty black hole in her once-pretty face. For one long, awestruck moment, James could not look away. She gave him that moment. It was the public price that tradition demanded she pay, and she lifted her chin as if to invite James to gape his fill. The corner of her mouth twitched. For an instant she terrified him with the threat of a smile. He blanched, and when he gained control of his legs, he turned and fled, his stomach churning.

James sought Lone Bear out to tell him what he had seen.

"What would you do with an unfaithful woman?" the old man asked. It was another hot, dry afternoon, and Lone Bear had rolled up the walls of his tipi on two sides and was lounging in the cross-breeze.

"I wouldn't have betrayed her in front of the whole community if I had been the one to dally with her in the woods," James insisted. "Runs His Horses should have kept his mouth shut."

"I see that you are of one mind with the lover, not the husband."

"No, I don't say that I would ... Runs His Horses's behavior was hardly exemplary when he ... But he compounded it by divulging his indiscretion in public."

"The deed was done. The woman had been unfaithful to her husband. It was Runs His Horses's duty to say that White Otter's Tail did not belong in the circle of virtuous women. It was Four Strike's right to cut off the nose of his unfaithful woman, for in that way he can be certain that no other man will want her."

"Why didn't he simply leave her or send her away?"

"He could have divorced her," Lone Bear agreed. "He chose not to. She is free to leave him if she wishes."

"He could as well have shot her," James muttered. "It might have been kinder."

"Such things have been known to happen. I have also known men to kill one another over women." He shook his head. "These things are not good. They cause hearts to harden and cousins to take sides against one another. Better to cut off the woman's nose and have done with it. The women will think about this for a long time to come." He offered James a strip of jerky to chew on and keep the mouth moist. "How does the white man punish the woman who is unfaithful?"

It was an embarrassing question. "We don't cut off her nose," was the best James could think of to say for his kind. He ripped off a bite of the chewy meat and held it in his mouth, savoring the gamy flavor.

"There is no punishment, then?"

"I wouldn't say that. Adultery is certainly not..." He would have to confess that most men would assert the right to mete out some punishment before they left the faithless baggage and shot the lover, but somehow none of that seemed as bad as cutting off the woman's nose. "But, you see, we are permitted only one wife—one at a time, that is—and we try very hard to keep that wife quite satisfied."

"And are the white men satisfied with one woman?"

"Well, yes, they are." He rolled the jerky to the other side of his mouth. "Most of them. Some of them."

Lone Bear laughed. "A warrior is always questing, is he not? It is for the woman to guard her virtue. That is what the women tell the young girls. A virtuous woman is honored by her people. She attends the feasts for virgins before she is married, and later, if she has been faithful to her husband, she sits in the circle with the most honorable women. One who defiles the circle will be denounced, as you have seen."

"It could have been Kezawin," he said aloud for the first time. "Anyone could have made a false claim against her, and who could have proven him wrong?"

"Make a false claim and bite the knife?" Lone Bear's expression indicated that the idea was too outlandish to consider further. "I had only one wife," he reported. "One wife was enough for me. She sat in the circle of the most honorable women all her life. One wife, if she is a good worker and produces children, is enough for most Lakota men. More than that—" He dismissed the notion with a wave of his hand. "Too much squabbling. As you say, keep one wife satisfied. Women are demanding. You can't please two. Four Strikes was asking for trouble if you ask me.''

One woman was all the trouble James could handle. She filled his mind and left room for little else. The summer celebrations wound down, and the Lakota began separating into smaller bands. James hoped that fewer people might mean more time alone with Kezawin as the Hunkpapa divided itself into smaller groups. But fall meant more foraging, more hunting, and in a lean year the tasks consumed all efforts. James had to content himself with working near Kezawin, watching her and thinking how good it would be to hold her again.

He made a fair showing in the fall hunt, bringing down two cows and a young bull from a herd that the dry weather and sparse grass had thinned. He stayed to help Kezawin and Lone Bear with the butchering and traded commentary with his neighbors over the work. The success of the hunt lent a festive atmosphere as the people labored over the carcasses that were strewn about the dull brown flat. Part of James's kill was claimed by tail-tiers, and he saw that it pleased Kezawin when he stepped back and invited her relatives to share.

Lone Bear boasted that his white protégé had finally acquired some useful skills, and that he also showed promise of becoming a medicine man, perhaps not a *wicaśa wakan* like himself, but a *pejuà wicasa*—a man of herbs. James might have taken exception to the idea that he was only "promising," since he was highly educated in that area, but he said nothing disrespectful. Coming from Lone Bear, "promising" was complimentary, and James was given the opportunity to bask publicly in the old man's approval. Again he saw the satisfaction in Kezawin's eyes.

The hunters feasted with their families, and everyone danced in celebration that evening. Buffalo dancers reenacted the day's events to the compelling heartbeat rhythm of the drums. For the first time, James felt that he, too, must dance to celebrate the people's good fortune. The power of the drum made his blood surge, and the life force within him was immediate in a way he'd never known before. Time and space were nonentities. James was not an individual. He danced as one of the hunters.

With thoughts of cold water on his mind, James stepped out of the circle of bright firelight and into the darkness. Someone wrapped in a blanket came toward him. Even before his eyes adjusted to the dark, he knew it was Kezawin.

"The women's dance circle is one short," he told her.

"I have been dancing." She nodded toward a spot just outside the circle. "You were too caught up to notice. That's good."

"I'm thirsty."

She led him to her lodge, ducked inside and returned with the buffalo's bladder that she'd filled earlier from a spring. He tipped it up and let the cool water run down his neck as he drank. In a moment he knew he would feel the night air's chill, but now he was hot from the dancing. When he'd had enough, he handed her the bag, but he wasn't ready to go back to the dance.

"There's been so little time for us lately," he said. "Couldn't we just talk?" He glanced around. White moonlight brightened the camp, and the conical lodges became dark shadows against the night sky. There were embers in several fire pits, and they were within view of a circle of four of the older men who were sharing a leisurely pipe. Down the way a pair of men's moccasins stood toe-to-toe with a pair of women's moccasins beneath a sheltering blanket. James's eyes glittered with childlike excitement as he looked down at her. "Let's try that."

With a smile she handed him her trade blanket, and he held it over their heads, surrounding them with a dark curtain. The drumbeat faded into the background as the duet of their breathing filled the improvised tent.

"It's a small blanket," he whispered. "Come closer and put your arms around me."

"It's not a small blanket." Still, she did as he asked.

"What are we permitted to do in here?"

"Talk."

"That's all?"

"Nuzzle."

"Nuzzle?"

"You know—" She stood on her toes, stretched her neck and rubbed her cheek lightly against his. Her eyelids passed across his lips, and her lashes tickled the corner of his mouth. He got the idea. They made circles and lazy eights over each other's faces with their noses, touched foreheads, inhaled the warmth of each other's breath.

"Nuzzling is nice." Her eyebrow was a small soft pelt for his lips to stroke. She pressed her lips, warm and moist, against his neck. Sweet torture, he thought. These people loved to test the limits of their endurance.

"Let us be prairie dogs," she whispered.

He glanced up. There was an opening above his head, and he could see stars. They could have been prairie dogs, bedding down in their tight, cozy burrow for the night. "You mean we are permitted to kiss?"

"Our feet are firmly planted on the ground, and no one sees our faces."

With his arms held high, he made love to her mouth, tilting his head first to one side, then the other. His kisses were alternately tentative and bold, and she responded with a shy nip or a flirtatious tongue. For James it was at once delicious and infuriating.

With a pathetic groan he broke off kissing her. "A man must have arms made of steel to court a woman thus."

"A Lakota man has mighty shoulders and strong arms," Kezawin said with a sigh. She slid her hands up to his shoulders and kneaded them. "When he can no longer hold up the blanket, the next suitor gets his turn."

James took a quick peek outside. "No competition tonight. It's a good thing, too." Lowering his arms was almost as painful as holding them aloft, and he groaned with the effort. "I think this is a sport for younger men."

"Is it so for white men, too?" He gave her a puzzled look as he draped the blanket around her shoulders. Pulling it snugly about her body, she explained. "Sometimes I think it is a sport for men, like a horse race, or...or even like a horse raid. Many parents tie a belt around their daughter's waist and pass it between her legs to discourage the young men. A maiden must be chaste before marriage, or she will be found out and bring shame upon herself and her family."

"And I have witnessed what happens to a married woman."

On a silent agreement they strolled at the pace of two who had no desire to be anywhere else. "I cannot help feeling sad for White Otter's Tail," Kezawin said.

"Why didn't she stay away from the ceremony?" It was one of the questions he'd pondered the most since the incident had happened.

"If she had, then Four Strikes would have challenged her. We all know who sits among the honorable women and who does not."

"She was trapped, then," James surmised. "I should think it would have been preferable to face her husband in private."

"Perhaps she hoped Runs His Horses would not be there. Perhaps the other women said, 'Come, White Otter's Tail. Let's go to the feast,' and there she was. Unable to hide. Unable to say that she did not hear the call. Trapped, just as you say." Kezawin shook her head sadly. "It must have been a bad time for her."

"Not as bad as what followed."

"Four Strikes has not divorced White Otter's Tail," Kezawin pointed out. "Her family would have little pity for her if she were sent back to them after such a disgrace."

"And there are no consequences for Runs His Horses?"

"He will not be considered for *akicita* membership. When men fight over women, it is not good for the people. A man who causes bickering and bad feelings loses face. A woman, too."

"Cutting off someone's nose seems a harsh punishment," James said, but the indignation he meant to express was lacking in his tone. The more he thought about it, the less willing he became to set himself up a judge.

"What would your people do?"

"Don't ask me that. I've thought about it a great deal since I talked about it with your father. My people don't compare favorably, I'm afraid. I put myself in Runs His Horses's place, and I cannot say that I would have played by the rules."

"The rules? You see, it *is* a game."

"Sometimes," he admitted. "And games are played for amusement. It's best not to let the game get out of hand—a lesson one learns as a child when things get rough and someone gets hurt."

The drum pounded out the rhythm of a grass dance, and Kezawin's heartbeat tagged along. "Are we playing a game?" she asked quietly.

"Last summer I was full of games. I thought you were beautiful and fascinating, and I wanted you. I thought that this dream of yours was the only thing keeping us apart. A year later..." So much had gotten out of hand, he thought. So many things had gone too far. For a scholar, he seemed to require many lessons, and he wasn't even certain what he had learned.

No, that wasn't true. He was sure of one thing. "I killed a man because he wanted you the same way I wanted you. I know now that I might have caused you more harm by loving you than his demands and accusations could ever cause. Your virtue protected you from the harm he would have done. I might have taken that from you."

"I might have given it up," she said. "If I had, it would have been my choice. I have no husband. No one would have cut off my nose." They had reached a stand of plum bushes, and she stopped and turned to look up at him. "I know that you spoke from the heart when you praised me before the people. I was honored when you said those things. When you called me a good woman, I knew that it was so."

"Never doubt it." He started to touch her cheek, but he sensed that the night had eyes, and he drew his hand back.

"Sometimes," she said in a soft shy voice, "the heart makes its own rules. I care for you, James. Respect is a good thing. Honor is a good thing. But I cannot close my eyes at night without recalling the way I feel when you touch me. And when I think of it, I try to feel that way again just by remembering. I try to bring you close to me in the darkness."

He stepped as close as he dared, instinctively protecting this intimacy. "I've done the same," he whispered. "In the quietest hours I've thought of going to you. I've told myself I wouldn't wake you. I would only watch you sleep."

"You would have found me awake."

"I would not have forced—"

"You would not have had to. I—" She lifted her chin and told her secret softly into the hollow of his neck. "Sometimes I think of you, and I touch myself because I—"

"Ah, Kezawin, I thought I was the only one who—"

"Would the deer woman make me do that?"

"If there is such a creature, she's going to make us both crazy by keeping us apart. I want to marry you, Kezawin." Once the words were out, he knew it was, indeed, what he wanted, even though he had dismissed it as an impossibility each time the idea had occurred to him. What could he promise her?

"You want to touch me, James. Beyond that, you have no vision."

"And you?"

"I want you to touch me, and beyond that . . ."

He drew her behind the bushes before she could say another word. Her blanket slid to the ground, and he caught her in his arms and held her close, because he wanted her to feel the extent of his need for her. If nothing else, their needs were complementary.

"I'm not playing any games with you, Kezawin. I can't go on like this. I keep thinking that we are inhabitants of two different worlds, but I can't think of living in either one of them without you anymore. I'll do whatever I have to do to prove myself to you. I'll have a vision, if that's what you want."

She drew back from him and laid her hands against his roughened cheeks. "There's nothing I require, James. I care for you, and that is that."

"Enough to be my wife?"

She closed her eyes and willed the deer woman to go away so that she could tell him yes. "I am barren," she warned in a hoarse voice.

"You had no children with your first husband. Perhaps I can give them to you."

She looked at him again, and she allowed herself to wonder whether it might be possible. In the dark she saw the spark of promise in his eyes. "You must perform *inipi* for your own sake, not for mine. Cleanse yourself, James. Be certain this is right for you."

Chapter Nine

He had tried it once before, and nothing had happened. He had nearly choked on the smoke and produced a bucketful of sweat. A year ago the *inipi* ritual had opened James's pores, but not his mind. But he decided to try it again, and when he did, he agreed to do it, not for Kezawin, but for himself. He had long held that something was missing in the context of his life, and no matter how hard he studied or worked or strove, it was still missing. Of late he had considered the possibility that something was missing within him.

He wanted it to be something concrete, something he could simply identify, acquire and add to himself. Something like a wife. Kezawin refused to let the solution be that simple. He believed that she cared for him, but there were times when he sensed that she also pitied him, as she might pity someone who was missing a limb. Even as his respect for her increased daily, so did her sympathy for him. He didn't like it. He knew damn well what she thought he was missing, and the fact that he even wondered whether there might be a shred of truth to this exotic idea made the scientist in him uncomfortable.

He had once scoffed at the notion that this medicine, this personal power her people prized so highly, might be something he lacked. His confidence had been unshakable at a time when he was certain he knew more than they knew about almost anything of real import. He had documents to prove it. In their primitive innocence they were unimpressed with his great wealth of knowledge. They were unenlightened, he told himself.

And yet, he was lacking something, and he had begun to feel the lack inside himself. The lack *of* himself. His life had been a series of severances, a chopping of ties, one by one. He was disconnected. He was drifting. There were times when he thought he might be within reach of a mooring, but he drifted away again. Finally he explained his frustration to Lone Bear and asked the medicine man to perform *inipi* for him once more.

It had been a warm autumn day, but the night chill was sharp. James had not been allowed to help with the preparation of the beehive-shaped sweathouse, and Lone Bear seemed to take each step with excruciatingly slow deliberation. James was anxious. He wanted to get on with it. But the placement of every detail was crucial to Lone Bear, and he would not be hurried.

The willow frame had been covered with hides, and a pit had been dug in the center of the hut. Lone Bear handled the dirt carefully, using it to form a path from the small round house and a little mound at the end, which Lone Bear termed *unci*—grandmother. He covered the floor of the hut with sage.

Kezawin had gathered the cottonwood for the fire, and it would be she who would tend the fire and roll the stones into the lodge, just as she had for James's first *inipi*. This time James gave more attention to the elements of the ritual, and Lone Bear responded to James's interest by explaining each step. He had chosen the stones carefully. He called them "bird stones," and showed James that they were dull, earthy, never shiny, and that they had designs on them like quillwork. They were too hard to burst in the hot fire.

The lodge's entrance faced west, and on that side Lone Bear placed a buffalo skull and built a small rack where the pipe would stand. James was told to place six small bundles of red willow bark tobacco near the skull as his personal offering. Kezawin filled a quilled deerskin bag with spring water. Outside the lodge, the coals in the fire pit burned red-hot, and the stones were ready. James savored the night breeze on his face as he waited for Lone Bear to call him into the lodge. He shivered with anticipation. When the word was given, he set his breechclout aside, crouched and entered the earth's womb like one of the four-legged ones. The flap dropped behind him, and the world became small and dark.

Lone Bear had purified the interior with an incense of sweet grass. Six rocks came in under the flap, one by one, glowing in the dark like red meteors on their way to the center pit, the very core of the earth. Lone Bear chanted as he tossed finely ground cedar, which made a shower of minute white sparks over the rocks. He lit the pipe, smoked, then passed it to James. They rubbed the smoke over their bodies. Lone Bear's chanting continued while he dipped sage into the cold water and sprinkled it over the heated rocks. The steam hissed as the rocks exhaled earth's breath, and Lone Bear sang," *Tunkaśila*, grandfather, *hi-yah, hi-yah*."

James relaxed in this dark private place while the smoke crept up on him. Lone Bear talked with him of mundane things, then chanted and sprinkled more water. Kezawin pushed more rocks inside, and the process continued until James was suddenly overwhelmed by smoke and steam. His first instinct was to defend himself against it as he had a year ago—to take shallow breaths and concentrate on getting through this with a minimum of discomfort. But this time was meant to be different. He took a deep breath, and the heat seared every organ in his body. He coughed and groaned, but he refused to give in to his body's protests. Slowly he sucked in another breath. This time he felt the soothing penetration of something warm and moist, something life-giving. He exhaled and filled himself again.

Lone Bear recognized the sound of one who had just re-lived his first breath. It was at once painful and exhilarating, and the newborn one would gorge himself like the man parched for water, until he fell on his face. Before that happened, Lone Bear lifted the flap and gave James a breath of cooling air.

"When you need air from the outside," Lone Bear instructed, "say *mitakuye oyasin*. All my relatives. Say that when your lungs are ablaze, and we will help you."

Lone Bear's singing continued, and James joined in. They smoked and spoke of the good feeling it gave them to be there together. Each time Kezawin pushed a rock beneath the flap, they said *pilamaye* in recognition of her participation.

"She shares this with us," James said.

"Yes. She is with you."

"*Mitakuye oyasin.*"

Each of the four directions was honored with smoke and beseeched in prayer. James had a sense that the earth breathed power into him. Each breath seemed to inflate him, both physically and mentally, so that there was more room inside him for meaningful things.

Hope. He wanted to offer what he had learned in some useful way. Lone Bear prayed for this.

Sorrow. He told Lone Bear that he had taken two human lives, and the faces of those men haunted him. Lone Bear prayed for this.

Joy. James spoke of Kezawin and the life he wanted to make with her. Lone Bear prayed for this, also.

Gratitude. He had looked death in the eye four times that he could name, and his life had been spared.

"Recite them," Lone Bear instructed.

"I contracted an illness as a child," James recalled. "Many died. I lived."

"Tunkaśila."

"A man came to my room to take what was mine. We fought. He died, and I lived."

"Tunkaśila."

"I fell into the hands of an enemy. A man who was with me died at their hands, but a friend risked her life to save mine."

"Tunkaśila."

"A man threatened to take my woman's good name. We fought. He died, and I lived."

"Tunkaśila."

Naming his closest brushes with death gave James a heady feeling. Four times. Was it four escapes, or four times delivered? Lone Bear credited God. Was it God or luck? James had never been much of a gambler. If it was luck, then there was no order, no guide, no reason, but if there was a divine hand in all this . . . why? Why James Garrett?

"Will it come to me here?" James asked. "Tonight?"

"Will what come to you, my good friend?"

"Some kind of answer."

"Not if your question is 'why?' Such an impudent question will echo in the hills, and *Tunkaśila* will shake His head, and the *Taku Wakan*, the kindred spirits, will not speak."

James bit off the question and laughed. "Maybe 'why' isn't the right question this time. Maybe it's 'who' and 'what.' Who am I? And what am I supposed to do?"

"Those are two questions, my friend. You seek a vision, and for that, you must go to the hill. *Hanble ceya*." In the dark there came another steamy hiss. "First things first. Here you cleanse yourself. You prepare. When you are open to the answers, they will come to you, but be ready. Sometimes we are unprepared for the answers we receive, and we want to throw them back."

"It would be a relief to know."

"A relief from what?" Lone Bear asked.

"Uncertainty."

"Your vision will not make you *Tunkaśila*. You will always be uncertain because you wear the fragile flesh of a man. But there are four living parts to your soul, and one of those parts will allow you to be the best man you can be if you understand it properly. You have been given great gifts. When you know those gifts, as I believe you truly do, you know who you are. Go to the hill and find out how to use them."

Both men left the lodge together and bathed in the spring-fed pool that was just down the hill from Lone Bear's tipi. James's heart was as light as his head, and the cold water made his skin sing. "I'm ready now," he said, his voice charged with enthusiasm. They wrapped themselves in wool trade blankets and returned to the tipi, where they found Kezawin waiting.

It was as though she had known James's decision before he had made it. That didn't surprise him. This night, all sounds seemed to harmonize, and all thoughts seemed to point in one direction. She had made a fire and had meat simmering. Lone Bear would eat, but James would not. They all went inside together.

"I have made this for you." The buffalo robe Kezawin held up for James's inspection was decorated with strips of quillwork done in red, yellow and black geometric designs.

"It is the hide from your first kill. It will keep you from the cold."

James let the trade blanket slide to the floor. He was naked, but this was not a time when it mattered. Kezawin walked behind him and wrapped him in the robe. She came back with another gift.

"I have filled this gourd with four hundred and five small stones," she said. "One stone for each different kind of tree. Take your brothers with you." She handed him the gourd, and James's academic mind automatically raced to count species of trees. Another part of him, a part he had only recently begun to heed, told him to stop counting. Trust that there are four hundred and five trees in the land the Sioux bands walk, and believe that Kezawin knows every one of them.

She unsheathed her skinning knife. "You will take something of me with you, also."

She pushed her wide sleeve up, hooked it over her left shoulder and poised the knife on her upper arm.

"Kezawin, no!"

Lone Bear laid a steadying hand on James's arm. "Hold the gourd and let her fill it with her sacrifice. She will give forty pieces of her skin to help you."

She had already sliced one small bit from her arm. James extended the gourd and watched her take the skin from the point of her knife and add it to the collection of tiny stones. She repeated the process until her arm ran red with streams of blood. In his anguish, James felt each bite of the blade. In her self-denial, Kezawin did not.

Lone Bear led James to a hilltop not far from camp. It was not the hill that he had used so long ago, for they were far from the campsite where many Lakota medicine men had gone to the hill for their first visions. But it was a place that had been the site of other *hanble ceya*, for the small pit had been dug and dug again so that even the harshest elements never completely erased it. Lone Bear gave James a pipe before he turned and made his way back down the hill. Wrapped in his robe, James nested in the earth's curved palm. He listened to Lone Bear's footfalls until they faded in the night, and he thought he was alone.

He sat still, cradling the gourd with its precious contents against his naked belly. The night wind whispered in the grass. A small creature scurried across a barren stretch of ground just below him, and suddenly a winged silhouette swooped from distant heights, stretching clawed feet to snatch and hold. There was a squeak of terror, but the night bird, wings outstretched, hardly broke stride as it pushed off with a single unruffled stroke.

James's head was still light from the sweat bath, but he was no longer empty. The wind, the grass, the small gopher and its powerful predator had each taken a place in him. But there was room for more. He smoked the pipe, praying to the four directions and the earth and sky as Lone Bear had instructed him to do. Then he cleaned the bowl carefully. His belly was empty, and the bowl reminded him of food. He realized that he had no physical hunger. His head was lighter now, airy with the smoke. Smoke was *wakan*, Lone Bear had said. It rose from the pipe to the spirits, taking a man's prayers, but the man draws its power back through the stem of the pipe and into his body.

James wrapped his robe close about him and buried his face in the curly hair, curving his body around the gourd. He felt warm and secure, as though he had returned to a safe place, one that he had known long ago. He made himself still and quiet, and he listened. He heard the sound of rushing air and the flapping of wings. Something brushed the back of his neck. Wait, he told himself. Be still. Let him come to you. Welcome him. Welcome him.

It was not a hawk or an eagle. It was a gray owl with yellow eyes, and it perched on the bare brown bones of a winter cottonwood. While James watched, the owl presided over a parade of specters. Among them James recognized the two he had killed by the gaping holes he had made in their bodies. He braced himself for their censure, but they went their way without regard for his presence.

Then his mother appeared, and she led a procession of people who followed in a human chain with their hands firmly linked. They were Lakota people, old and young, and he was filled with an overwhelming sense of dread. He felt himself moving toward them, trembling all the while. He reached for his mother, but she slipped through his fingers and sped away like a wisp of smoke. Her diaphanous form disappeared into a hole in the ground beneath the cottonwood tree. Desperately he grabbed for the others who followed after her, but too many of them were made of air. Only a few hands of solid flesh touched his. He saw only hands. He avoided looking at faces.

"Garrett."

Lone Bear's voice was a splash of water that washed the whole tableau away, and James raised his head. He peered into the dark. "Lone Bear, have you come for me?"

But for the rustle of wind in the grass, the night was quiet. James clutched his knees and waited. His head felt heavy now, his eyelids leaden. He dropped his forehead on his knees and closed his eyes.

"Don't look for me, Garrett," came the voice in his ears again. "Listen. Have you seen the white deer?"

"No," James replied into the center of his body. "I've seen only death. I want to go back to camp."

"It is as I told you, Garrett. Wait for the white deer. Let him come. Welcome him. Welcome him. *Hi-yay-yay-yay. Hunh.*"

James waited. He had no sense of the passage of time. He was beyond time, and his only connection to anything tangible was through Lone Bear's voice and Kezawin's flesh. Within the buffaloskin sac Kezawin had made for him, he curled himself into a tight ball and made a womb of himself for the gourd. It felt warm and alive, balancing there against the sac between his thighs that held his seed. He thought of a toy wooden chicken he'd once owned in which a succession of smaller chickens nested. The smallest one held the egg. Generations. Reflections inside reflections. Begin with the egg. End with the egg. Shield the future from the night and begin again tomorrow. Begin with the egg.

He waited. When fear struck him hard, he held fast to the warm, dark, safe place. In such a place, he had prepared himself. In such a place he had cleansed himself. In such a place he could be still and listen. Then he would hear Lone Bear's song, faintly at first.

"Let him come. Welcome him. Welcome him. *Hi-yay hunh hunh. Hi-yah. Hi-yah.*"

And James was no longer afraid.

The darkness receded. The world became light. When the white deer appeared in the bright mist and came forward, he carried a bag made from the skin of a badger. He trotted around James, round and round like a creature from a carousel, and James circled with him until he got so dizzy that he sat down hard in the dewy grass, laughing. Thoroughly elated, he flopped on his back and watched the blue sky revolve overhead.

The white deer came to him, nuzzled him and dropped the bag next to his ear. Inside the bag James found a collection of plants, a trowel and a pen, and a few gray feathers that had been gathered together. At the bottom of the bag he found the deer amulet that Kezawin had given him, two black stones and a small bone whistle.

"You are White Deer's Brother," Lone Bear's voice said. "You may not eat the flesh of your own kind. You are a healer. Use your gifts well, and lives may be spared. You know many things, but there is more. Even death can be your teacher. Listen to your heart, White Deer's Brother."

When James opened his eyes, it was raining. He tilted his head back, and the first drop hit him in the eye. It was gray daylight, and the raindrops were multiplying, waking him, washing his face. He opened his mouth and let the cold rain slake his sudden thirst. He felt as though he'd been out of his body for a while, but now that he was back in it, it was making demands. His stomach rumbled roundly as he forced aching muscles to move still joints.

"Garrett!" The voice was Lone Bear's. James settled back once more like a turtle in his shell, prepared to hear more instructions, but this time the old man came walking up over the hill. "If you have seen nothing yet, you might as well come down and try again another time. You will soon be sitting in a mud pit."

James pulled his robe around his shoulders and rose from the vision pit on unsteady legs, but when Lone Bear saw his face, he knew his young friend had experienced something so beautiful and overpowering that it would be called *sa—red*.

James tried his voice. "How long have I been up here?"

"This is the fourth sunrise."

Among the Lakota, every momentous occasion required a feast no matter how lean the hunting season had been, and a wedding, no matter how unlikely a pair the bride and groom made, was a momentous occasion. Thunder Shield's wife and his parents, his closest relatives, would remain in their lodge during the festivities, but the rest of the camp had turned out to witness the marriage of Double Woman Dreamer and the strange white shaman.

James had experienced a successful *hanble ceya*, returning from the hill with a song, and Lone Bear had interpreted his vision and proclaimed his medicine to be strong enough to withstand the power of the deer woman. Many people were skeptical, but Lone Bear had Bear Medicine, which was the most powerful kind. Within days after James's vision, Lone Bear performed the *Hunka* ceremony, the waving of the horses' tails, in James's honor. In the ritual taught the Hunkpapa by their Oglala cousins, Lone Bear made James kin to the Lakota and promised to help him in all things, as was proper for a blood relative.

James had, at Kezawin's suggestion, gifted his prospective father-in-law with the buckskin horse that he had stolen on their way home from Pawnee territory, formally announcing that he wanted her for his wife. Now he waited for her to be brought to him. The marriage was called *Wiyan he cinacaqupi*—"He wanted that woman, so they gave her to him." The guests were satisfied that this was true when they saw the look on his face when he first glimpsed his bride. Standing there in the white elkskins that she had made for him with quillwork in black-and-gray symbolic designs, he had only one horse to offer, but he wanted her. And so they gave her to him.

Her father had put her in a fine saddle on one of his own best horses, and he led her through the camp with great solemnity. James's heart thudded like late-summer thunder as he watched them approach. Her black braids were wrapped in white ermine, and her forehead was painted with a strip of red, the color of great promise. She glistened like a jewel in the golden rays of the autumn sun, even though her eyes were shyly downcast. James wondered in that moment who he thought he was to claim such a regal bride. He waited for her beside Lone Bear's lodge, which was the closest thing he had to a home. He was an impoverished interloper, a small man, an unworthy man. And then she lifted her chin, and her lashes unveiled onyx eyes, which found him unerringly. The loving look she gave him made him worthy.

She, too, was dressed in white elkskin, and he had seen her in the dress before, although she doubted he would recognize it. She had added some quillwork and elk's teeth, as befit a bride, but it was the same dress she had been wearing the first time they met. He looked almost as surprised by the sight of her now as he had then, but this time she saw so much more. He was James, and she would be his wife. Her heart soared as she beheld his sun-brightened hair framing his dear, handsome face and the promise of a clear summer's day in his eyes.

Lone Bear handed James the horse's reins and stepped back, giving his daughter away. James had been instructed to picket the horse beside what served as his family's tipi, but he instead stepped up to the horse's side and reached for Kezawin in a totally indecorous gesture. She laughed and slid off the horse and into his arms. Her eyes bright with joy, she lifted her chin, inviting his own sign of approval. He dipped his head and covered her mouth with a kiss that would tell the world, "This is my wife."

Let them see, he thought, and if she turns into a deer this very moment, I will follow her to some secret bower where I can live with her and protect her from all slings and arrows.

Let them see, she thought, that this is the man who is not afraid to touch his tongue to mine, taste my love and be my husband.

They saw the strange gesture, and some even smiled and nodded their heads. Others shrugged and followed their noses to the food, mumbling that it was the kind of behavior one might expect from a white man and one who had dreamed of the deer woman.

After all the guests had been fed, gifts had been given and relatives had been honored in the traditional rites, there was still the dancing. As soon as the sun had slipped behind the hills, the air had taken on a seasonable chill. The women wrapped themselves in blankets and took to their side of the huge festive fire to do their sedate form of dancing, but the men, mimicking the prancing prairie chicken or the hunter in pursuit, easily expended enough energy to throw off the night's chill.

James stomped circles in the dry grass with the rest of the men, vigorously displaying his style for his new bride. Proper decorum demanded that a man make a pretense of being unaware of the women's dance line, but James glanced Kezawin's way, caught her attention and smiled. He would gladly have traded his new moccasins for a single waltz. He was tempted to snatch her away from the line of solemn-faced women and whirl her about the camp fire to a tune he was conjuring in his head.

Kezawin understood the eager look in her husband's eyes. She had no notion of stepping across the grass with him in three-quarter time, but she saw his need to hold her, and she wanted nothing more at that moment than to be held by him.

But the drum demanded the dancers' attention, and when the beat wound down, the men signaled with their dance whistles that the music must go on. When next James checked the women's dance line for his bride, she wasn't there. He went looking for her, but each person he asked either covered her mouth with her hand and giggled, or slapped him on the back and asked him whether the celebration was over for him so soon.

Finally he followed his instincts and headed toward the edge of camp, and there he saw that a fire burned inside her lodge. He could remember no other dwelling that had beckoned him to come home the way this one did. The dew cloth doubled the thickness of the lower fourth of the structure and formed an opaque, shoulder-height tier of dim shadow. Above that the cone glowed with the warmth of a tan lamp globe. And the sooty peak took on a darker tone again, as though it had been drizzled with an icing of ash. A wisp of white smoke escaped through the top flaps to welcome him. A mountain with a molten interior, he thought as he stretched his stride. A sweet confection. A woman's breast. Feet, move faster; it's our wedding night.

He could smell sweet grass smoke when he ducked through the door. Kezawin sat with her sleek legs and her small feet tucked demurely to one side as she fanned her hair with a quill brush in the heat of the small fire. James's mouth went dry. He straightened slowly and watched the damp silky hair cascade over her shoulder as the brush released it bit by bit. She looked up and smiled, and he swallowed hard. As an afterthought, he pegged the door shut.

"I became somewhat nervous when I couldn't find you," he managed to say as he took a tentative step on the soft carpet. "I thought maybe you had changed your mind and gone a-hiding."

"You gave me that man-look," she reminded him, and her eyes danced with the memory. "I wanted to bathe myself in sweet-scented water." She had also put her wedding dress aside and was dressed in a supple, unadorned elkskin shift.

James laid his hands on his chest and felt the dampness of his shirt. "I should have thought to do the same, but I saw the fire, and I could think of nothing but—"

His face colored, and she longed to lay her hands against his cheeks and see how warm they felt. "I shall bathe you, if you will permit me to."

He laughed as he skinned the damp shirt over his head. "I would permit you to drown me, my love, if that be your wish, but I must touch your hair first and smell this sweet-water scent."

"You would spend your wedding night touching your wife's hair, James Garrett?" she teased.

"I would wrap myself in your hair," he told her as he untied a long pouch from his waist, then undid ties and thongs and sent his moccasins and leggings the way of the shirt. He stood before her, naked now but for his breech-clout, displaying the lean length of his body made golden tan by the Lakota sun. "I can think of no more luxurious way to dress myself after a bath. But here—" He held up the pouch for her inspection. "I have a surprise for you."

From the pouch he produced a long, suggestively shaped cedar flute, which bore an adjustable pitch changer carved to resemble the headless torso of a horse. Each of the five finger holes was painted red, as was the acornlike mouth-piece. James tossed the leather sheath aside and held the flute aloft.

Kezawin's eyes lit up. "A Big Twisted Flute. Where did you get it?"

"From Buffalo Dreamer, of course. The only one who makes them. He says that when I play this for you, you will be unable to resist me." He walked around the fire and sat beside her near the sleeping robes. "He was amazed at how quickly I mastered the music." James had neglected to mention his previous experience with wind instruments. As he made himself comfortable in a cross-legged sitting position, Kezawin slipped a braided wreath over his head and arranged it around his neck. He held the leafy gift to his nose and smelled the tangy fragrance of calamus.

"Muskrat food," she called it. "Do you like the scent?"

He chuckled. "I'm sure it improves my own."

"I saw how well you danced," she offered with a smile. "You are learning so many things. Did Buffalo Dreamer teach you any songs?"

"Your husband is not such a dolt that he doesn't know the price of the flute includes the love song." She smiled while he positioned his fingers on the stops. "Prepare to be properly wooed, sweet woman."

She sucked her own lip between her teeth as she watched him place the knoblike mouthpiece in the center of his lower lip and carefully close his mouth around it. The minor key was reminiscent of an erotic whistling, like a lilting night call from a heart in hiding, a lover's hopeful entreaty. The plea was one that drew the heart from a woman's breast.

Kezawin moved behind him, took a piece of soft chamois and dipped it into the infusion of warm, scented water she had prepared for his bath. She washed his back while he played, and the woody scent of the water combined with the calamus to form a fresh masculine scent. She scrubbed in soothing circles over the long, corded muscles in his back, and then she rose on her knees and gave the same attention to his shoulders and upper arms. She dampened the sun-lightened hair that had grown to reach his shoulders, before nestling her mouth near his ear as she reached past his shoulder to tend to his chest.

"Those who might be returning from the dancing will hear your music and think that Buffalo Dreamer himself is playing," she whispered. "Maidens must cover their ears and hurry home tonight—no, please, play on." He smiled around the mouthpiece before closing his lips around it again. In the distance the dance drum added its persistent ta-tum, ta-tum, a cadence inspired by the loping buffalo, but James's love song softened the sound.

"The young men will be on the prowl," Kezawin whispered. "And husbands are saying to their wives, 'I ache for you, *mitawin*. Ease me.' Such is the power of the Big Twisted Flute. The horse, you see—" she pointed to the small carving on the flute, and even through her shift he felt her breasts press against his back "—is most eager among the four-legged creatures to mate. Don't stop playing yet. Your music has magic. I would hear more."

She replenished the warm water on her cloth, forked her thighs around his buttocks and reached beneath his elbows to wash his thighs. She started on the left side, working from the outside and moving gradually toward the inside, and down and down, achingly close, perilously, preciously close. The tune warbled, and Kezawin moved to the right side.

She touched the ridge of scar tissue, his badge of honor from his first buffalo hunt, and she thought, later I will touch my lips here, and he will know how much I respect his courage. She slid her cloth over the inside of his thigh, and when she had come as close as she could, she dropped the cloth and slipped her hand into the place where his breechclout gapped away from his body. When she cradled the softest, most vulnerable part of him in her palm, the music stopped.

She untied the thong at his hip. The clout fell away, and she stroked him until he groaned. "Ah, Kezawin, you have all the magic."

Magic. Deer magic. She pressed her forehead into the center of his back and wrapped her arms around his chest. "I am too bold. I must not be too—"

"Kezawin, no." As quickly as he could manage on unsteady knees, he turned to her and took her in his arms, crooning, "No, none of this. I am your husband now, and I won't let you—"

"*Don't* let me, please." She took his face in her hands and felt the heat she had caused. "Swear to me, James. If I become a wild thing—"

"I shall match your wildness with wildness of my own," he vowed, and turned his face to press his lips into the center of the gentle palm that had held him a moment ago.

"No, no, you must promise me. If I should change . . . if you see anything, if you hear any strange sounds, you must leave this place as quickly as you can. You must not—"

"I promise," he whispered as he guided them both to their knees. Filling his hands with her hips, he slid the soft leather up and down, teasing himself with the knowledge of her nudity underneath the shift. "You'll not hurt me this night unless you turn me away. I ache for you, *mitawin*."

A mixture of fear and desire cavorted in circles inside her head, but the dizziness was not something she wanted stopped. "I want to give you ease. I could not turn you away, and that is why you must—"

"I must see you." She lifted her arms and let him peel her dress over her head. Her hair spilled over her breasts, and he thought, yes, a little at a time. He trailed his fingertips up the sides of her thighs, over her hips, across the small, soft curve of her belly. "I must put my child there, Kezawin. I believe we are meant to have children."

"You have seen this?" she asked hopefully.

"I feel it now." He moved the curtain of hair, tucking it behind her shoulder, and admired one fine, full breast. "You will suckle my child here," he promised as he lowered his head to sample her lovely nipple himself. "Like this."

Something inside her strained to give him nourishment in response to his lips' gentle tugging. She plunged her fingers into the rabbit-soft thickness of his hair and held his head close even as he exposed her other breast and treated it the same arousing way. "Our babies will have to share their mother's breasts with their father," he told her as he took her in his arms and eased her back to the bed he could now call theirs. He settled over her and stroked her forehead. "Put aside these worries and love me," he whispered between kisses. "You cannot harm me with love."

"You would make love with me face-to-face?"

"I would make love with you any way you want. Put your arms around me and whisper your wishes in my ear."

"Face-to-face is good," she said as she flattened her hands at the small of his back. "That way you can watch...to make sure—"

"To make sure I give you pleasure," he finished for her. His hands strayed from her breast to her belly. "I want to see it on your lovely face. Don't be afraid, Kezawin. I love you, and I will be gentle and make you ready for me."

"I'm not afraid of you," she whispered.

"Not afraid?" He took her hand and placed it on the would-be invader that waxed tumescent with his need. "Then you are a brave woman, and you deserve a brave husband. Have you a place for me?" He searched carefully, as a blind man might, learning each curve by texture, until he reached his destination with two sentient fingers. "Yes, you do. Small and round and warm. A man must tread lightly here. Lightly, gently, like this."

He stroked her as though he had feathers for fingers, tended her until she moaned, and he smiled against her temple and whispered, "You will cleanse me. Yes, there, you see? Your body makes this for me. For your husband. You will take me inside and make me clean."

She opened herself for him, and he knelt between her thighs and pressed himself against her, rotating his hips to tease until there could be no more teasing. He wanted her to tell him, but she held back. She must not entice. She must not seduce.

"Don't let me—"

"I won't," he ground out, and with a slight shift of his weight, he sheathed himself inside her. He pinned her hands on either side of her head and laced his fingers with hers. "I won't let you be anything less than a woman. Five fingers, Kezawin. Five on each hand. They'll stay that way. I promise you."

He stroked her inside, and she rose, rose, rose. She flowered for him, and he moved deeper. She felt something different. Something inside her was changing. Too much feeling. Too many flowers. "James!"

"Wrap your legs around me," he commanded. "Yes. Beautiful. Let me fill you ... fill you ..."

"Please open your eyes," she whispered. She had no control. It was up to him. "Watch me ... watch me ..."

He saw her through the white haze of his pleasure. Her eyes were glazed with ecstasy and wide with fear. "I see a woman," he whispered. "A woman's face, a woman's body ... taking her man's seed."

They nested in curly buffalo hair and explored each other in wonder, delighting in the contrasts between two bodies—one male, one female; one light, one dark; one large, one small—that had come together, each adding to the other. Together they were so much more than they had been separately.

The shadows of a dying fire flickered over the slanted walls. Kezawin moved her fingers through the fine smattering of hair on James's chest, and she dreamed of one possibility after another, while James wondered how much of her belonged to him.

"What if I decided to go back East?" he wondered idly. "Would you go with me?"

She lifted her head and stared at him. "Back to where you lived as a white man?"

He laughed. "I live *here* as a white man. You could live there as a Lakota."

"I could *die* there as a Lakota."

"I would protect you," he promised. "What would you do if I decided to go?"

Carefully she laid her cheek against his cheek and pushed back her fear. "I am your wife," she told him. "I would go with you. If the *wakincuzas*, the ones who decide, chose to move the camp tomorrow, and you would not go, I would stay with you. And we would die together."

She had promised him complete devotion. No Lakota wished to be separated from his community. He rubbed her shoulder, telling her that he understood. "There are things I would show you," he said quietly. "Just to amuse you, I think. I would like to see the world that spawned me through your eyes. But I don't belong there anymore. The part of my soul your father told me I would find—that part of me would die there."

"Then you will not take me away?"

He shook his head and combed his fingers through her hair. "And I will not go without you."

She turned her lips to his chest in gratitude, then snuggled against his side and watched the flickering fire again. "In the winter you must paint your achievements on the dew cloth," she said lazily. "And I shall paint them on a robe. You must paint with pictures, and I shall use designs to tell the stories."

"What makes you think I can paint pictures?" he asked as he wrapped his hand with her hair.

"Men make pictures, and women make symbols."

"Why?"

She kissed his flat nipple and lifted her head to see whether she had changed its shape. "Because it has always been so."

"Then I shall paint a picture of my greatest accomplishment directly across from the door," he decided. "A picture of the woman I have wooed and won...and undressed."

"No!" She laughed again and pinched his leg with her toes. "You must paint the buffalo hunt and the horse raid—those things."

"Ah, *those* things. If I'm to spend the winter painting, I should be permitted to paint what I want. I could make a picture of the time we saw the white deer."

"Was he part of your vision?" she asked as she braced herself up on her elbows and watched him play with her hair. "My father said that you had a powerful vision."

"Did he tell you about it?"

She nodded toward the badgerskin bag that hung on its own special rack. "He only told me how to make your medicine bag."

Lone Bear had told him that White Deer's Brother was his secret name, the name the spirits would call him. Its power would be broken if James told the name to anyone. He must heed the white deer's warning. His brothers would help him feed his family, but he, himself, must never again taste venison. James's vision was more than a personal dream, Lone Bear told him. It was a vision for the people, and even Lone Bear seemed troubled by the fact that a white man had been given such a vision. It was for that reason that he had performed the *Hunka* rite and waved the horses' tails over James's head, declaring his kinship with the Lakota.

It troubled James, as well. Why him? Lone Bear called him a healer, and with that much he could be comfortable, for he was a naturalist, and with Kezawin's teaching he had become an herbalist. It was the specter of death that left him with a terrible feeling of foreboding. Lone Bear reminded him that death would come, and no healer would ever change that final truth. But James's gift would help many people, and he must search for the wisdom to use it properly.

He knew that Kezawin did not expect to be told the particulars of his vision. He smiled at her as he spread her hair across his chest. "He also said that my medicine was strong enough to withstand the threat of the deer woman, but you were terrified the whole time we were making love.

"Not the whole time. Something happened that made me feel too wonderful to be terrified."

James's chest swelled with pride. "Your first husband was a boy. Now you are married to a man who can make that happen whenever you—" The cloudiness crept over her face again. "Forget about all that, Kezawin. Please. I'm sorry I mentioned him."

"Three men now," she reflected. "I want to believe my father's judgment, but the deer woman is powerful, too. Three men have died."

"You aren't counting Thunder Shield, are you? I'm the one who's responsible for his death, not you."

"It concerned me. You fought because—"

He touched two fingers to her lips. "There is something I would tell you about myself, Kezawin. Something I should have told you before." He took a deep breath and let it out slowly as he searched for the words he needed. "I have taken the lives of two men." He looked into her eyes and did not find the shocked expression he expected. "The first one I killed in a fight last winter. This man came to my room to steal my journals, and I caught him. We struggled. He had a knife, and I ended up killing him with it. It's a story that seems to be repeating itself with me."

"Have you made amends to his family?"

"There were witnesses who saw that I was defending myself. I was not charged with any crime."

He had not understood her question, and she reminded herself that he must learn this for himself. One day he would acknowledge the need to untie himself from these deaths, and he would know what he must do.

"This is why you came back?" she asked.

"The dead man's father has much power. I was relieved of my..." He realized that "teaching post" would mean nothing to her. "I was no longer welcome in the place where I have lived and worked."

"Were you cast out?"

He knew that banishment was the most severe form of punishment among the Lakota, and he heard the note of sympathy in her voice. "Not exactly."

"Then surely your relations would help you."

"There is no love between my father and me. My work was my life, and my life there was over."

She pillowed her head in the hollow of his shoulder and put her arm around him. "And now it begins here."

"Yes, it does." Indeed, he could think of no better place.

"I believe your medicine must be strong. Our lovemaking was wonderful and red, was it not?"

He turned her in his arms and smoothed her hair back from her face. Anything red was the finest there was. "It was the truest red I've ever known," he told her. He touched her cheek, then trailed his fingers along the side of her neck.

"And I did not change, did I?"

"I saw nothing but Kezawin," he assured her as he slipped his hand beneath one full breast and lifted it slightly, just to admire. "And Kezawin is all woman." He ducked his head to taste one puckering nipple, which reminded him of a dark ripe plum. ''My woman,'' he whispered.

And he knew that it was he who would never again be the same.

Chapter Ten

James fancied himself something of a writer and a passable musician, but he had never had any interest in painting, and with good reason. The frustration it caused made him want to throw things. He held the bone brush up to his face and examined the sharpened tip through the fine mist of his breath. The rib was porous enough to hold the paint, but it wasn't pliable. He wondered how good a dart the thing would make.

"The horses are wonderful, James. See how the buckskin chases the others toward the door."

When he turned from his work on the dew cloth canvas, the look on Kezawin's face chased the scowl from his own. The quills, which she held in her right cheek as she softened them with her saliva, made her smile sweetly lopsided. "I'd kiss you for the compliment," he said, "but your mouth looks lethal right now."

Her laughter overrode the melancholy echo of winter wind. She selected one of the points protruding from the corner of her mouth and pulled out a root-dyed quill. "The male porcupine would know the way to avoid his mate's quills," she teased.

"The human male may soon pull the pricklers from his mate's mouth and give her something better to soften."

"Ayyy," she scolded good-naturedly as she feigned wide-eyed shock. "The male porcupine has better manners."

"The male porcupine isn't expected to paint pictures on the walls of his den." He waved his bone brush at the stylized figure he was working on. "Look at this. This doesn't look like a deer. It looks more like a jackrabbit with horns." She giggled. "If you choke on your quills, woman, your insolence will be well-served."

"But the horses are wonderful," she reminded him. "They're headed straight for the door. I can imagine them tearing outside, rearing up and plunging into the snow."

"Hmm." He studied his painting of the previous week. "They'll never be museum pieces, but you're right; the horses will pass."

"You must paint a man with yellow hair riding the buckskin."

"I'm not finished with it yet," he told her. He took up the tortoiseshell paint pot again and dipped the tip of his brush into a close approximation of white, which he'd achieved by mixing boiled hide scrapings with light clay. He studied his horse again. He'd be satisfied if he could get the deer to look more like a colt than a rabbit. One more try, he thought as he began applying the paint.

"I'm not sure I can make anything resembling a man," he continued absently. With his nose inches from the wall, he was concentrating on the deer's head. The slant of the wall didn't help matters much, but he thought it was probably easier than painting the ceiling of a church. "I've been trying to remember the painted markings of the buckskin—some sort of dots, I think, and something else. I want to get those on there."

He leaned back for an assessment. Much better. *Much* better. Garrett, you might just impress them at the Louvre after all. "You must remember those markings. You were quick to wash them off."

"I do remember them."

"Good." He added a touch to the albino deer's antlers, dropped the bone brush into the pot of white paint and shoved it aside. He took up the pot of black. "Let me get this right. How did those markings go?"

"It might not be good to show everything you saw on that horse," she suggested without looking up from the quills she was splicing into her design.

"Why not?"

"Because the owner would be identified by those markings."

"I became the owner when I stole the horse." He would never have thought he would discuss his own theft with pride, but he'd learned there was a kind of art in that, too. Here it was legal if you got away with it. In his world, it was only legal for people who had enough wealth and power to make it so.

"Besides, the original owner is not apt to come calling and see the evidence on our walls." Her silence brought him up short. "Is he?"

Kezawin went on quilling.

James backed away and surveyed his horse fresco in a new light. "Kezawin, whose horses did I steal?"

"They were not close relations. Just some Brûlé cousins. They should have been watching more closely."

James groaned as he set the pot of black paint next to the white. "Brûlés! They would have *given* us a horse to get us home."

"It was very dark that night."

"And you never told me."

"It was a fine coup, James. They would have killed you if they could have, but you were too clever and too quick.

You got away." She nodded toward the painting. "Put yourself on that horse where you belong. Just leave off the markings."

It took him a moment to get over feeling foolish. Then he laughed, remembering how pleased he had been with his narrow escape. Among the Plains tribes, stealing horses was almost a game. In the white world—again, it depended on whose horses were stolen—a man could get himself hanged for his trouble.

James grabbed several pieces of firewood from the pile near the door and added them to the fire. "I don't want to be around when your cousins meet up with Lone Bear if he's riding that buckskin."

"They will be too embarrassed to admit that they were so careless."

Taking a robe from their sleeping pallet, he moved to sit beside her to enjoy the heat from her body on this dark and lazy winter's day. He draped the robe around them both. "I think I shall decorate our walls with ink drawings of plant specimens," he suggested. "That I can do well."

"What kind of story would your drawings tell?"

"The story of what brought us together."

She thought this over, trying to imagine how such a thing might take shape on their dew cloth.

"Something a bit different," he suggested. "It would look just like a piece of work that hung in my mother's bedroom. Like you, she enjoyed doing needlework." He remembered the strip of embroidered tapestry that had been his first botanical text. He had committed the herb sampler to memory many times over as he'd listened to his mother read aloud to him.

"But you wore such plain clothes when you came here." She slipped another quill from her mouth and talked around the three or four still poking forth. "The woman you speak of died long ago, and you had no wife. I thought it was sad that you were without a woman to apply designs to your clothes. You seemed . . . *unśica*."

"So you thought me pathetic, hmm? Just like a woman to pity the single man, while most of us manage to be unaware of our pitiable state." He touched the strip of quill-work on his shirt. "But you have dressed me well."

"You have brought me many hides."

He knew she was being generous. A Lakota hunter might have brought home twice as much game as he had, but James figured he had done well enough by his small family. "When I lived among the whites, I used to pay a tailor to make my clothes. Even if I had a wife, I would have worn those plain clothes. That's the way white men dress, particularly—"

"How do the white women dress?" she asked.

He thought back and realized that his own tastes had changed. "Their dresses are long, with big skirts. They like more decoration than men do, but it's different from what *we* wear—you and I. For instance, they wear brightly polished stones."

"Stones?"

"Polished. The kind that glitter. They make necklaces and bracelets out of them."

"Shells and teeth are not as heavy as stones, and they make much prettier decorations. Perhaps the white women use pony beads like the ones the traders bring on their pony pack trains."

"I don't know. I never paid much attention to fashion. I used to see beads sometimes in shawls or maybe hair coverings, but, no, I don't think they do much of that."

"Many of our women have changed to the beads." Kezawin held out the unfinished moccasins and touched the even row in a feminine gesture, giving them both a chance to admire the orange-and-yellow design. "I prefer to use quills."

"It makes a more handsome design."

"Of course, it takes more skill." She glanced up at him, her eyes twinkling.

"Indeed, far more skill," he agreed. Her eyes met their match when his danced to her tune. "Only a lazy woman would use beads."

"And those white women can't even do that much."

"They're ugly, too, most of them."

"I suspected so, although I've never seen one. If they're so lazy, they must be fat, as well."

"Fat as cows."

She giggled. "And they must quarrel with their husbands when they want more food." He nodded. "And they must have voices like crows and skin like—"

He laughed and nodded, remembering how Raleigh Brown's older sister, whom he'd once thought to be the incarnation of Venus, had broken his adolescent heart by getting married. She had inadvertently mended it again by putting on twenty pounds almost immediately thereafter.

"Now tell me what they are really like."

"They are like any other women, I suppose." He moved to sit behind her, scooting close to her back so that he could watch over her shoulder. "Some plain and some beautiful, some lazy and some ambitious. There are those who would have been anxious to tell the whole world what a fool I'd made of myself by raiding our ally's camp. Others might have let it pass with a quiet little dig. 'Oh, incidentally, that was my cousin's horse you stole.' A few..." He adjusted his robe around his shoulders, making a warm shell of himself for her. "The pearls among them would do nothing to diminish a man's heroic moment. A man would be crazy if he found one of those pearls and didn't marry her.''

She turned to look up at him. "It *was* a fine coup."

He smiled. "Especially if that pearl of a woman happens to use quills instead of beads."

"You tease me," she said, and made a pretense of going back to her work. She was down to two quills in her mouth.

"Tease you? I tell you truly that I have never seen such a quiller. If I had, I would have married her long ago. It amazes me how quickly—" one quill was now left in her mouth "—you work those things into the design."

"These are swallows," she pointed out. "The sign of the deer woman. It is thanks to her that I have this skill."

"And your healing touch. I don't think she's such a bad old girl." Kezawin tossed back a warning glance. "I'm not taking her lightly," he added quickly. The sharp end of the last quill looked mean. "Obviously she has power. Look how good this is. What kind of a dream would I have to have to improve my painting?"

"I think practice would be the best thing."

"Mmm. That's the hard way." James smiled secretly as the last quill came out of her mouth. "You may have to be satisfied with a mediocre artist. My talents lie in other directions."

Kezawin carefully folded the quill around the sinew, smiling to herself in just the way her husband did. "What directions would those be?"

"Shall I take out the Big Twisted Flute?"

"Only if you plan to accomplish nothing else the rest of the day."

"I plan to accomplish my most sacred duty." He took the moccasin out of her hands and set it aside with her awl and her bladder pouches full of quills. She turned, and both smiles were discovered. "Getting you with child."

"You have taken this duty quite seriously," she said quietly as she touched his bristly cheek.

"It is one that demands my constant attention. Now that you've removed the weapons from your mouth—"

"I have no defense against these quills on your face."

He kissed the corner of her mouth. "I'll shave again in the spring," he promised. He wondered whether it was his promise or his kiss that precipitated the sweet mewling sound she made beneath his arresting mouth.

"My brother's injury ails him today."

The announcement came through the door like a whoosh of cold air. James lifted his head and stifled a groan at the sight of Kezawin's softly parted lips. She consulted with a look. He gave an almost imperceptible nod.

"Bring Mouse Face Boy," she invited loudly enough to be heard outside. "We will try to help him."

On the end of a long, slow, helpless sigh, James went to unpeg the door.

Blue Heels kept his post beside the door as always, wrapped in his robe and keeping close watch on the proceedings while Mouse Face Boy chattered away. Blue Heels wondered at the power of the white man's medicine. After all, he had taken Double Woman Dreamer as his wife almost four moons past, and there he sat, strong and healthy as ever. Blue Heels had been certain the man was doomed. Double Woman Dreamer was simply too beautiful to be a wife to any mere mortal. Blue Heels had thought it fitting that she remain chaste, and that he might follow her example, keeping himself pure in honor of his secret love for her.

He hated the way the white man looked at her. It was wrong to look at her in the face; everyone knew that. Blue Heels had stolen many glimpses and thought for sure he would die while he was looking at her. Looking the other way also made him feel as though he might die. Her power was awful. Her beauty was awful. The way he ached inside every time he thought of her was almost unbearable.

And here was his brother, showing off Sapa, the crow, and chattering like a magpie with both of them as though they were just ordinary people.

James made every effort to preserve Mouse Face Boy's modesty, keeping his breechclout in place while he treated his hip with hot and cold wraps. The effectiveness of the treatment was evident in the child's elevated spirits, but James could have done without the flapping crow.

"Say your name," Mouse Face Boy coaxed. The thick leather wrapping that protected the boy's hand from the bird's claws was in tatters. A crippled wing prevented the crow from flying, but not from flapping each time its owner pet its breast. "Say 'Sapa.' Show my friends what a smart boy you are."

"Rawwk! Raaawwwk!"

James dodged an undulating wing. "Almost said it that time."

"He really can say his name," Mouse Face Boy insisted. "He doesn't like to make mistakes in front of people, so he just makes crow sounds. Come on, Sapa. You know how to say it. Sahhpahh. Come on."

"Perhaps this will help." Kezawin offered Mouse Face Boy a handful of meat tidbits.

Blue Heels broke his customary silence. "You'd better not spoil him." Three heads turned in surprise, and Blue Heels wanted to pull his robe up over his head. Instead, he stretched his neck and cleared his throat, hoping to steady his unpredictable voice. "My father says we might have to eat that bird before this winter ends."

"No, we won't," Mouse Face Boy countered. "There are plenty of dogs around, and *Ate* thinks he knows where he can find deer. He's going out tomorrow."

"And I'm going with him." Blue Heels risked a quick glance to see whether Double Woman Dreamer was impressed. *Haho!* She was smiling. He squared his shoulders, adjusted his robe and prepared for the worst.

"Look, Sapa. Meat. Now say your name, or I won't—" the beak was quicker than the hand "—or I won't give you any more. Sahhpahh."

When the treatment was done, Kezawin sent the boys on their way with a parfleche of dried meat, which they were invited to take to their mother. After they had gone, she put a ration of meat and dried turnips into her boiling pouch while James cleaned up from his painting. She could feel his displeasure, but she asked nothing. She knew that he would tell her what bothered him when he had the words ready.

Finally he took his place at the back of the tipi, seating himself against the willow backrest. "It isn't just ourselves, you know." He realized he'd begun in the middle, which indicated even to him that he was uncomfortable broaching the subject. "We have your father to provide for, as well."

It was his way to start by telling her something she already knew. She took her place at the willow backrest to his left and waited. After this curious announcement he would surely get around to saying what was on his mind.

"I don't think you ought to be giving so much food away," he said flatly. "Lately it seems that anyone who comes to you for medicine goes away with some of our food."

"Food is growing scarce."

"That's exactly my point. I don't mind your giving the children something to eat, but you gave them a good portion of what we had left."

"You remember that Many Plums spoke for me first and bit the knife when others hesitated. She has many mouths to feed."

"I know." He took up a coyote pelt and arranged it on her lap with the hair side next to her. "I remember well how she spoke. But the drifts are waist deep out there in some places. The last two times I went looking for game, there was nothing. Even the wolves have gone elsewhere."

"It's a bad winter."

"I know I'm not the best provider, Kezawin, but I am trying to keep meat in the kettle."

"It's the same for everyone." She laid a comforting hand on his thigh. "You've done well. Better than many of the other hunters. It pleases me to honor you in this way."

"What way?"

"By giving away meat. And you must know that sooner or later we shall receive what is owed us. When the weather is warm again, they will remember us for the medicine we have provided."

"When the weather is warm again, we won't have this problem." He stared into the fire, avoiding her eyes. "For right now, I just think we should hold back a little more. Things could get much worse before they get better."

"Hold back?" The concept was foreign to her. "You mean, keep it for ourselves?"

"I mean not give so much away," he clipped.

"As long as one of us has food, we all eat."

"I'm not suggesting we let anyone starve."

"We have enough for now. You'll find something soon, and we'll have fresh meat. I gave away venison, James. You have not eaten venison, so we have much to share."

"You and Lone Bear eat venison." He sighed impatiently. "I'm just saying we need to save enough so that we don't go hungry."

"Have you never gone hungry?"

He thought for a moment, then shook his head. "Not for any length of time."

"There may be hungry times before the warm winds come to take the snow away. The place where you lived as a white man must be wonderfully bountiful if the white people never go hungry."

Never covered too much ground, but he wasn't sure how he could explain the reality of haves and have-nots. "I haven't personally... not myself, nor my own family. You see, my family was fairly wealthy. We owned quite a large... Not that there aren't some—quite a few, really—poor people, people who have little. I, myself, lived a very simple—"

"Then your family would help the others, wouldn't they? You would sponsor feasts and give many gifts."

"Some, yes. There is charity, of course, but you can't help everybody."

"Why not?"

"Because then you would have nothing left."

"When you have given until you have nothing left, you will be highly honored. Then people will give you what you need, and it will be said that you are a generous man." She shifted her legs, tucking them to the other side of her seat, and adjusted the coyote robe. James had a capacity for generosity, she thought. Someone had neglected his training.

He scowled as he studied the yellow flame. The whole idea sounded almost biblical. Idealistic. People didn't live that way. Finally he shook his head. "No, I can't... Then you've become a charity case yourself. You can't give *everything* away."

"It is a bad sign when a man has too much. It means that he has not sponsored feasts or ceremonies, nor has he helped his relations. It means he has not given."

"But if we give until we have nothing left, and no one else has anything left—"

"We will all be hungry for a time." She saw that this frightened him more than other dangers he had faced. She moved closer and linked her arm with his. "But the Moon of the Birth of Calves will come. It always does. And imagine how green the grass will be after all this snow. *Tatanka* will eat and eat, and he will be so slow and fat that he will say, 'Take some of my flesh, Lakota brothers. I have plenty.'"

James ran his finger along the edge of her hair, smiling as he lifted it away from her face and smoothed it back. He often asked her not to braid it, and often she indulged him. "I will not have you go hungry. I shall go out again tomorrow. If I have to find enough meat for the whole camp, I *will* keep you fed."

They were brave words, she thought. Proud words. They had lived at the edge of camp, always a part of it but never completely included. They were more independent than most, but Kezawin knew that they were not self-reliant. Without each other, they would be like two hollow drums, but without the people, they would die.

"It is not for one man to feed the camp," she told him. She knew this time he would be gone for many days. It was so hard to forget the way her first husband and her brother had gone off full of youthful confidence. The deer woman had seen to their deaths. James must not go alone. "In times like these, small hunting parties may have better luck than a single hunter."

* * *

James swallowed his pride and paid a call on Catch The Bear, Many Plum's husband. The winter hunting parties were mostly family affairs for just a few men. But Kezawin was right. It was not wise to hunt alone in the deepest part of the winter, and one man alone was less effective than a small group. He told himself that Catch The Bear owed him something, but he made no such suggestion to the beefy man who was father to the slight, sickly Mouse Face Boy. He simply asked to be included with the party. Catch The Bear agreed without hesitation.

The camp had moved farther west in its quest for retreating game. In recent years, the Lakota had expanded their hunting grounds into what had once been Crow territory. As the rivalry continued, the Crow people were pushed west of the Greasy Grass River. This season, it seemed, so had the game. Catch The Bear's party followed signs for days, covering more ground when they chose to lead their horses and travel on snowshoes.

Winter hunting was an arduous, methodical task that involved none of the frenzy of the summer buffalo surround. It was a hardship to venture so far from the main camp. Even if the weather held, the days were often sullen and dim, the nights long and frigid. Long-distance tracking required stamina and determination. Trapping required unlimited patience.

Catch The Bear led a party of five, including his two brothers, Painted Shield and Two Broken Arrows, Blue Heels and James. James soon learned the value of group effort, and although much of the game was small, the hunters managed to take what they could find. One man was always left with the cache and the horses, while the rest competed with the wolves for the deer or antelope that still roamed the eastern slopes of the Bighorns, grazing near the underground seeps where they might still find forage.

James hated being left with the job of guarding the camp, especially in the waning daylight when the cool white sun threw a splash of pink and gold in the sky, then slunk behind the mountains. It was a time when the eerie lack of sound made his skin crawl. He was tempted to watch the sun, give it a parting curse for deserting him, but when he noticed a pricking of horses' ears and heard movement in the brush on the slope below him, he stretched out on his belly and cocked his rifle.

Anyone from his own party would have called out. He scanned the slope and picked out the offending brush. If it were an animal, it was soon to be meat. A man—well, he'd better be saying his prayers. Another bush moved. More than one man, and they were waiting for dusk, when they would make shadowy targets.

If they were Crow, James realized that for every one he detected, there were probably two who had not given themselves away. He figured they were just out of range, and he decided he would not wait for them to come to him. The only cover was a stand of three or four cottonwoods between him and the brush, and that was where the horses were tied. James concentrated on that destination and pushed all distractions from his mind.

He sprang to his feet and fired at the first bush as soon as he darted within range. The return fire came just as he dove for the trees. One horse backed up, loosening the half hitch at the end of his rein and breaking free of the tree. James braced his back against a tree and reloaded his rifle while the horse took off, drawing more fire. Within seconds he had mounted another of the horses and was charging the second scruffy bush. The Crow warrior tried to dive clear of James's charge, but his efforts caught him a bullet in the face.

Catch The Bear, on his way back from the hunt, heard the fracas. On snowshoes he skimmed the crusty snow, topping the rise above their camp in time to watch James ride over the heads of his would-be ambushers. Delighted, Catch The Bear shed his snowshoes, mounted up and joined James in chasing the last two Crow braves into the draw, where their own horses waited. James was more interested in the two extra Crow horses, and he rounded them up while Catch The Bear gave a rousing whoop and a halfhearted chase, letting the two outrun him in the deep snow.

"Two scalps and two Crow ponies!" Catch The Bear shouted to James as he trotted back. "That's a good day's work, my friend."

"I can use the horses," James said. "Taking Crow scalps would weaken my medicine."

"Since I backed you up, I shall take them myself."

James nodded. "Be my guest."

Catch The Bear dropped to the ground near the corpses, which lay in a macabre sort of tête-à-tête. James watched him deftly slice away the top of the scalp and wondered how Catch The Bear would reconcile his actions with regret for taking a life. Of course, Catch The Bear had not killed the men. James had.

"We travel tonight," Catch The Bear announced when the other three hunters returned to camp. "You missed all the excitement."

James finished tying his captured horses in a pack line, nose to tail, and made sure his hands were steady before joining the others. He had acted without hesitation, almost as though he had practiced his move in advance, but when it was over, the trembling had started on the inside and worked its way out. He'd had to make himself busy with the horses while he brought it under control.

Catch The Bear gave him a congratulatory slap on the back. "Our cousin, Garrett, turned the Crows' surprise back on them, and two of them paid the price. But now we'd better move quickly, since our enemies may come looking for us."

"It's been a good hunt," Two Broken Arrows attested, and he looked at James. "You'll go with us next time."

James had been gone for ten days, and Kezawin had counted every heartbeat of every one of them. She had battled against despair, but with each passing day she lost ground. When the news came that the hunting party was on its way into camp, she ran back to their lodge, changed her dress, brushed her hair until it crackled and raced back outside to welcome her husband. The village rejoiced at the sight of fresh meat, but Kezawin's private joy was for James's safe return. In the midst of the excitement all she knew was that he was there, alive, whole and healthy.

The other men offered reserved greetings to their wives, but restraint was unthinkable for James. He saw Kezawin making her way through the snow to meet him, and he urged his horse in her direction. When she stood beside his knee and looked up at him as though he'd brought her a trove of treasure, he slid off his horse and caught her in his arms.

"You're all right?" she asked, almost as though she'd gone shy on him. "You're not hurt?"

"Not at all." She was an armful, bundled up to her chin in her wearing robe, and all he could do was shower her face with kisses. "I missed you. Oh, I missed you."

"Such a long, long time. I was afraid—"

"I'm fine." He took a moment to inspect her face. "Have you had enough to eat? You look tired. Is your father well?"

She smiled and took the reins from his hand. "I shall see to the horse." She had many things to tell him, but they would wait for a private moment.

"Horses." He grinned as he put his arm around her shoulders to keep her close as they walked. "They're Crow this time, not Brûlé." He saw all the anxious questions and the belated fear in her eyes, and he shrugged them off. "We had a little tussle with another hunting party. I ended up with a couple of extra horses." It was the explanation of a man who hoped his woman would never know how terrified he had been or how close he had come to being the corpse rather than the victor.

"There will be a victory celebration, then, and you will be honored."

"It isn't something I want to celebrate. It happened—you know, all of a sudden they were there, and it was either... I was lucky, that's all. I want to celebrate being home." He gave her shoulders a hard squeeze. "And I want to celebrate with only my wife."

But the community celebration was unavoidable. Three fur traders had stopped to trade in recent days, and they were invited to participate. There was not the jubilation of a summer festival, for the hibernating earth preferred not to be disturbed during the long winter's night, but there was feasting. In the wintertime, when the Lakota bands broke up into smaller camps, the council tipi at the center of camp was large enough to accommodate most of the people. Stories were told, first eagerly, then more leisurely until finally the children slept with their heads in their parents' laps and the tales were coming fewer and further between.

Pipes were passed, and James caught up on three-month-old news with the visitors from Missouri. There was a fever growing, they said, a fever to move West, and it wouldn't be long before the population spilled across the Mississippi.

James found it hard to imagine, but it came from the mouths of the traders as a dire prediction. Settlers would undoubtedly threaten the fur business.

Could it be true? James wondered as he and Kezawin returned to their lodge. Could there be appreciable numbers of his kind edging closer to the great river? Surely this land, with its unbroken expanse of grassland and its formidable mountains, would not interest a nation of farmers. There was plenty of good land for them east of the Mississippi— land that had never been touched by a plow.

When the fire had warmed their tipi, Kezawin undressed her husband. He'd hardly spoken since they'd left the council lodge, and she knew he was troubled. She wanted to bathe him and caress the trouble away from his mind. He was content to give himself over to her and let her try.

Her hands eased ten days' tension away. He closed his eyes and willed that all thoughts and recollections be gone as he leaned against the willow backrest and absorbed the heat of the fire into skin he'd thought would never again be truly warm. The mint-scented water she used in washing him made him tingle all over. When he opened his eyes again, Kezawin was letting her dress slip to the floor. He watched her buff herself with the wet swatch of deerskin until her skin gleamed like burnished copper in the firelight. The long black hair framed her shoulders. Enchanted, he started up from his seat.

"Stay there," she ordered softly. "Let me make you more comfortable."

He gave her a lazy smile. "I don't think you can make me any more comfortable."

"I think I can," she said huskily as she straddled his lap. Then, as he eased himself inside her, she whispered. "It's good to have you home."

It was good to be home. It was good to taste her sweet breast, to tongue her nipple into a hard bead and then pull it into his mouth and suck gently and make her moan and hold her hips and make her move them against him and make her moan and make her take more of him, all of him, and ride him higher and higher and make her moan and moan and moan....

So good.

And then it was good just to hold her sweat-slick body against his chest and watch the fire burn.

Finally, it was good to be two in a sleeping robe again.

"Where did this come from?" James asked as he tugged on a red blanket that had been added to their bed.

"I got it from the fur traders. But I didn't trade food for it," she hastened to add. "Just a pair of winter moccasins."

"Your work is too good to trade away for blankets."

"Oh, I hadn't done much to those moccasins. And these blankets make good wearing robes, don't you think? Many of the people gave pelts for them."

"It's just a blanket," he said as his attention drifted toward the flames again. She remained silent, stroking the hair on his chest, and he knew she wouldn't ask, wouldn't coax him to tell her anything he didn't want her to know. He didn't want her to know the bloody details—the way a man looks when his face has been blown off or what it sounds like when someone hacks off the top of a man's head. Maybe she had seen it all before, but he wanted to believe she hadn't. He wanted to believe he could keep her from ever having to see and hear and smell such things.

Catch The Bear had announced at the feast that they had counted coup on the Crows and that James had handled himself like a true Lakota warrior. The song that had been sung in his honor couched his deed in poetic terms, and the details of the event had been discussed among the men. Kezawin knew what had happened, but James needed to confess it.

"I killed two men," he said tonelessly. "Two *more* men."

"The Crows."

He nodded without taking his eyes off the fire.

"They attacked you."

"They were ready to ambush me, but I made the first move. I was alone at the time, standing watch over the camp, and I didn't figure I had much of a chance unless I acted quickly."

"And you were spared."

"Again." He turned to her, and she saw the pain in his eyes. "I can still see them, Kezawin. Four of them now. Am I becoming some kind of an executioner?"

"No one kills without regret," she reminded him. "Even as you celebrate your victory, a part of you mourns because you have taken life."

"I must perform *inipi*," he decided. "Tomorrow. I must rid myself of this awful image of death—so much death."

"You did not seek this, but it came to you. You must regret it, then let it go. You have much to do with life." She turned her lips against his muscled chest, kissed him and whispered. "You have started a life where it was thought no life would grow."

For a moment James lay very still. "I have done... what?"

Kezawin took his hand and placed it over her firm, feminine belly. "You have done your sacred duty, beloved husband." She looked up to see the wonder in his eyes. "Your child grows inside me."

Chapter Eleven

Kezawin had reminded her husband that gathering wood and carrying water were woman's work, but he took a perverse pleasure in ignoring her protests. There was always a chance of finding some game near the spring, he said, but they both knew what a slim chance it was. He loved to walk the draw with her on mornings like this one, when the air was clear and crisp with cold. The winter sky was pale and delicate, like a bird's eggshell cast high overhead. The barren, windswept hills marked the shell's jagged edge, but the barely blue canopy was uninterrupted from horizon to horizon.

Tough slough grass poked its evergreen blades through the snow and ice in the bog below the spring. On the rise above, the morning mist hovered above a small pool, indicating the warm spring's location. Water seeped over a gentle grade and froze, creating a natural ice playground. The children were already out sliding over the gentle slope and on the glassy pond below it. The same bitter wind that had kept them inside for two days had cleared much of the snow off the ice.

There was wood to be found in the stand of cottonwoods on the high ground beyond the spring. It wasn't long before Kezawin had amassed as much as she could bundle up and carry on her back, but James's pile did not grow as quickly. The children were too delightful a distraction. They laughed and shrieked at one another as they skidded on the ice, sliding over the little hill by the handiest mode—most often on their bottoms. James shivered as he watched, but even the toddlers seemed impervious to the cold as their older brothers and sisters dragged them over the ice on old hides or slabs of rawhide.

James forgot about the sticks in his hands as he watched one small girl's stubby legs slide out from under her several times. She picked herself up each time without a whimper. He imagined holding his arms out to catch a tiny version of Kezawin, and the image made him smile.

Kezawin's heart swelled when she glanced up from bundling her pile of sticks and saw the direction of her husband's attention. What a good day it would be when she presented this man with a child of his own. She made her rawhide loop secure and went to James, leaving her bundle on the ground. Together they watched one little boy slide across the ice and bowl his brother over. James laughed as he tossed a few sticks atop his own little wood pile. They exchanged a look that said, *Imagine this! We have a child coming.* He drew her closer, protecting his whole family within the warmth of his embrace, and slid his hand up and down her back as they stood watching the children.

"They must think you're a very strange man," she teased when they caught the brief notice of a pair of the boys. "Holding your wife as though you were a suitor with no courting robe."

At the sound of her voice, another boy looked up at them, then politely glanced away. James laughed and rocked Kezawin back and forth until she laughed with him. "We have a right to be strange," he reminded her. "It's expected. People would be disappointed if we were not."

"Then seeing that you also gather wood will keep them happy."

"They will say, 'It's just that crazy white man.'" He slipped his hand beneath her robe and laid it lovingly over her flat belly. "But when they see the reason for my strange behavior, this time they'll understand."

"They would understand the way you spoil me if I were heavy with child." Smiling up at him, she put her hand over his and squeezed it. He wore the badgerskin helmet she'd made for him, and the white center stripe ended at the bridge of his nose. Beneath the edge of the gray-and-white pelt his blue eyes twinkled at her. "But I'm still small," she said quietly.

"By summer you will be fat and irritable, and I shall be thin and anxious."

"I won't have you getting thin and anxious." She tucked her face into the warm hollow under his chin. The badgerskin touched his shoulders and made a little tent around his face, and she felt as though she had crawled inside. "Do all white men carry wood and water for their wives?"

"Only this one." To his knowledge, it was true. "You did all right, Mrs. Garrett. Crazy husbands are hard to come by."

"I know." She smiled. "As are crazy wives."

They tied James's pile of wood into a bundle, but he refused to let Kezawin carry even the smaller of the two burdens on her back. She protested his gallantry less this time and led the way to the spring. The winter sun cast sharp shadow images on the ice—a tall man with a bundle of sticks on his back, and a small woman, a bundle herself, who stood beside him. In blue shadow, they were a perfectly complementary pair. All around them the sunlight was caught, crystalized in the ice and snow, and the tiny rays of light winked at them.

Kezawin drew out the water bladders and lowered the first one into the small ice bowl full of continuously running spring water. As she watched, the air bubbles started doing a funny dance, while the ring of thin ice blurred into the water. She squeezed her eyes shut for a moment, and the ground seemed to tilt beneath her feet. She made a stumbling attempt to steady herself and lost her grip on the bladder's rawhide harness just as a strong arm kept her from falling into the sloshy snow.

"Steady, there. Did you slip?"

The rawhide string floated as the bladder slowly sank. "The water bag!" Kezawin started to reach for it again, but it dissolved before her eyes as she tried to regain her footing in the snow.

"Let it go." He caught her before she crumpled. "What is it, Kezawin?"

"Nothing. Just a little . . ." She used him as a mooring as she struggled to make muscles work in legs that seemed to be failing her. She managed a thin laugh. "A little craziness is all."

James slipped his arms out of makeshift straps and let the bundle of wood clatter to the ground. "Oh, no!" Kezawin cried as he swept her up into his arms. "Now they will talk. When they hear that I am growing strong with child, they will say that Double Woman Dreamer cannot carry a child the way other women—"

"They will say that Double Woman Dreamer married a man who will not let her carry his child alone." He knew that the buffalo robe accounted for at least half the weight he'd lifted. He had noticed how little she'd been eating in recent days, but if she'd been sick, she had succeeded in hiding it from him. He feared she might have done just that, for the Lakota word for pregnancy meant "growing strong," and sickness would seem a weakness to her.

"You see? I can easily carry you both."

"Oh, but it is for the woman—"

"Oh, but it is for the man, when the woman's head is light. I shall come back for the wood and water."

He carried her back to their lodge and laid her in their sleeping robes. She protested, but when she tried to get up, he eased her back down. "Stay put while I get a fire going. And then you'll stay here and get warm while I go back to pick up the wood."

"After the spectacle we just made, I won't have you carrying all my wood for me, James."

He tossed an arm load of wood next to the fire pit. "We may be in for our first marital spat, Mrs. Garrett." He took flint from the little strike-a-light bag Kezawin had recently quilled for him and built the fire as though he had eyes in his hands. Kezawin's complexion had taken on a strangely yellowish cast. There had been a time when he would have said, as any man would, let women take care of women's complaints, but not now. This was Kezawin, who never complained, and if she was inclined to do so now, she had no one to complain to but James.

She tried to lie still, but even when she closed her eyes, the lodge kept spinning. *I shall not be sick in my husband's presence,* she told herself. *This will pass.* The heat from the fire and the heat within her met and mixed, swirled and churned...

"What troubles you?" he asked gently.

She opened her eyes, found him hovering over her and wondered when he had moved. "It's the child. I shall brew a tea to clear my head and make my stomach behave properly. Then I shall finish—"

"I'll take care of the tea. And don't tell me—I know exactly what to put in it."

She closed her eyes and smiled only slightly. "You have stolen all my medicine, James Garrett. You have written my soul into your journals."

"Impossible," James mumbled as he arranged the boiling pouch on its tripod and maneuvered several stones into the hottest part of the fire. "Not even Will Shakespeare could find words to do you justice."

"Is he your *kola*, this Will Shakespeare?"

"He's one of the old ones, long dead, but we have saved his songs and stories in our books, and we—Kezawin, what is it?"

She was pulling at her clothes as he moved back to her side. "Too warm," she muttered. "Do not speak a dead one's name, James. Not now. Not . . . with the child . . ."

He cupped his hands around her face. She *was* too warm. He'd had little experience with pregnant women, but this worried him. Fever always worried him. "When did this start?" he asked.

"When we were at the spring."

"When was the first time? Has it always come in the morning like this?" He covered her with the red trade blanket and gently squeezed her shoulders. "Kezawin, when you're sick, you must tell me. I won't be—"

"I have not been sick," she insisted. "This was the first time. But I'm a strong woman, and I can bear you children, James. This will pass. I promise."

"It's just a little morning sickness," he assured her as he tucked the blanket around her. "You'll be fine if you'll stop trying to prove how strong you are and let me take care of you."

She closed her eyes and nodded. "I'll be fine." Her eyes felt like two small fire pits. "Please," she whispered. "I'm very thirsty."

"A little water, followed shortly thereafter by your own magic tea," he promised as he took up a pair of sticks and pulled one of the heated rocks from the fire.

"No magic."

"Fine. No magic." The water hissed as the rock hit the water with a plunk. "Just good medicine."

When the tea was ready, Kezawin wrapped herself in the red blanket and sat near the fire, using her willow backrest for the support that was more necessary than she wanted James to know. Her back ached, and the fire inside her burned as hot as the one James had made. Within her spinning thoughts there was one going round and round, telling her to cover her own fire. Smother it. Make it burn itself out. Douse it with tea. Make it go away. It must not touch the child.

James sat next to her and sipped tea from a wooden bowl. "It's normal for a woman to have sickness at this time." He glanced up and added quickly, "From what I've heard, I think it's normal. I've had precious little experience with these things, I'm afraid."

"You are a man," she said. Four words that explained everything. She was a woman, and she would have known about these things had it not been for her dream. She had treated women for menstrual difficulties, but no woman who carried a child dared get too close to one who had dreamed of the deer woman.

It was a woman's duty to protect the child in her womb, and Kezawin would do the same for her child. She was glad that James was there to treat the crippled ones, like Mouse Face Boy, whom she must avoid during the growing-strong-time. She would avoid eye contact with the *heyoka*, the one who had dreamed of thunder and was obliged to do everything he did in the reverse of the way it was normally done. The *winkte*, the man who wore women's clothes, must also be avoided lest she bear a son with the heart of a woman. Such a one was *wakan*, both respected and feared, and lived a lonely life.

Kezawin had known that life. She had accepted it, but now she had a husband, and a child was coming. She would not be sick, she told her spinning head. She wasn't certain whether this was normal, either, but it felt too much like weakness to her, and she would not permit herself to be weak. Not now. She would do all the right things. She sipped her tea. Douse the fire, she thought. It must not burn where the child was living inside her.

"I am a *strange* man," he reminded her. "*Wakan*. I behave as I please. I do what I want. And I want to help you grow strong."

She raised her heavy head with some difficulty and looked at him tenderly. "You already have," she said. "Now I must not disappoint you. I must—"

Her stomach rebelled and would not let her rest until its contents had been eliminated. James held her head and spoke to her quietly, telling her that he was with her and that all would be well. But the heat of her skin seared him with fear. This was something more than morning sickness.

Whatever his doubts about Lone Bear's medicine, James had the utmost respect for the old man's wisdom. He was a pipe-bearer, one of the *wakincuzas*, "the ones who decide." James knew that a man was neither expected nor permitted by the women to involve himself in life's exclusively female provinces, but Kezawin had kept no food down for two days. Herbal infusions had little effect on her fever, and she could not hide her pain. James had kept the two of them to themselves, but it was time to seek Lone Bear's counsel. If Kezawin suffered from influenza, others might have it, too. That was his first question.

"There are others who are ill," Lone Bear said after they had smoked together. "I heard of two yesterday and one today. Winter maladies, I guess. You must see that my daughter eats soon, and give her only fresh water." He wagged a finger in the air. "Do not let her drink stale water. If she has fever, a spirit must have built its fire near her. Have you been speaking of the dead?" James glanced away, and his father-in-law sighed. "Burn sage, and keep the lodge fire high. Perhaps a sweat would help to purge the evil."

"I would not have her get chilled."

"A little cold air makes the body stronger. No one shies away from the cold but those with weak blood, who cannot endure." He tapped James's thigh with a finger. "You have your *pejuta*, Garrett, your herbs and roots. Use them well. Let her sweat and pray. She will find strength. You'll see."

When James returned to the lodge, he found that she still slept. He added fuel to the fire and tossed a few sprigs of sage into the flames. He gathered all of the medicine bags in front of him and paged through his journal. He had tried everything. He had had some success with easing her headache—at least so she told him. Perhaps even in her illness she sought to comfort him. He had to find a way to control her vomiting. He chose dried prickly pear, willow bark and bee balm and reached for the water bag. Then he paused. Fresh water. When had he gotten water last? He couldn't remember.

He hurried to the spring, trotting most of the way. Squatting beside the little pool, he lowered the tawny translucent buffalo's bladder into the water and surveyed the late-afternoon sky while he waited for the pouch to fill. It had been days since any new snow had fallen, but there was snow in the air. A low gray cloud cover flowed overhead like a stream rushing from the western mountains toward the eastern rivers. Snow tonight, he thought. He popped the wooden stopper into the bladder, draped the rawhide strap across his chest and gathered a bundle of wood. By the time he got back to the lodge, his hands were stiff with the cold.

His heart leaped into his throat. There was Kezawin, wrapped in her red blanket and huddled near the fire, shivering like a small animal cornered by the hunter. He dropped the firewood and threw off his robe.

"Forgive me for being gone so long, love. Your father warned me against stale water, and he's right." He knelt behind her and surrounded her with his embrace. "I must be careful about the water," he said close to her ear. Her little body trembled in his arms, and he felt sick inside. "You're cold now?" he whispered. "I am, too. We'll be warm in a moment. Now that I'm here with you, we can both get warm."

She tipped her head back against his shoulder and closed her eyes. His cheek felt like a snowball next to her cheek, but it didn't matter. Her body was at once cold on the inside and hot on the outside, and he was all that was steady. "Your hands are cold," she said. "Don't get them too close to the fire. They'll hurt."

"I need to thaw them out and get them working on some new medicine."

"Have you had a new vision?"

"No. Only a new idea."

"I trust you," she said, her voice raspy.

He shut his eyes tight and pressed his lips to her warm neck. "I know."

James made the tea and fed her small sips while he held her across his lap. She dozed in his arms, then awakened to ask him if he'd eaten anything. He told her he would, and she dozed again. He ducked outside and found that the gray afternoon had become an ash-white evening, luminous within a cloudy cocoon. Something was coming, and the camp waited quietly for the onslaught.

One thin, eerie cry rent the night. James was struck by this solitary night sound, in part because it was the voice of a child, and Lakota children never cried. Crying was discouraged from infancy. It touched him, too, with hollowness and hunger. He couldn't remember his last substantial meal. But there was something else in that cry, something elusive and frightening. Something was coming, riding in on the wind, and there was nothing to do but wait for it.

Kezawin was awake when James went back inside. He cooled her face again with his hands, and she made a smile for him that did not reach her eyes. "What have you eaten?" she asked.

"Nothing yet," he told her. "I've been soaking Cheyenne turnip and breadroot. And I've boiled some dried cherries. I thought you might try a little cherry soup."

"You must have meat."

"I plan to ask your father to stay with you while I go out hunting. There is *wasna* here and a little venison." He shrugged. "I cannot eat venison."

"I know. The *wasna* has only buffalo meat." She covered his hands with hers. "It's different being married to a white man." She thought it over again and shook her head. "Being married to *you* is different."

"Different from what?"

"Different from anything else. You do things differently. You must hunt whenever you see fit to hunt and not worry about leaving me. The others are close by."

He brought her fingers to his lips and kissed them. "Does 'different' mean better or worse than anything else?"

He had a way of not hearing what she said sometimes, but she smiled again anyway. "It's good being your wife. Your ways are different, but you love me well."

"You must let me have some of my own ways," he said, "even while I learn to practice some of yours. I will always be a white man, and there are those things I cannot change."

"And I will always be Lakota."

"Our child will look different from the other children," he told her.

"Our child will be beautiful, just like the others."

"But I shall be his father, and there will be things for me to teach him."

"And things for his grandfather to teach him."

"And his mother." He nibbled her fingertips again. "Or *her* mother. This child may have the best of both our worlds."

"I would have you do something for me," she whispered.

"Anything."

"Play the Big Twisted Flute for me." His eyes widened in a teasing suggestion, and she gave a wan smile. "I think the music will not have its usual effect tonight, but it would soothe me."

The music became part of the winter night, a melancholy whistling on the wind. From some distant corner of the camp came the slow, steady throb of a medicine drum. James remembered their wedding night, when his lilting music had entwined itself with the beat of the dance drum— two entities, like a man and his wife, becoming one. He played for his wife now, not to seduce but to comfort, because she was as dear to him as his own breath. He was tired and hungry, and his eyes rested on her and fed. In this moment, too, he was one with her.

The medicine drum stopped, and James put his flute down and dipped out a bowl of the cherry soup for Keza-win. He grabbed a handful of *wasna* from a parfleche and nibbled at it while Kezawin drank. The drumbeat resumed.

"Someone else is ill," she said.

"It must be some winter complaint that's going around. If we could rid you of this fever, I think you'd be back on your feet. I'm going to sponge you down."

"Mmm, I would like that," she said with a sigh. "Almost like music."

He took the red blanket from her and moved her closer to the fire. She helped him remove her soft buckskin shift, and he dipped a piece of chamois in warm water. He wished he had thought to add some aromatic herbs to the water as she had done for him. It was then that he noticed the rash of red spots on her chest. He glanced down and saw that her abdomen was covered, too. He could not draw breath as he touched her gingerly, his hands trembling with his disbelief.

The medicine drum threaded its rhythm through the steady howl of the wind as memory took him back.

A pale blond woman turned vacant eyes upon a child, and a man responded with a wretched groan.

"God, not this. God in heaven, not this."

Out of the corner of his eye he saw red, and the pieces fell together in his mind. With a predatory growl he snatched up the trade blanket and pitched it into the fire. The red wool smoldered, smoked, then lit up like a pool of oil.

"It had to be the traders," he muttered. "Damn their putrid souls, it *had* to be them."

Kezawin gripped a handful of curly buffalo hair and elevated herself on one elbow. She understood nothing but James's anger, for he spoke in English. As her head spun with nausea, she tried to make her burning eyes focus on the towering figure of her husband. "What is it, James?"

He took a deep breath and exhaled slowly, summoning some measure of reason. "I could be wrong," he said, but the words were devoid of hope. He knelt beside her and gathered the buffalo robes close about her as he examined the dark red spots closely. It had been a long time, but he had not forgotten how they had looked on his mother's skin—and his own.

Kezawin. This was Kezawin. He lifted his gaze from the swell of her spotted breasts to her face and read her question again in her eyes.

"This rash," he began carefully. "Have you seen anything like this before?"

Her dark eyes plumbed the depths of his. She did not need to look down. She knew what was there on her body. "It's a strange thing. I think it's a bad sign."

"I thought perhaps it was something you knew about," he suggested. "Something you had seen and treated before."

"It's something *you* know about. I see it in your eyes. Tell me what you know."

Tell her what? Tell her the word that was uttered in whispers lest it turn order into chaos? He had not learned the word in Lakota, and the only synonym he knew was death. "When I was a child, I suffered from an illness. My mother contracted it, too, and many other people also suffered from it. You see, when one person—"

"Your mother died."

He nodded solemnly.

"And the others?"

"Many...some recovered." He kissed her hand and pressed it against his chest so that she could feel his heartbeat. "I did, as you see. I'm healthy. But this disease is very... We call it smallpox." The word brought a bitter taste to his tongue. He carried her hand to his forehead and placed her fingers on the two small pits hidden beneath a sweep of tawny hair. "I wear the scars from the spots. They were like the ones you have now."

Lovingly she touched the small dents in his skin and thought of the child he once was, and then she glanced away. "This may be the same spirit that visited one of the Brûlé camps several winters past. We heard about it, but little was said. No one wanted to disturb that spirit again."

"It's not a spirit, Kezawin. It's a disease. Your father has told me that there are others who are sick, but the spots—a person gets sick first, and then the spots appear a few days later. That's how we know what it is."

"The medicine drum," she acknowledged.

"I think the traders may have brought the disease. If they did, it's in their blankets and every other filthy thing they palmed off on the people."

"I washed the blanket," she said, closing her eyes against the burning. Her mouth was dry, and she was tired, but she didn't want him to think that she would put a blanket on their bed that smelled of white traders. Everything that came from them had to be washed and flown in the air, even in the winter. The smell was . . . She opened her eyes and saw the blurred shape of her husband's white face, and she smiled a little. He was different. He was not a white man; he was James. "I did wash it," she repeated.

"It doesn't matter. If the traders carried the disease and the blankets were contaminated—"

"I don't understand." Kezawin shook her head and sighed. "Illness comes to the body, not blankets. It's an evil that dwells—"

He raised his hands in protest. "This thing comes from my world, and I know it well. We must burn everything they brought and keep the sick people away from those who are well."

"Why?"

"Because it spreads from one to another. I have seen this, and I know."

She pulled at the buffalo robe, trying to draw it closer to her chin. "Then you must leave here, James. You must take my father and the others who—"

"No." He touched her cheek, and she flinched, trying to draw back. "It's all right," he soothed, brushing her hair back from her face. "I've had the pox. I can't get it again. I'm the only one who should tend the sick."

"You must tell my father," she said. "You must tell the *wakincuzas* of your experiences with this pox."

"I'll tell them they must order the healthy families to move and put those who are sick together in—"

"James." She laid her hand on his arm and struggled with fading senses. "Don't tell them what they must do. They won't hear you. Tell them...what you know. What you have seen. Tell my father first. Let him... I'm so thirsty...so tired..."

He hated leaving her alone, but he had no choice. She had taken a little more soup and gotten sick again. She tried some tea, then slept while he sponged her with tepid water. The wind howled, and a fine cloud of snow swirled about him as he stood before Lone Bear's tipi and asked for admittance. Lone Bear was stretched out on his side, enjoying a smoke.

"I'm tired," he said. "There is too much work for an old man. The north wind brings on too many complaints."

James took his place to Lone Bear's right, but he left a six-foot space between them. Then he committed what he knew to be an unpardonable breech of etiquette by refusing the pipe. "Your daughter is very ill, Lone Bear. I cannot smoke with you. I cannot smoke with anyone."

"Is this part of your medicine now?"

"Yes." It was not untrue, although it was not part of his vision. Lone Bear had given him an explanation that would serve him well. "I must touch no one who is well now. I may touch only the sick, and I know that my wife is not the only one."

"I have been in three different lodges just tonight," Lone Bear said. "It's too much for an old man. Buffalo Dreamer is busy, too. Something bad is afoot here."

"I know. I have seen it before, and I know what must be done."

Lone Bear saw the fear in his son-in-law's face. Out of respect for the young man, he turned his attention to the fire. "Is this a thing that comes from the white man?" he asked.

"Yes, I believe it is."

"Have you brought it here?"

"No. I had the disease when I was a child, and it will not come to me again."

Lone Bear considered the news and nodded. "That is powerful medicine."

"Yes, it is. And because I'm the only one who has this medicine, I must use it to help the people. And I must speak with the *wakincuzas* and tell them what I know."

Lone Bear looked at James again. "I remember your vision."

"Yes," James said softly. "So do I."

"They will listen to you because you have been to the hill. You need not tell them everything you saw there, but they must know that your *šicun* guides you in this matter."

Lone Bear instructed the *epapáha* to announce a gathering of the ones who decide in the council lodge. Four men gathered, and James cringed as he watched them pass the pipe among themselves, but he said nothing. Lone Bear explained that James's medicine dictated that he keep his distance and refuse the pipe for the present time, and the explanation was not questioned.

"A number of people have become ill in recent days," James began. "They have fever, pain in the back and head, and they cannot keep their food down. Some may have spots." He passed his hand over his face and chest. "Dark red spots all over them. I have to come to talk with you about this illness."

"Ohan," said Red Elk, the eldest of the four, nodding his approval as he lit a twist of sweet grass and laid it over a rock in the fire pit. "My grandson is sick."

"Then what I have to say comes all the harder. I have seen this illness before. My mother died from it. I suffered from it, too, but I recovered, and it will not plague my body again. The only way to prevent it from spreading throughout the camp is to keep those who are sick far away from those who are well."

James waited while the pipe was passed again. He wanted to say his piece and get back to Kezawin, but he knew that the deliberations would not be rushed. There would be no voting. The decision would be made by consensus, which took time. James rubbed his hand over his stubby beard and tried to recall his last shave.

"This illness comes from the white man, then," Meets The Enemy said. "It is the one that killed the Brûlés."

"I think it's the same one," James concurred, "although there are other illnesses that come with spots on the skin. My wife is a healer, and she has not seen spots like these. I think the traders brought it here."

"There is an evil among us," said Meets The Enemy. "Perhaps *you* brought it here, Garrett. You have been with the whites and the Pawnee. You married one who has dreamed of the deer woman. You killed my nephew."

"I have helped many others when they needed medicine, as has my wife," James said evenly. "All of you know what happened between me and Thun—the one you speak of. It was not my wish to kill him, but neither was it my wish to die.''

The pipe was passed again before Cry Of The Crow contributed his thoughts. "Tunkaśila would never protect us if we abandoned our sick ones."

"The new camp need not be far away," James said. "I would tend the sick, and those who are healthy would bring us food, water and wood. Everything that came from the traders must be burned, and nothing that the sick ones have used must be taken to the new camp. The illness abides in their bedding and on the bowls from which they drink."

"I cannot think that I would leave my grandson and make a new camp," Red Elk said.

James leaned his elbows against his knees and stared at his own hands. "When my mother and I were ill," he said, barely audibly, "my father left us. I remember the sound of his footsteps as he walked away."

"What did you do?" Cry Of The Crow asked.

"My mother died, and I lived to hate him for it." He lifted one shoulder as if he could shrug off all those years. "But I lived," He looked up. "My father lived, and so did my older brother. There were many who died."

"And so it will be," Red Elk said. "Some will live and some will die, but the Lakota will stay together in all things."

"You have separated into smaller camps for the winter," James pointed out, "because it's easier to feed a smaller group and because... because survival—*our* survival—depends upon our doing what's best for all of us. We would have two small camps, close but not—"

"Everyone in one of the camps would be sick," Red Elk countered.

"Except me," James replied. "I will not get sick."

Meets The Enemy turned to Lone Bear. "Did you interpret this one's vision?" Lone Bear nodded. "How do our people fall ill while this man does not? How does he avoid the deer woman's power? Is he a man of true vision, or does he trick us?"

"His medicine has grown stronger since he came to us," Lone Bear said. "I have seen that he has a vision of the people, and for this I waved the horses' tails over him and made him a *hunka*. He would not deceive us."

"I am *wakan*," James said. Hearing the words from his own mouth brought him a sense of inner strength. "I know that now. Something brought me here. Perhaps this *śicun* my wife speaks about. I don't know. But I know now that I'm not lost. I'm here because I am supposed to be here. I have seen this in a vision, and I know that I have medicine. Beyond that, I bring the memory of an experience that no one seeks, but because of it, I can be useful to the people."

"What you suggest is impossible," Meets The Enemy said. "If the traders brought this thing, I think you must be one of them. They will come back and murder the helpless in the camp you 'tend.'"

James stared into the fire. "My wife is growing strong with child," he said quietly. "She is also sick with this disease."

Again the pipe was passed, and the spark at the end of the slow-burning sweet grass glowed its last. "We must think about this," Red Elk said finally. "We must watch and wait. That is all I have to say."

"Ohan," was chorused in agreement. Lone Bear only grunted. Red Elk tapped the ashes from the pipe, and the five men went their separate ways in the cold white night.

The more time they took to think about it, the worse things would get, James told himself as he trudged homeward. With his badgerskin over his head and his buffalo robe dragging behind him in the snow, he wondered at the strange figure he would have cut on the Harvard campus. How his life had changed in a year's time. Something had brought him here, he'd said. The real wonder was that he'd believed everything he'd said. He was not the same James Garrett who had walked the wintery streets of Boston in top hat and billowing black cloak a year ago. And the man he was now, no matter what the apparel, no longer belonged there. But Meets The Enemy—and there were surely many others—was not ready to grant him a place here.

The wind whistled in his ears as he bent to unfasten the lodge door, but as he pulled the peg, the sound of his wife's pain cut through all else. It was a breathlessly shallow, desperate grunting sound. He tore through the door and fastened it against the howling wind with unsteady fingers. His robe and his badgerskin hat crumpled in a heap on the floor. He tossed two pieces of wood on the fire on his way to her bedside.

"I'm sorry I was gone so long, but I had to..."

She saw a yellow beacon through the fog of her pain, and somewhere in the core of her brain she knew that it was wrong for him to be there. He was a man, and this was a woman's time. She tried to push him back with a trembling hand. "Go, James. When it's over—"

"When what's over? You're going to be—"

"It's the child," she gasped. "When it's over, then we shall grieve together, but now..."

He swallowed hard and glanced down, then away. The buffalo robe covered the length of her, but underneath that... Again she panted, voicing only the slightest hint of her agony with a low grunt. He took her hands in his. She squeezed them with more strength than he'd thought she had left.

"I'll make a poultice for the bleeding," he whispered.

"It's too late. The child has slipped from my body."

The pain subsided for the moment, leaving her dark eyes glazed with grief. "There will be more children," he promised. "You will grow strong again."

"But I lost *this* one."

"We," he amended. "We lost him."

His eyes, once blue, now gray, were sorrow itself. That much she could discern through the mist that filled her head. "You must go," she said, rasping. "However different, you are still a man, and this is a woman's—"

I am your husband, his brain cried, but calmly he said, "I am a shaman, and I have learned much of what I know from a woman. You will not send me away."

The poultice he used was her medicine. The snowpack he put around her middle was his. The pain finally dulled, and the flow of blood became manageable. He cleaned up the bed, made some broth and got her to drink a little before she fell asleep. He was about to take some food when a voice outside summoned him to the council lodge.

There were only three of the *wakincuzas* there. James seated himself as he had before, and waited while the pipe was passed.

Lone Bear spoke. "Red Elk's grandson has died, and his wife and daughter are both sick. The *eyapaha* will announce the new camp at daybreak, and those who are untouched by the disease will move. We have decided upon a place on the far side of the ravine where there is windbreak."

James nodded. "How many would you say have become ill?"

"Maybe eight or nine."

"Move this lodge closer to mine. It's large enough to accommodate those and more." James sighed. "I'm afraid there will be more. Every person who is not sick must leave, but whoever becomes sick must return."

"There will be some who will not leave," Lone Bear said.

"But they must be ordered to leave. If they aren't sick, they must not be allowed to stay."

"Each person must decide for himself if someone close to him is ill," Lone Bear said. "I would not separate a mother from her child or—"

"If that mother has other children, she must think of them." James glanced from one wizened face to another, but none of the three would agree with him. "I hope you will explain to them what the consequences might be if they stay."

"We will tell them all that you have said. Red Elk has decided to stay," Lone Bear said. "As have I."

"Your daughter would not have you stay. I shall care for her and the others."

"It is too much for one man." He tapped the ashes from the pipe, and all four unfolded their legs and stood to leave.

"Lone Bear," James pleaded. "Please set an example for the others. Those who are well must look after themselves, and they must supply us with water and wood and . . . and offer prayers for this pox to leave us."

"I am not well," Lone Bear said quietly. "Meets The Enemy and Cry Of The Crow will go to the new camp. The *akicita* will collect those things that must be destroyed and see to the burning."

In the dim firelight James looked closely and detected the first sign—the yellowish cast of the old man's face. "I will bring your sleeping robes to my lodge, *Tunkanśi*," James said, calling him father-in-law. Lone Bear nodded. "There is something else," James added, turning to the others. "The corpses must be burned along with all that they have touched.

"That is not our way," Cry Of The Crow protested.

"In this camp, Red Elk and I shall decide," Lone Bear said. "When the time comes, we shall decide. But the four of us have agreed that you will keep no sick ones on the far side of the ravine."

Meets The Enemy's lip curled as he glanced at James. "How soon before everyone is back here, I wonder. Will the white man watch the last of the Lakota turn to smoke and ash?"

"I saw that some would die, and others would live," James answered. "But I did not see their faces. Already I have lost—" he turned to Lone Bear and gentled his voice "—my unborn child."

Chapter Twelve

Some of the people could not be persuaded to move to the new camp and leave sick loved ones behind. Many Plums was one who stayed behind with her sons, both of whom had contracted smallpox. James knew that all he could do for them was to treat the symptoms—the fever, the nausea, the pain—with herbal medicine and cool sponge baths, and to try to get them to drink as much as possible. Red Elk, who said that the years had tanned his hide and made his skin too leathery to become spotted, spent nights as well as days ministering to the sick. Lone Bear contributed smoke, prayers and supplications until he collapsed in James's arms and had to be carried back to his daughter's lodge.

Kezawin continued to weaken, but each time James returned to the lodge to see to his wife, coax her to take some tea or broth and tell her she was getting better, she resolved to live through the night to hear him tell her that the sun had risen on another day. Then she would close her eyes, and the deer woman's laughter would ring in her ears and keep her from succumbing to a deeper, more restful sleep.

When she rested that way, her breathing so slight and shallow, James would hold her in his arms, listen to her hallucinatory murmurings and chafe her fragile hand between his rough palms to remind her that there was life in her limbs. "You cannot leave me," he would whisper, hoping she could hear him through her pain. "You once told me that I needed to discover what I value, and I have done that. It's you, Kezawin. You're my partner, remember? My teacher and pupil, my *kola*, my lover, my wife. It was not by chance that we found one another. You know that. We came together like two halves to become whole, and I will not become that pathetic fraction again. I don't know what I would do or where I would go if you left me now."

He pressed her hand to his mouth, willing her to feel the bonding between them. He wanted her to draw on his strength, his breath, his body's immunity. If ever such a thing was possible between two people, it had to be for them. Two halves of a whole. Two of the world's misfits, one concave with loneliness, one convex with unfulfilled promise. Across half a continent God—or *Tunkašila*, who were one and the same to James now—had brought them together and found a perfect fit.

"You'll not leave me now, Kezawin." There was a hard edge to his softly spoken demand, as if he thought repeating it more firmly would make it be true. "If you go, I swear I'm going with you. I'll not stay behind to bury the dead. I'll not be the white man who shovels the dirt over the faces of the people. Let me be one with you, Kezawin. Stay with me. If I have a purpose, I cannot fulfill it without you. Stay with me," he muttered as he brushed his lips over her sweat-dampened temple. "Stay."

Each morning James met a messenger from the *akicita*, who brought wood and water, food if there was any to be found, and the newly sick. He stood at the rendezvous place and watched Catch The Bear approach this time, leading a horse loaded with wood and paunches of water. The morning's fog had lifted, and it floated overhead like a length of shimmering gauze, reducing the sun's power to a round soft glow. In his heavy wearing robe and his plush coyote cap, Catch The Bear mirrored James as the two men faced each other across the established twenty-foot quarantine space.

"Can I hope that you bring me no new patients today, my friend?" James asked.

"I bring only water and wood. Perhaps the end of this nightmare is in sight."

"We need food here, Catch The Bear. Fresh meat. Some are so weak—"

"I will bring the next kill. The snow is so deep, all the creatures are sleeping or gone." He studied the length of reins he held between his hands. "How is it with my wife and sons?"

"I think Blue Heels has come through the worst of it," James said. "Many Plums . . . has fever now."

Catch The Bear nodded without looking up. "What news must I take back to the others?"

"During the night we lost the mother to Runs His Horses and Four Strikes's young son."

"I will tell them today's smoke belongs to them." He raised his head, and James saw that the man's eyes glittered beneath the silver fur of his cap. "What of my son, Mouse Face Boy?"

"Keep him in your prayers, my friend. He is very weak."

"It's hard being separated from them. If the *akicita* were not needed here, I would cross over and die with them."

As he heard the anguish in his brave friend's words, James remembered a similar vow he'd made to Kezawin earlier. Catch The Bear would carry on for the good of the living even if his heart crossed over to the camp of the dying. Would that he, James, could find such courage of his own, he thought to himself. "I will care for them as I would my brother's family," James promised.

Catch The Bear turned and trudged away.

* * *

Lone Bear was dying, and there was no help for it. James had lost track of the days. Six, he believed, for Kezawin. The spots on her body had turned to blisters. Three, he thought, for Lone Bear. He had just broken out with the rash, but the fever had taken a heavy toll on the old man.

"No more," Lone Bear protested, shaking his head at the sight of the bowl in James's hand. "I cannot swallow."

"You must tell me what to do, *Tunkanśi*. I've tried my medicine. Let me try yours. Tell me..."

Lone Bear lifted a bony hand and pressed his dry lips together. "When the time comes, you get the drum. You play slow...you play easy. I shall sing my death song."

"Your daughter still lives. Are you not as strong as she? Look at her." James knew that in his condition Lone Bear couldn't see that far. But it was for Kezawin's sake that he became angry with the old man. There she lay sleeping, her breathing shallow, but each time he brought her something, she drank. "She won't give up, *Tunkanśi*, and I don't want her to wake up and find you gone."

Cracked lips stretched in a lurid smile. "I won't go far, you know. Don't speak my name."

"Don't try to scare me, old man. I'm not as naive as I once was."

"You've learned some," Lone Bear acknowledged. "When you have patience...when you have wisdom..." He closed his eyes, struggled with a few labored breaths, then surprised James with a faint dry cackle. "Then you will be as old as I am."

"I haven't time to become as wise as you. There are not enough suns and moons and summers to accomplish that."

"You know how to fill an old man's heart." Because he could no longer drink, he sucked at his cheeks, seeking enough moisture from within to finish out his life. "Think of this," he said. "There are some moments so packed full of life, like a woman nearing her time. They make up for a hundred summers. Those are the moments that make you . . . the man you are."

Surely this was one of those moments, and James searched for some important thing to say, something that would keep the old man there with him just a little longer. "I will dance this summer and gaze at the sun," he promised hastily. "I will pierce my breast. You must be there to see this, *Ate* to guide me, to show me the way."

The graying head rolled listlessly from one side to the other, but the thin smile was there. James had called him *ate*—father, not father-in-law—and Lone Bear understood. "You will know the way. You must make your vow . . . but not to me. *Tunkašila* will hear you. Say, 'All my relatives.'"

"*Mitakuye oyasin.*"

"Yes. We shall hear you, also. Rest assured." He opened his eyes suddenly and lifted a glazed stare toward a point beyond the smoke hole. "Welcome him," he intoned. "Welcome him. He comes. He comes."

James snatched Lone Bear's small medicine drum from its place near his bed and took up the beat of the old man's chant.

"I am an old man.
I have made much medicine.
I am content to follow my relatives.
He comes, *hey hunh*. He comes."

The chant became thready and weak, and finally it drifted on a trail of smoke toward the night sky.

Kezawin had listened to her father's death song, but she hadn't the strength to mourn him properly. She had seen tears standing in her husband's eyes, but she could not make them herself. Her body had been drained of the new life it had nourished and of the fluids that nourished her own life. Her body burned. Her father's inner fire had consumed him quickly, but hers burned slowly while her life evaporated. She had at least a dim awareness of everything around her, but it was all a part of the burning. When James spoke to her of sorrow, she felt none. She hadn't the strength. She said nothing as she watched her husband take her father's remains from the lodge.

James carried Lone Bear's body to the little knoll that was already black with charcoaled wood and ashes. He arranged a bed of wood and laid the shell of the man, wrapped in his sleeping robes, to one side. Stalwart old Red Elk added the small bundled corpse of a child, and together they watched the past and the promise of the Lakota go up in flames. The heat from the fire seared James's eyes, and he let them be soothed by a gathering of tears.

It was not until he returned to the lodge that he truly saw how it was with Kezawin. The pulse beat in her wrist skittered against his fingers, and her breathing came in erratic puffs. She had held out this long, he thought, and if he could bring strength into her blood, she would survive. He had shared what food they had, and there was little left. He'd long since come to terms with his own hunger and made his peace with dried vegetables, but Kezawin needed fresh meat. Her people were hunters, and the blood of all prairie creatures flowed together in one communal vessel.

He offered her a sip of tea, but she refused. For the first time since she'd been ill, she turned the bowl away and curled up within herself. Panic pierced his gut like the hunter's lance.

"You have to try, Kezawin."

She seemed not to hear. Her lips were taut and unnaturally gray, and her eyelids were puffy. He adjusted his arm beneath her head and touched the bowl to her lips again. Her eyes and her lips remained closed.

"You can't die," he said flatly. "There's too much ahead for us. I know it. I can feel it. We have things to do, a life to live together. We have..."

The painting of the white deer claimed his attention. The light from the flames flickered over its stylized profile, the form he had not finished painting. The form itself was stiff and lifeless, but the cherry-hued eye gleamed with soft, unstinting compassion. Strange. He couldn't remember painting that eye. Perhaps Kezawin had finished it for him. But he had left other forms unfinished on the dew cloth. Why had she finished that one? And how did it come to look so...human?

He settled Kezawin back on the bed, rested his head in his hand and pressed his fingers against his eyes. Hunger and fatigue did strange things to the mind, he thought, but when he looked up again, the eye still looked down at him with the same haunting expression.

"Why?" he whispered to the painted form. "Did you bring me here to watch these people die? I'm no good to her. I'm no good to any of them now. Me and my kind." He stared steadily at the eye while he stumbled to his feet, the blood suddenly pumping through his body with growing, audible force. "Don't bring any more of us. Do you hear? Look what we've done!"

His head was filled with a terrible pounding, a sound and fury like the buffalo surround. Something compelled him to take up his robe and his rifle, even while he watched the painting, almost expecting it to move. He backed toward the door, taking a moment's worth of sanity to glance at Kezawin and see that she was sleeping. A moment's worth was all he had. He left the lodge without purpose or reason, his legs walking without direction. Something pulled him past the smoldering pyre on the hill and deep into the night. He heard nothing but the staccato pounding, the awful rush of pure energy. He saw nothing but black sky and white plains glistening, stretching into eternity. The Milky Way was the Lakota trail to eternity. Perhaps this was his journey.

He came to a grove of cottonwoods that stood beside a frozen creek. The roar inside his head faded away, and he heard the quiet of winter. He peered into the trees, but the grove was deep and dark as death. Then a breeze moved among the topmost branches, and they rustled like the medicine rattle. He took another step and stopped. Something didn't want him in the grove.

All right, he told himself. I'll wait here.

He watched, and as he waited, his mind was filled with the need for food. Not his own need, but Kezawin's and the others who were weak from the illness. He smelled meat, but he had no hunger for it. He saw himself as provider. Squatting in the snow, he loaded his rifle and balanced it over his knees, wondering how he'd satisfied himself on willow bark and calamus root. Perhaps he *had* become a brother to the deer. He pulled his badgerskin down over his forehead and waited—for what, he didn't know. He only knew that he was here, where he was supposed to be, and that something was coming.

The white deer, a shining, regal creature, stepped from the grove. James froze with his last breath caught deep in his chest. This area had been hunted and picked clean months ago. Where had this deer come from? His rump was round and ample, and his hindquarters were well shaped. He looked as though he'd been grazing in a cornfield all winter.

He could not be shot. No hunter would shoot such an animal, even if it meant that his family would go hungry. Even if James didn't believe that such a creature was *wakan* and that shooting it could bring about calamity, he knew that the albino was rare. He was enchanted by the wonder of the creature, who should not have been there at all. He should have fled the vicinity with his kind long ago.

James sat still and waited. The white deer sniffed the night air and took another step in his direction. Something spoke in his ears, telling him that Kezawin could not live another day without fresh meat. And there were others. Blue Heels, Mouse Face Boy and Many Plums. Poor noseless White Otter's Tail and old Whirling Water. All of them needed fresh meat.

Welcome him. Welcome him. He comes. He comes.

James gripped the barrel and the stock of his rifle, and his eyes became wide with horror as he watched the white deer approach. No! He could not do this thing. He stood abruptly and waved his hand. "Run!" he shouted. "Keep running till you reach the mountains!"

The deer stood still. James could see his eye now, soft with a compassionate gleam. "Run away," he whispered, his voice hoarse. "I can't shoot you."

Tears blurred his sight, and he heard the death rattle in the trees. His vision was no longer limited by his eyesight.

You are White Deer's Brother. You cannot use your brother selfishly, but he will share his flesh to help you feed your family.

"Send me something else," he pleaded as he shouldered the rifle. He trembled violently inside himself, but his hands were steady. "*Tunkaśila*, send me something else. Not this beautiful . . . prophetic . . ."

Welcome him. Welcome him. He comes. He comes.

The white deer stepped closer, then stood ready.

James aimed for a clean, quick kill and pulled the trigger. The deer dropped heavily in the snow. The tears that coursed down James's cheeks as he drew his knife were as much for those at home as they were for the brother who lay at his feet. They were for Lone Bear and Kezawin, Mouse Face Boy and White Otter's tail—all who suffered. He sang his apology in a surprisingly steady voice and knelt to gut the sacrifice.

James's stomach churned, but he knew that real sickness was not the cause. The odor of boiling venison made him queasy and spared him from any consideration of eating it himself, no matter how hungry he was. He cooled a bowl of the broth he'd made from the meat and one select herb. Sliding his arm beneath Kezawin's head, he prepared himself for her initial refusal, but not for her question.

"There is no more venison. Where did you . . . get this?"

He thought for a moment. He knew he could not lie to her, but to tell her what he'd done . . . "This was given to you by your *šicun*," he said.

"The white deer?"

James nodded, still holding the bowl for her.

"You did not . . . hunt him down."

"Drink this, and I will tell you how my brother provides for my family tonight."

She glanced at the bowl, and when she looked back up at him, he saw trust. She sipped at the blood of his brother.

"He must have been real," James said as he slid his leg beneath her back to lend support. "Meat cannot be made from dreams. Yet the whole time I was butchering, I expected it all to vanish into the frigid night air. I was led to the cottonwood grove," he marveled. "By what or whom, I don't know, but I simply followed . . . something. And he came to me. I couldn't chase him away. And that voice . . ."

It seemed strange to talk about it. Ordinary human words made the whole experience sound preposterous in his own ears. He'd killed the white deer, and that was that. Right or wrong, he'd done it.

"You knew the voice?"

She doubted nothing he'd said. He could see that in her eyes. The mystery was perfectly acceptable to her as a mystery. It didn't have to be solved. He was grateful for that, because she took the soup on faith, and there was no stronger case he could have prepared to persuade her to eat.

"It sounded to me like your father's voice, but, of course, he's very much on my mind, and I might have imagined, distraught as I was..."

"The soup is good," she whispered.

He smiled. A tight bud of hope began to open within him. "I don't know where he came from. He was as fat as a corn-fed calf."

"The Mandan had no corn to speak of this year. Perhaps he visited the Pawnee."

There was a spark in her eye, a light he'd not seen since the morning she fell ill. His heart soared. "I made a vow to pierce myself and gaze at the sun," he told her. "I told your father this, and I shall keep my word."

She nodded.

"You will recover now, Kezawin. You'll get strong again."

"And the others?"

"I'm encouraged by the fact that we have no new patients from the other camp. Red Elk has miraculously not been stricken. The fresh meat will help the others, at least some of them, I'm sure."

"You knew what to do," she said. "That's why you were brought here by my *śicun*."

"Perhaps." She finished the broth, and he laid her down and covered her with the buffalo robe. "Rest now and let the blood of my brother do its work."

Her eyes were drifting closed when she asked, "What was the herb you added to the soup?"

"That was the red root plant."

Mouse Face Boy was little more than a remnant of what he'd once been. His small crippled body had wasted away, having had no real muscle to feed on. Blue Heels had rallied, and he sat with his brother, trying to get him to drink some of the broth that the white shaman had made for the sick ones. But it was no use. The soup ran from the corner of Mouse Face Boy's mouth. He could not swallow. He muttered unintelligibly. Part of him had gone on its last journey already, and soon his breath would follow.

Blue Heels himself had been strong enough to partake of the meat of the deer the white man had killed. Over the course of the day his body had cooled, and the nausea had subsided. He had few spots on his body, certainly fewer than his mother, Many Plums, whose bed lay opposite her sons' on the woman's side of the lodge. Her breathing was labored. She, too, had been unable to take any nourishment. Not far from where she lay, Red Elk was making a bundle of White Otter's Tail's corpse. The woman without a nose. Perhaps she could be at peace now, Blue Heels thought. Surely she had paid the price for her bad behavior.

When the white man entered the lodge, Blue Heels stiffened. He held his dying brother's head in his lap, and he needed to be angry with someone. The traders had brought this evil upon his people, and the traders were white. Mouse Face Boy loved this man, but Blue Heels could not share in that devotion. He scooted back toward the dew cloth and glowered as the man approached.

"My brother is dying," Blue Heels announced defiantly, as though James might be getting his wish.

James knelt beside the frail little figure, took his pulse and touched his face. He sighed, hoping to expel the debilitating sense of helplessness he felt, but it was still there when he took another breath. He looked at Blue Heels and saw his anger. "You know your brother better than anyone," James said. "If you say death is coming to him, I believe you. How shall we prepare for this?"

"I don't want him to die."

"I know. Have you told him this?"

"I have told him, but I don't think he can hear me anymore."

James brushed the loose fall of hair away from the inert boy's face. "Perhaps not. Perhaps he is already at peace."

"It's the white traders," Blue Heels said. "And others like them."

James looked up, and this time he saw that the hatred was for him. "I'm sorry, my friend. You're right. I'm afraid we've brought trouble."

"I should kill you," Blue Heels ground out. Lightning sizzled in his dark eyes.

"If it would help Mouse Face Boy, I would say, go ahead." All the sadness he had known gathered in the grayness of his eyes. "I have killed, and I know that nothing is solved when the killing is done. It is a burden I would not wish upon a friend."

"I am not your friend."

"But I am yours." He touched Mouse Face Boy's cheek with the back of his hand. Another child, he thought. He remembered how hardy they had seemed as he'd watched them time and again, playing on the ice. Immune to the cold, but not the pox. "I lost the child my wife carried," he said quietly. "I lost my father-in-law. Years ago I lost my mother. All to this evil disease." Again James delved Blue Heels's dark eyes with his. "I grieve with you."

Finally Blue Heels permitted the pain, but he denied himself tears. "It should be me," he said. "The accident that crippled him many years ago—that was my fault. My brother should live in my body, and I should die in his."

The haunted darkness in the boy's eyes seemed worse than tears. James cast about for words, and suddenly they were there. "I have known this feeling you're experiencing, but what you suggest is not within your power. My father-in-law would tell you that there are other sacrifices you can make."

"What good will they do?"

"I don't know," James said. "We listen to those who are wiser than we are, follow their good examples, and then we watch and wait."

The next morning Blue Heels came to James's lodge. Out of respect he kept his eyes from the sleeping robes at the back of the tent as he took the crow that was perched on his shoulder and offered it to James.

"Since we must burn his belongings, we have nothing of his to give away except this bird. He would want it to go to you, James Garrett."

James nodded and offered his forearm as a perch.

"My mother is gone, too," Blue Heels said. "We're taking them up to the hill now."

"I shall join you there."

After the boy left, James found a perch for Sapa, the crow, on the top of his willow backrest. He added wood to the fire and gathered up his robe and his hat, all the while avoiding Kezawin's eyes. He had thought he could become hardened to all this after so much death, but he had not. If anything, it seemed he had gotten softer. Inside his chest his heart was breaking, and he could not look up. One look at her face would be his undoing.

"You must help me, James."

His resolve disappeared as he turned to find her sitting up in bed. She held her hair to one side, and with her skinning knife, she was sawing it off.

"Kezawin, what—"

"I would go to the hill with you," she said. "It is time I grieved, too."

In two long steps he was by her side. "You're as weak as a fledgling sparrow," he protested. "You can't even stand."

"You will help me," she said calmly. "If I falter, you will carry me. If you refuse, I shall proceed on hands and knees until I reach the place where they have all gone."

He watched the lovely black hair fall to the floor in discarded disarray. "He would not want this, Kezawin."

"He must be mourned properly. Four days, and then no more crying." She lifted her chin, and he saw the first tears he had ever seen standing in her eyes. "I have not yet had my four days."

"Please, love," he whispered. "You've been so sick. Have a care for yourself . . . for your husband."

"I do." She touched his soft, sleek, golden beard. "Your heart breaks, just as mine does. Mine will not heal until it has wailed in sorrow. And you must do what your way demands."

He dressed her warmly, but it was to no avail. Once they reached the bleak, white, windswept hill, she threw off her robe and scratched bloody furrows in her arms while she keened. Kezawin's voice rose highest above the crackling flames. Red Elk chanted, and Blue Heels, who had gashed his legs, covered his head with ashes and took a stoic stance. James allowed his heart its own expression. Tears rolled down his cheeks as he watched his wife rend her clothes and shower herself with ashes.

And the shrill sound of her keening echoed in the hills and became one with the wretched winter wind.

Chapter Thirteen

The long, cold, hungry winter was past. On the hide that bore Red Elk's winter count, the spiral of symbols through which he tracked the life of the band, it was memorialized simply as Smallpox Winter. The old man sensed that this would not be the last time the symbol was used, but he hoped it was the last time he would paint it himself. The measures they had taken to prevent the evil from jumping from one person's body to another's may have saved lives, but they had been unsettling. Children had been separated from parents. It was wrong to do this. People had been sent on their final journey without raising their bodies toward the sun. This was wrong, too, and Red Elk's instincts had shouted against it. But it was done to banish the evil, and soon after James had brought fresh meat, the evil had moved on.

For now, summer had come to the prairie once again. The deep snow had nourished earth's deepest roots and brought forth lush spring grass, and the early-summer rain had kept it green. The Hunkpapa journeyed southward. The small winter camps had come together, small creeks flowing into a larger stream. By the time the sun had reached its solstice, they would join the rest of their Lakota cousins in the sacred *Paha Sapa*, the Black Hills, where those who may have suffered less during the hunger moons would honor their cousins' endurance with gifts and songs. There would be feasting and ceremony in celebration of the promise of life's renewal.

There were always many vows made during hard times, and this summer there would be many dancers who would gaze at the sun. Young men like Blue Heels would dance for the first time, and older men would seek new levels of vision. A few of the women would dance in behalf of people who were absent from them, but they would not be pierced. In all cases, the dancers had offered the pipe and made a vow. They journeyed now toward a rendezvous in the majestic pine-covered hills with, as they were wont to repeat ceremonially, all their relations, including those who had been and were yet to be.

James had made the vow as well, first to Lone Bear, and then in the formal, proper way. Kezawin lived, and in his mind the Sun Dance was something he could do to show his gratitude. Red Elk had agreed to sponsor him, to be the instructor that Lone Bear would have been to him. But as James rode beside his wife within the moving stream of people under the warm summer sun, he felt bereft by Lone Bear's absence and a reluctance to participate in the ceremony without him. The bird riding with him on the wooden perch he'd fashioned reminded him of another absence.

Kezawin sensed her husband's restlessness, and she knew that he would choose his time to speak his mind. They made camp, shared food and walked together in silence. There were women playing the plum pit game, girls wrapping strings around their fingers in a version of cat's cradle, and men swapping stories around camp fires. A young woman great with child ducked into her tipi when she saw James and Kezawin coming, but there were others who greeted them warmly. Catch The Bear, on his way to his Kit Fox Society gathering, stopped to suggest that James join Blue Heels and him for a hunt.

They walked beyond the camp toward the hills where the horses grazed. Kezawin had grown accustomed to the way James would take her hand sometimes as they walked, especially once they had left the camp behind them.

"I found more red root plant this evening while you were getting water," he told her, breaking the silence.

"You seem to find it only when I'm not with you."

He'd never thought about it before, but he realized it was true. "Coincidence, I'm sure."

"I think it calls to you. Haven't you noticed?" The fringe of her dress tapped her legs softly as she walked. "It happens to me with some plants. My favorites, like food-of-the-elk."

"Maybe it does, in a way. I was watching a fight on the hill, and afterwards—"

"A fight?"

"A badger and a rattlesnake." He chuckled with the memory. "The snake was enjoying a nice warm rock and the badger's den must have been underneath it. You've never heard so much spitting and hissing. The badger puffed up like a billowing sheet, leaping into the air when the snake struck. Neither took his attention off the other as I crept up on them. I got pretty close before the snake fell back and slithered away."

"The badger won the battle?"

He nodded. "For the time being. He scooted under his rock to lick his wounds, I suppose, but the rattler had left him to his den. Then I found the red root plant, just down the hill near the creek bank. I went right to it."

"Your medicine bag is made of badgerskin. He shares his victory with you."

"A part of me said, this is interesting. I must observe. I must make notes. Another part said, this is significant. I must find someone who is wiser than I am and ask him what it means."

"What did you do?"

He shrugged. "I gathered some of the red root plant and came home."

"Some?"

"I left some to reseed, just as you always do. And I, uh, I made my apologies." He didn't know why he hesitated in reporting the latter. There was a feeling of rightness about making his peace with the plants.

They had walked into the privacy of the night, veering away from the horse herd, which was guarded by sentries. Crickets sang in the tall grass. "Shall we sit together in the cottonwood grove by the creek and talk of—"

"No, let's find another place. The other side of the hill, perhaps." Since the night he had followed his instincts to the grove where the white deer waited, he had not entered a grove of trees after dark. He remembered the strong feeling he'd gotten that the grove was inviolable, at least to him. It wasn't the thinking of an educated man, he told himself. Nevertheless, he hiked over the hill with his wife, and she took the blanket from her shoulders and spread it out for them.

The blanket created a cozy nest in the grass, a place to while away the night and enjoy the star-studded sky. He told her his names for the constellations and recounted Greek myths. She countered with her names for them and the legends the Lakota told. It surprised him that on opposing sides of the planet people had for centuries looked up at the same sky and seen the same shapes—bears, dogs, hunters, those who had dared to dream or dared to disobey.

"I'm afraid of the Sun Dance," he confessed finally without preface.

"It is a demanding ordeal," she said. "You must be prepared for pain."

"I'm not afraid of pain. I'm afraid of..." He searched the patterns of stars, looking for some hint. "I suppose it's all those things I haven't the capacity to understand. I'm afraid of being at their mercy, of hearing and seeing things that I cannot explain but dare no longer ignore."

"Don't white people have mysteries?"

"Yes, we have mysteries, but we feel compelled to solve them, and if we can't, then we just don't live quite so closely with them, I guess. We attend to them only on one day of the week."

"That seems very strange," she decided.

"Yes, it does...now." He turned over on his side and propped himself up on his elbow. "Kezawin, what if I don't belong here? What would happen if I were to see something or hear something while I dance that tells me I must not stay with the Lakota people?"

"Is this what you fear?"

"Yes. It is my worst fear."

"Where would you go?"

"I don't know. I'm not sure where I belong now."

"Would you take me with you?"

He let a moment of silence pass before asking gently, "Would you go?"

"I am your wife," she said. "We have starved together. We have shared the loss of our child, and whether we have another or not, I will be faithful to my husband."

He knew the full import of her vow. She would not marry again. "I would not take you from your people. They need you."

"Then you would throw me away?"

"No, never. I would never divorce you." He slid the backs of his fingers over her cheek. "I don't know what I would do. I keep thinking I should just leave well enough alone and not ask for any more visions. The last one was...so full of death."

"But it saved many lives, James. This smallpox came from the white man, and only a white man would know what had to be done to break its power."

"But what if there's more?" He rolled over on his back and considered the stars again. Half a continent away there were so many people. How many of them looked up at these same stars even now and wondered about charting a westward course for the chance at a better life?

He sat up, and she followed his lead. A bit of moonlight lit like a moth in her raven hair, which hung just past her shoulders now. He plucked a piece of grass and stuck the end of it in his mouth. "I told you once that I didn't think the white people would ever come here to live. They have their frame houses and their farms and cities, and I cannot think they would try to take this place with its ceaseless wind and flat, unforgiving terrain. But if they do, I cannot think that there will be anything but more trouble."

"But you are not trouble."

"All I wanted to do was study plants. Now it seems all I want to do is love my wife." He smiled. "And study plants and learn their special uses."

"The Sun Dance is a personal matter," she told him. "It is between you and *Tunkaśila* whether you rescind your vow."

"What would you think of a man who rescinded his vow?"

"I don't know whether that's ever been done." She was quiet for a moment. "I would think that he knew himself and knew what he had to do."

He chuckled. "You refuse to be a nag, don't you?"

"A female horse?"

"A woman who is always reminding her husband to do this and that."

"Oho! Such a woman might find herself twinkling in the heavens as a reminder to the others. Perhaps the scars from my spots would become the stars."

He touched the twin spots that rode high on her cheeks, one on each side. "These beauty marks," he said. "They remind me that I don't ever want to come that close to losing you again. I need to be more wary. As you say, a white man should know the kind of threat the whites may pose."

"The Lakota are a strong people, James. If there is a fight—"

"This plague we had wasn't a fight," he said. "It was certain death for most of the clan if we had not quarantined the sick."

"What is certain death? Death comes when it comes. Even *Iktomi*, the trickster god, cannot trick death. James Garrett cannot trick death, either. Something *wakan* came to you, just as surely as something *wakan* came to me. We must listen and watch. The white deer is a powerful *šicun*."

"I shall honor my vow," he said with assurance, and then in a less confident tone, "I shall attend closely. Let come what comes. I want to know where I belong."

She laid her head against his shoulder. "I think tonight you belong in my arms."

He plucked the stock of grass from the corner of his mouth, and a grin slowly spread across his face. "What makes you think that?"

"Once the preparations begin, you will have to abstain."

"For how long?"

"Red Elk will determine that." She gave a flirtatious laugh as she sat up and looked at him. "I think it may be the hardest part of your sacrifice."

He pushed her hair back from her neck and murmured, "I don't doubt that," as he dipped his head to take a nibble.

"Returning to your wife will be a joyous occasion." With her promise she slyly slipped the knot on his breechclout thong. Her femininity responded even to the warmth of his breath in the hollow of her neck.

He moved his hands along her thighs, pushing her skirt up as he went. "I don't need a vision to tell me that," he whispered.

"But in your weakened condition, you may be unable to—" he groaned when she touched him "—make this warrior stand straight and tall."

"I shall trust him to you." He eased her down into their nest and moved over her.

Only from the vantage point of the hills, which protected the valley like the sides of a cradle, could the real circle be discerned. It was formed by a great multitude of tipis, almost as though they had been tossed into the outstretched hollow like a handful of sand. But the arrangement was prescribed by tradition, and each *tiośpaye*, or clan, had its designated place. Among the Lakota, everything was done in its proper way. When the people gathered for the summer ceremonies, there was a wealth of ancient tradition to be observed. At the center of it all was the Sun Dance, the most solemn and most essential ceremony, because it celebrated the wholeness of the people and made the connection between the flesh and the spirit of the Lakota.

The *eyapaha* rode among the circles within a circle of tipis and announced the choosing of the *can wakan*, the sacred pole. It had taken four days to prepare the campsite and four days for the medicine men to instruct the dancers. The third set of four would be devoted to the dance itself. Trusted scouts had searched for a worthy cottonwood tree and had made their report to the medicine men. The whole camp was abuzz with excitement, and all hearts pounded to the beat of the drum as men, women and children, some riding horses that were painted and draped with leafy chains, went out to bring the chosen tree back to the pit that had been carefully prepared for it.

The tree was cut down by those men and women who had been deemed worthy of the honor. With great care it was stripped of all but the fork and the uppermost branches and leaves before the procession escorted it to its place in the center of camp. There it was erected in the center of a huge circular bower, the Sun Dance lodge, which was made of poles and pine boughs to provide shade for the onlookers. A crosspiece between the forked branches at the top of the pole was outfitted with lengths of rawhide thong, one for each dancer.

For the rest of the people, the preparations had been marked by visiting with old friends and relatives who'd been distant over the long winter months. For those who had vowed to make the Sun Dance sacrifice, the time had been spent together in one lodge receiving instructions. Then came three days of solemnity throughout the camp as the Sun Gazers danced together as one from sunrise to sunset, blowing on eagle-bone whistles and pushing their bodies past the point of exhaustion. On the fourth day the dancers purified themselves in the sweat lodge and made ready for the final step.

James was certain that he had lost all the weight he had gained back after the first good spring hunt, but as Red Elk helped him dress for the climactic portion of the ceremony, he knew that he was ready, both in his mind and body, to meet unusual demands. His every sense seemed unusually keen, and he felt clean and strong. Although many of the dancers wore red skirts, Red Elk wrapped a blue blanket around James's waist to show that, as a wearer of the color of the heavens, he was engaged in a sacred undertaking. He carried a hoop covered with otterskin to symbolize the sun and the cycle of the seasons. He wore the deer amulet Kezawin had given him, and his medicine bundle was suspended around his neck. Arm bands and anklets proclaimed James's love, his strength and his cleverness.

He knew there would be pain, and he was prepared for that. Red Elk had explained to him that he must learn joy in pain and pain in joy, for such was life's greatest truth. After three days of dancing and purification, he had cleared his mind, and he was like the guileless babe who did not question whether the lesson he was about to receive was one he wanted to know.

The dancers followed the medicine men from the Sun Dance tipi to the center of the circular Sun Dance lodge. Babies were brought to the circle, and the mothers called upon those men who exemplified courage and wisdom to pierce their children's ears. When a man's name was called, he stepped forward and told of his exemplary deeds so that all might learn from him and the infants might follow his precedent.

It was time for the piercing of flesh. James lay on the painted buffalo hide. Red Elk placed a piece of wood between his teeth, and James watched the gray head dip toward his chest. The first pain came of caring. Red Elk bit the flesh above James's heart to make it numb. Then quickly, surely, Red Elk pierced James's flesh with a sharp awl and inserted a sage stick and an eagle's claw, which were tied to one of the braided thongs. He moved to James's right, bit him again, and pierced him a second time. The pain became a dull ache, which throbbed with the beat of the drum.

James got to his feet, and Red Elk pulled him back to make the thongs taut. Blood streamed down to his belly. Catch The Bear helped Blue Heels to his feet and stood him next to James, who now faced the sun. The others, twelve in all, became one with him in this until they no longer needed to look at one another or harken to the sound of one another's presence. They were together, all "gazing at the sun leaning."

The thongs pulled the flesh away from his chest. James looked down at himself and saw two tipis, like a woman's pointed breasts. For a time he would be both man and woman. He remembered the way Kezawin had endured the loss of her child, her father, very nearly her life, and he hoped he could be female courage, as well as male, at least for this brief time. Red Elk put the eagle-bone whistle into James's mouth, and each breath became an offering.

The sun burned deep into his brain until the interior of his head was sheer brightness. At first it had seemed impossible to stare and keep staring, dance and keep dancing, but now it was impossible to look away. The beat of the drum kept his body moving, made his feet shuffle in the step that had become a part of him in the past few days. The singers' voices became distant as the shrill sound of his own whistle filled his ears. Red Elk was always nearby, reminding him to pull back, keep the thongs taut. The flesh would tear, he said. The brave man would bear the pain.

The bright light was filtered now through a soft haze of pain. Kezawin came to him, smiling. He saw that wonderful expression in her eyes, and he remembered she'd always looked at him that way whenever he'd brought meat for her cooking pot. She rubbed something soft over his sweat-streaked face. He could smell the pungent sage.

"I am permitted to clean your wounds," she said. "If thirst threatens to overtake you before you break free, call for water, and I will bring it. There is no shame in this. It is a sacred thing you do."

He knew she tended somehow to his chest, but he could not tell exactly what she did. Her touch soothed him, and he wanted to beg her not to take it from him, but he held his tongue. Afraid that he would disgrace himself, he said nothing while she daubed his face with grease.

"You endure this pain for me," Kezawin said quietly. "For I am one of the people, and you are one with us. You are our *hunka*."

"*Hunka. Hunka. Hunka.*" Another voice superimposed itself upon Kezawin's last word. The voice of the drum. The voice of a man. Not Red Elk. It was Lone Bear. James squared his shoulders and pulled back so that the old man would see his courage and be proud.

The sun blistered his brain, and from the blisters came rattlesnakes. Blue rattlesnakes with fangs that spat bullets faster than any rifle could shoot them. The badger flew from his rocky den and drove them back, but they doubled their numbers and came back to worry the badger from all sides. He bared his black claws and his flashing white teeth, bit off one head, broke the spine of another. But the rattlers struck and struck, hacking at the badger's silvery hide. He backed into his den, and the snakes surrounded him and kept him there.

Welcome him. Welcome him. He comes. He comes.

It would have to be a cool place. The sun blistered and scorched, and the cave would be a place of refuge. James stood at the entrance and asked for permission to enter. Kezawin appeared. "The badger is tired," she said. "He has tried everything, but they have no ears. They cannot understand. They make so much noise sputtering and hissing and spitting bullets. How do they hear *Tunkaśila* when he tells them who they are and what they must do?"

"I don't know," James said. "I don't remember. I only know that the badger must not give up. If he does, they will consume him, and the hoop will be broken. There will be no children."

"No children? You must talk to them. You must tell them who we are." She stepped closer to him, and her hair caught the sun's bright rays and glinted, nearly blinding him. "You

know who we are now, don't you? You know what makes
us Lakota."

"I believe so."

"Then you must tell them."

"There are no words to tell them."

"You must try."

He nodded, and already he felt the badger's weariness
creep into his bones, too. "Let me come inside. When they
come, I shall meet them at the door. I shall tell them who
you are."

Welcome him. Welcome him. He comes. He comes.

The face of the white deer waited for James. His cherry-
hued eyes, full of compassion, beckoned. He was made of
light, so bright that he made a man's eyes ache just to look
at him. So beautiful that a man could not bear to look away.

"You are White Deer's Brother
He provides for your family,
The people at the center of the earth.
Welcome him. Welcome him.
He comes. He comes."

Filled with a sudden rush of power, James leaned back
against his tether. His flesh broke away, and he fell back to
the earth with a euphoric sense of absolute freedom.

James had a vague sense of the feasting and celebration
that followed the Sun Dance, but his participation was
minimal. He was grateful for food and water and the attention given his wounds. He sought the cool dark cave of
sleep. When he woke, he found that Red Elk had cared for
him. Like the other sponsors, he waited for the dancers to
recover so that the medicine man could interpret their visions and the sponsors could see them home.

But in James's mind no doubts lingered. Lone Bear had seen him through his ordeal and let him know where he belonged. He spoke of it to Kezawin later when she tended to his bandaged wounds.

"*Tunkaśila* would not have me lose the part of myself that I have found," he told her. "I have work to do here. I am to be something of a bridge. If I cannot make my people understand when I speak with them, I will write it down, telling them what I have experienced, what I know to be true."

"You were not able to understand when you came to us, stumbling around the prairie looking for plants."

He laughed at the mental picture she painted of his former self. "I had to be changed," he said. "All the time that you were expecting to change into a deer, I was the one who was undergoing the transformation."

"Perhaps there are things that I have yet to learn about the deer woman. She gave me gifts."

"That she did." He could no longer doubt her. There were too many inexplicable mysteries, and for all his education, he was just beginning to understand what mystery meant. "But I think I am at peace with her. I don't think she'll harm me."

A grating screech sounded the warning a moment before a flapping black wing brushed James's face, and Sapa landed on his shoulder. "Impossible beast!" James grumbled as he slid his hand beneath the bird's breast and moved him back to his perch. "I'm speaking with my wife here. Wait your turn. I'll speak with you later."

"Sahhpahh," the crow intoned.

"Yes, I know. You are such a wonder." The bird reminded him of other news. "Catch The Bear spoke to me today of Blue Heels's wish to learn my medicine, which, of course, is *our* medicine. What do you think?"

"Blue Heels must have been touched by this wish while he gazed at the sun."

"Then he must have the opportunity," James concluded. "I may never be accepted completely, especially not by the relatives of the one I killed, but I think the people will grant me a place among them."

"You must certainly rid yourself of the burden of that one's death," she told him. "You must make restitution in the proper manner and be done with it."

"Is there a way?"

"Of course there is a way. There must be a way to put hard feelings and guilt aside. Without some way to release one another from these things, where would we be?"

Where, indeed? he wondered. Who dared call these people savages? "Show me the way," he said.

She smiled. "I shall. Tomorrow." Touching his wounds with feather-light fingertips, she asked, "Is it too soon for a joyous reunion with your wife?"

He returned a smile more mischievous than hers. "You are testing that question on the wrong part of my anatomy."

"Shall I ask the warrior?"

"He is most anxious to give his reply."

Kiciyuskapi, the Untying Each Other Ceremony, was announced throughout the encampment by the herald. James had performed *inipi* the previous night and expressed his need to release the burden of Thunder Shield's death. The following morning he and Kezawin waited near the council lodge while Red Elk went to Meets The Enemy, who was the eldest male in Thunder Shield's family, and told him that James was anxious to atone for the part he had played in his nephew's death. The relatives gathered at the council lodge before all the people. Red Elk lit the ceremonial pipe with a buffalo chip and handed it to Meets The Enemy.

"Take this pipe. In smoking it, bear no ill will toward anyone."

Meets The Enemy smoked, and then the pipe was offered to James with the same admonition. Red Elk then sent Catch The Bear and two other *akicita* members to lead the donated horses to the council lodge. James and Kezawin had pledged all but one of their horses to the cause of peace. Many of the horses had been given in payment for their medicine. Red Elk indicated that Meets The Enemy should mount one of the eight horses. When he did so, Red Elk led him back to his lodge, and the *akicita* brought the rest of the horses along. That done, Red Elk announced that the Untying Each Other Ceremony had achieved its purpose. "They are free," he said.

The Friends of the White Deer, a society of two, left the village together on the back of the one horse they had not given away, a stout buckskin. They were headed for an afternoon of gathering plants on the slopes of *Paha Sapa*, and they could be heard laughing as they went. It was unseemly for a man to ride his horse thus, with a woman sitting behind him. Unfitting, too, for a woman to laugh in such an unrestrained manner. But no one turned his head. No one sought out a friend to spread their names in gossip. It was Double Woman Dreamer and her husband, the strange white plant-taker. No one denied the fact that their medicine was powerful. Their behavior was sometimes odd, but like the *winkte* and the *heyoka*, they were *wakan*, and without them, the circle would not be complete.

*   *   *   *   *

Author's Afterword

Medicine Woman began as a personal challenge to write a love story about a Lakota woman and a transplanted white man—the reverse of my own situation—and set it in a time when the Lakota culture was dominant in the land that would be named North and South Dakota. The Dakota Territory was named in ironic tribute to those from whom the land was to be wrested by hook and by crook. The greater loss was not the land, but a way of life in which the individual lived in harmony with the environment and balanced the temporal and the spiritual aspects of life as a matter of course rather than design. The "noble savage" concept is as simplistic and ludicrous as any idea born of limited vision.

My research began with interviews, and continued with the tales my brother-in-law, Philip Eagle, told at a family reunion. He kept his audience entertained with stories of the *wanaġi*, the spirits, interspersed with funny anecdotes, which were fast becoming local folklore. But the stories that interested me most were those of the deer woman. "I know of three," he said. "I didn't see them myself, but they said..." Intriguing stories, as was the story of the albino deer, which brought good fortune to the people as long as it was permitted to graze peacefully in the Grand River bot-

tomland. I thank him and my husband, Clyde, for the sou
of this story.

I researched this further with as many early interviews a
I could find, realizing that most of the literature about In
dians was written by non-Indians. Much is undoubtedly lost
in translation, but late-nineteenth-century interviews re
corded by apparently trusted non-Indians were the best
source documents to be found. My aim was to bring as
much authenticity to the Lakota in this story as I could. I
apologize in advance for the degree to which I may have
fallen short. In all fiction, there is an element of fantasy.

In my research I found precious little evidence of the kind
of hero I wished to portray—a man whose mind was not too
narrow to learn, not just intellectually but spiritually, from
a native culture that was trivialized in his world. Happily, it
seems that there were such people, though they were few and
far between. There were those among the white immigrants
who studied and transcribed the Lakota language, who
pleaded the cause of justice for the Indian people before
deaf Congressional ears, who photographed and recorded
for posterity. There was even one case of a white man who
stayed with the people through one of the many devastat
ing bouts with smallpox. Such is the stuff that a cross
cultural romance may be made of.

Finally, the reader should know that the Sioux Nation has
three branches and three dialects. The Santee, who speak
Dakota, and the Yankton—as well as the Yanktonais—who
speak Nakota, were located east of the Missouri River. The
Teton, who speak Lakota, were west-river people made up
of seven bands, or council fires: the Oglala, Brûlé (Si
cangu), Miniconju, Blackfeet (Sihasapa; not to be con
fused with the Montana Blackfeet), Sans Arc (Itazipco),
Two Kettle (Oohenunpa), and the Hunkpapa.

Lakota Words and Phrases

Lakota was not a written language until the white man applied the symbols of his alphabet to the cause. Hence, the spelling of Lakota words and the use of diacritical marks will vary from source to source. Besides the Lakota dialect, there are also the Dakota and Nakota dialects, and within each there are variations from band to band. When the U.S. government assigned people to reservations in the last century, Standing Rock Sioux Indian Reservation became the home of the Hunkpapa, one of the Lakota bands, but also of a small group of Yanktonais, who speak the Nakota dialect. To the government, they were all "Sioux."

I do not claim to be proficient with Lakota, but with the help of my husband's family and friends, I have gained some small knowledge of the language. I have used *Lakota-English Dictionary* by Reverend Eugene Buechel (Red Cloud Indian School Inc., Pine Ridge, SD, 1970) as my primary language reference. It is a language that is packed with connotative meaning, much of which is being lost as the language falls further into disuse, thanks to culture-killing educational policies that were implemented both by mission schools and the Bureau of Indian Affairs through the first half of this century. I hope that my attempt to describe the pronunciation of the words and phrases used in *Medicine Woman* and to list them here with admittedly limited definitions will help give the reader a feel for this wonderfully lyrical language.

akicita (ah-KEE-chee-tah)—policemen; a society of men who serve as peacekeepers

ate (ah-TAY)—father

can tarca winyela (chan-tarcha WEE-yay-lah)—the female white-tailed woods deer

eyapaha (AY-yah-pah-hah)—one who announces news to the village

Haho (hah-HO)—look at this!

hanble ceya (Hahn-BLAY-chay-yah)—to cry in prayer for a vision

heyoka (hay-YO-kah)—a contrary; a clown, considered sacred, who does everything in reverse

Hoka hey (HOH-kah hay)—Pay attention! Heads up!

hunka (HUHN-kah)—kin, relative; relative by ceremonial adoption

Iktomi (ick-DOE-mee)—a trickster spirit, generally evil

inipi (en-EE-pee)—purification rite performed by itself or in preparation for another ceremony; sometimes called the sweat bath

kiciyuskapi (kee-CHEE-yoo-skah-pee)—the untying each other ceremony; a ritual of putting aside guilt and resentment between two parties

kiniknik (kin-NICK-nick)—Indian tobacco made from such ingredients as pulverized willow bark

kola (KOH-lah)—friend

mahto (mah-TOE)—bear

mitakuye oyasin (mee-TAH-koo-yay oh-YAH-sihn)—all my relatives mitawin (mee-TAH-wihn)—my wife, my woman

ohan (oh-HAHN)—Yes! (emphatic)

onsila (OHN-shee-lah)—Poor thing!

Paha Sapa (pah-HAH sah-pah)—the Black Hills

pannunpala (pah-HUHN-pah-lah)—milkweed plant; "two little workbags of women"

pejuta (pay-JOO-dah)—medicine; "grass roots"

pejuta wicasa (pay-Joo-dah wee-CHA-shah)—man who uses herbs for healing; one kind of "medicine man," or shaman

pilamaye (pee-LAH-mah-yay)—thank you

sa (shah)—red; a very good thing is described as red

sapa (SAH-pah)—black

sicun (shee-CHUHN)—a spiritlike guardian, which may be derived or envisioned through the *ton*, the spiritual aspect of another being, especially an animal

taku (DAH-koo)—What?

tatanka (tak-TAHNK-kah)—the American bison, commonly called buffalo

Tiipasotka Wakansica (tee-ee-PAH-shoht-kah wah-KAHN-shee-kah)—Devil's Tower, Wyoming; "evil tower"

tiospaye (tee-OH-shpah-yay)—band or clan

tos (dohsh)—yes; used only by women

tuki (doo-KEE) Is that so!; used only by women

tunkansi (tuhn-KAHN-shee)—my father-in-law

Tunkasila (tuhn-KAHN-shee-lah)—grandfather; God

unci (uhn-CHEE)—grandmother; earth mother

unsica (UHN-shee-kah)—poor, pitiful

wahpehatapi (wah-PAY-yah-tah-pee)—lavender hyssop plant; "leaf that is chewed" wakan (wah-KAHN)—holy, sacred

wakincuzas (wah-KIHN-shoo-zuh)—leaders of a clan, "the ones who decide"

wanaği (wah-NAH-chee)—spirits of the departed

waśicun (wah-SHEE-choohn)—white man

wasna (wahs-NAH)—pemmican made from pulverized jerky and tallow; dried berries might be added

waśte (wash-TAY)—good

wicaśa (wee-CHA-shah)—man

wicaśa wakan (wee-CHA-shah wah-KAHN)—a holy man; the highest level of "medicine man," or shaman

winkte (WINK-dah)—a man who dresses and behaves as a woman, considered to be sacred

winyan (WEE-yahn)—woman, girl

Winyan he cinacaqupi (WEE-yahn hay chin-AH-chak-pee)—"He wanted that woman, so they gave her to him." Describes a marital agreement between families, based on the love between the two who are to marry.

Harlequin Historicals ®

COMING NEXT MONTH

#31 TEXAS HEART—Ruth Langan

Young Jessie Conway would stop at nothing to find her
missing father. And although she suspected Cole Matthews
was a veteran gunslinger, she would risk his company
along the Chisholm Trail for her family's sake. But Jessie's
fear melted when she learned her brooding companion
possessed a noble heart she alone was destined to claim.

#32 DELTA PEARL—Maureen Bronson

Jena Veray was alone and penniless, but free at last from
the sadistic clutches of her fiancé, and determined to make
a new start—somehow. But lighthearted Andrew Wade
had plans of his own, and Jena found herself swept up in
the rags-to-riches schemes of Andrew and his
unconventional friends.

AVAILABLE NOW:

JAYNE ANN KRENTZ
WINS HARLEQUIN'S
AWARD OF EXCELLENCE

With her October Temptation, *Lady's Choice*, Jayne
Ann Krentz marks more than a decade in romance
publishing. We thought it was about time she got our
official seal of approval—the Harlequin Award of
Excellence.

Since she began writing for Temptation in 1984, Ms
Krentz's novels have been a hallmark of this lively, sexy
series—and a benchmark for all writers in the genre.
Lady's Choice, her eighteenth Temptation, is as stirring
as her first, thanks to a tough and sexy hero, and a
heroine who is tough when she has to be, tender when
she chooses. . . .

The winner of numerous booksellers' awards, Ms Krentz
has also consistently ranked as a bestseller with readers,
on both romance and mass market lists. *Lady's Choice*
will do it for her again!

This lady is *Harlequin's* choice in October.

Available where Harlequin books are sold.   AE-LC-1

Harlequin American Romance®

SUMMER.

The sun, the surf, the sand...

One relaxing month by the sea was all Zoe, Diana and Gracie ever expected from their four-week stays at Gull Cottage, the luxurious East Hampton mansion. They never thought they'd soon be sharing those long summer days—or hot summer nights—with a special man. They never thought that what they found at the beach would change their lives forever. But as Boris, Gull Cottage's resident mynah bird said: "Beware of summer romances...."

Join Zoe, Diana and Gracie for the summer of their lives. Don't miss the GULL COTTAGE trilogy in American Romance: #301 *Charmed Circle* by Robin Francis (July 1989), #305 *Mother Knows Best* by Barbara Bretton (August 1989) and #309 *Saving Grace* by Anne McAllister (September 1989).

GULL COTTAGE—because a month can be the start of forever...

COMING SOON...

Indulge a Little

Give a Lot

An irresistible opportunity to pamper yourself with free* gifts and help a great cause, Big Brothers/Big Sisters Programs and Services.
*With proofs-of-purchase plus postage and handling.

Watch for it in October!

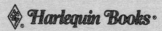

IND